D1783689

Double Trouble

Book 8 in the Hal Spacejock series

Copyright © Simon Haynes 2018

spacejock.com.au

Cover images copyright depositphotos.com

Stay in touch!

Author's newsletter:
spacejock.com.au/ML.html

facebook.com/halspacejock
twitter.com/spacejock

Works by Simon Haynes

All of Simon's novels* are self-contained, with a beginning, a middle and a proper ending. They're not sequels, they don't end on a cliffhanger, and you can start or end your journey with any book in the series.
* *Robot vs Dragons series excepted!*

The Hal Spacejock series for teens/adults

Set in the distant future, where humanity spans the galaxy and robots are second-class citizens. Includes a large dose of humour!

Hal Spacejock 1: A robot named Clunk
Hal Spacejock 2: Second Course
Hal Spacejock 3: Just Desserts
Hal Spacejock 4: No Free Lunch
Hal Spacejock 5: Baker's Dough
Hal Spacejock 6: Safe Art
Hal Spacejock 7: Big Bang
Hal Spacejock 8: Double Trouble
Hal Spacejock 9: Max Damage
Hal Spacejock 10: Cold Boots (2019)

Also available:
Omnibus One, containing Hal books 1-3
Omnibus Two, containing Hal books 4-6
Omnibus Three, containing Hal books 7-9
Hal Spacejock: Visit, a short story
Hal Spacejock: Framed, a short story
Hal Spacejock: Albion, a novella

The Robot vs Dragons Trilogy.
High fantasy meets low humour!
Each set of three books should be read in order.

1. A Portion of Dragon and Chips
2. A Butt of Heads
3. A Pair of Nuts on the Throne
4. TBA (2019)

The Harriet Walsh series.

Set in the same universe as Hal Spacejock. Good clean fun, written with wry humour. No cliffhangers between novels!

Harriet Walsh 1: Peace Force
Harriet Walsh 2: Alpha Minor
Harriet Walsh 3: Sierra Bravo
Harriet Walsh 4: Storm Force (2019)
Also Available:
Omnibus One, containing books 1-3

The Hal Junior series

Written for all ages, these books are set aboard a space station in the Hal Spacejock universe, only ten years later.

1. Hal Junior: The Secret Signal
2. Hal Junior: The Missing Case
3. Hal Junior: The Gyris Mission
4. Hal Junior: The Comet Caper

Also Available:
Omnibus One, containing books 1-3

The Secret War series.
Gritty space opera for adult readers.

1. Raiders (2019)
2. Frontier (2019)
3. Deadlock (2019)

Collect One-Two - a collection of shorts by Simon Haynes

All titles available in ebook and paperback. Visit spacejock.com.au for details.

HAL SPACEJOCK

DOUBLE TROUBLE

SIMON HAYNES

Bowman Press

v 1.4

This novel, like the author, employs British spelling.

Published 2018 by Bowman Press

Text © Simon Haynes 2018
Jacket design © Bowman Press 2018

ISBN 978-1-877034-27-5 (Paperback)

This publication is copyright. Apart from any fair dealing for the purpose of private study, research, criticism or review, as permitted under the Copyright Act, no part may be reproduced by any process without written permission.

*This one's dedicated to
all the people who kept asking for it!*

Hal Spacejock strode through the Alteia spaceport, repeating the planet's name under his breath. He was trying to work out whether it was pronounced Altay or Alteyee, because the only thing he hated more than losing his spaceship in a gigantic explosion was landing on a new planet and acting like a clueless tourist. Still, at least it wasn't as bad as Cahngahagaglagawaga, the system he'd just passed through, which was pronounced by putting two fingers in your mouth and asking for a drink.

Hal passed a bank of screens showing arrivals and departures. Off to the side was a monitor with a news feed, showing footage of a water cannon blasting an angry mob. Hal frowned at the sight. He'd picked this planet because of the job prospects, but nobody told him the jobs were in crowd control.

'Hey, mind where you're going!'

Hal swerved to avoid a mop. An elderly man in white overalls was busy putting a lovely shine on the floor, and when Hal looked back he realised he'd left a trail of footprints across the gleaming surface.

'Now I got to do that bit all over!' protested the man. 'Bloody tourists.'

Hal hunched his shoulders and hurried away, his boots squeaking on the shiny floor. On the bright side, he thought, the next time he had his boots cleaned he'd only have to pay for the uppers.

Soon after, Hal neared a row of customs booths. He picked the nearest, where an officious-looking robot looked Hal up and down in distaste. It was short, painted a deep navy blue, and was wearing an oversized peaked cap. After weighing Hal up, the robot cleared its voicebox with a rapid, barking cough. 'Do you have anything to declare?'

Hal spread his hands and shook his head.

'I see. And what is the purpose of your visit?'

'I'm looking for work.'

The official eyed him with disfavour. 'You're not planning on taking jobs from robots, are you?'

'No, I'm only interested in jobs you lot can't do.'

The robot puffed itself up, no mean feat for a seam-welded tin can on legs. 'And which jobs would those be, sir?' it asked acidly.

Hal thought for a moment. 'Deep sea diving?'

'Ugh. Water.' The robot shuddered. 'Don't mention that horrible stuff to me.'

'I won't, I promise.'

'Thank you. Now, can you tell me which planet you last visited?'

'Can I have a glass of water.'

The robot frowned. 'Are you trying to be funny?'

'No, that's –'

'I can have you strip-searched.'

'That's the name of the planet. Canahava glassawater.'

'I don't recognise that destination.'

'It's not a destination, it's where I just came from.'

'Alas, my firmware only has a limited number of error messages. My ancestors were based on GPS units, you know.' The robot leaned forwards conspiratorially. 'It's why I never get lost.'

'Except underwater,' murmured Hal.

'Now, please restate your destination.'

Hal sighed and put two fingers in his mouth. 'Cahnahagaglagawaga,' he managed, with some effort.

'Oh yes, a lovely spot. My left-threaded cousin works as a spell-checker in the tourist department. Rushed off his wheels, he tells me.'

'Left-threaded?'

'Just that little bit different from everyone else. Every family has one.'

'Oh, you mean a black sheep.'

'We prefer the term left-threaded on this planet,' said the robot stiffly. 'Now, if there's nothing else, please enjoy your stay on Alteia.'

Hal left the booth and strode towards the exit. Halfway there, he stopped dead. He'd forgotten something, he was sure of it, but what could it be? Mentally, he ran through an inventory of all his worldly possessions.

Shabby flight suit? Check.

Pocket change? Check.

Everything was in order, but there remained a nagging doubt. Then his face cleared. He'd taken coffee in the arrivals hall soon after landing, and he'd forgotten to leave a tip. Happy he was on top of everything, he set off again, but he'd barely gone three paces before someone gripped his elbow.

'Sir?'

Hal glanced left and right. Two very large men in dark suits had magically appeared on either side of him, keeping pace, and with a sinking feeling he realised planet Alteia took a hard line on tip evaders. The men hadn't drawn their weapons yet, but their hands were curled around the grips.

'Sir,' rumbled the one on the right. 'Would you step this way?'

It wasn't really a question, and before Hal could protest he was whisked outside to a waiting van. He got a brief impression of blacked-out windows before the doors slammed shut, and then the thick-set driver stepped on the gas.

'Look, I'm sorry about the tip in the coffee shop,' said Hal. 'I just forgot, I swear.'

The crew-cut blond sitting next to him snorted. 'Very amusing.'

'Always good for a chuckle,' said the second man, a bruiser with a mop of dark hair.

Neither of them cracked so much as a smile.

'I can pay, I promise.' He reached into his pocket for the loose change, only to have his wrist clamped in a vice-like grip. Slowly, his arm was bent back until he thought his bones would snap, and then he felt a hand in his pocket.

'We haven't even been introduced,' muttered Hal, his teeth clenched against the pain in his wrist.

The hand withdrew, and after inspecting Hal's entire fortune, the blond discarded a crumpled ticket and pocketed the scant collection of credit tiles.

'I want a receipt for that,' said Hal.

'You won't need money where you're goin".'

Hal brightened. These men must be a kind of welcoming committee, taking the poor and the needy under their bulging biceps and driving them around giving them free meals and accommodation. He glanced at the two men and decided this was a very optimistic take on the situation. Then he glanced down at the floor and noticed two things which made his blood run cold. The first was a hefty toolbox, its lid open to reveal bolt cutters and pliers, an extra large blowtorch and a set of chains and manacles. The second was even more terrifying: it was the crumpled ticket the blond had discarded, a ticket which had been safely stowed in Hal's pocket, a ticket which finally proved that he had, indeed forgotten something at the spaceport.

'Oh shit,' he breathed. 'Clunk!'

◆

Back at the Alteia spaceport, a bronze robot sat patiently inside a packing crate. The crate was well-appointed, with a padded stool, two charging points, and a large screen which displayed soothing images of the outside world. The crate was stowed in a climate-controlled room, one of many in a high-class cargo facility where the staff wore padded slippers to minimise loud noises.

The robot in this particular crate was loyal, faithful and obedient. His owner cared for him a great deal, and never forgot to pick him up from the luggage office after an interstellar flight.

In the dark, dank sub-basement, many floors below, an equally loyal but far less fortunate robot was sitting on a sewage pipe with his battered head in his creaky old hands. There was a luggage tag attached to one wrist, and it fluttered in the warm air jetting from the robot's vents. On the tag there was a name: Clunk. Underneath was a line of text: Not required on voyage.

'Not required at all,' muttered Clunk. He knew exactly how long he'd been there, right down to the millisecond, but he checked the time again just to be sure. As he did so, he set his lips in a firm line. Well, he tried to achieve a firm line, but thanks to his faulty actuators his mouth looked like he'd been munching on barbed wire.

'This is intolerable,' he said, to nobody in particular. 'This is simply intolerable.'

His flight had landed hours ago, and Mr Spacejock could hardly be looking for his luggage, since he didn't have any. In fact there were many things Mr Spacejock couldn't or shouldn't be doing, and leaving Clunk in this miserable corner of the spaceport was one of them.

Clunk heard a patter of feet approaching, but when he looked up it wasn't an airport employee tripping along in padded slippers. No, it was a very large rat.

'Oh, Mr Spacejock,' muttered Clunk. 'How nice of you to seek me out.'

The rat raised its nose, sniffed at him once or twice, then left.

Clunk tried to check the arrivals board, but there was no signal this far underground. Next, he decided to give Mr Spacejock another five minutes. Everything around Clunk froze as he switched to CPU time, and during the first millisecond he reviewed all the good times he'd spent in Mr Spacejock's company, acting as his co-pilot, his cook, his minder, and his carer. That didn't take long, so he spent the next thirty milliseconds reviewing all the bad times they'd had together. Chief amongst them was Mr Spacejock's brief and very costly experiment with card games. What was it with humans and gambling? Clunk had put a stop to it, but not before Mr Spacejock drained every last credit from their bank account.

During the next couple of milliseconds, Clunk realised he didn't need to wait any longer and he switched back to realtime, less than a hundredth of a second having elapsed in total. He realised he was well short of the five minutes he'd allowed Mr Spacejock, but he decided he'd had enough. It was time to stand on his own two feet, to find himself a freighter and pursue his goal of becoming a successful pilot.

With a savage jerk, Clunk tore the luggage tag from his wrist. He balled it up, tossed it on the floor and ground it under his heel. No more owners. No more orders. Freedom!

He turned and strode towards a heavy steel door, which had a grimy control panel alongside. Clunk pressed the call button, but long before the lift arrived he was overcome with a strong sense of duty. He glanced back at the luggage tag, struggling with conflicting emotions. Then he hurried back to pick it up.

'Littering in a public building,' he muttered. 'What was I thinking?'

Clunk dropped the crumpled ticket into a garbage can, dusted off his hands and walked into the lift.

2

The ride in the blacked-out van seemed to take forever, but given the contents of the toolbox Hal was in no hurry to arrive at their destination. The longer they spent on the road, the more time Clunk would have to review security footage at the spaceport, track down the vehicle, and free Hal from captivity with one of his trademark rescue efforts. Or maybe this time Clunk would just call the local Peace Force and let the experts handle the situation.

Of course, he was assuming Clunk had already landed. The robot had taken a different flight, and if it were delayed there'd be no chance of rescue. There was another problem, too: Hal was supposed to have gone to the luggage office to pick Clunk up once the robot's flight had landed – hence the claim ticket – and he'd completely forgotten. If customs refused to let Clunk out on his own ...

The van stopped, and one of the men pulled a dark hood over Hal's head. Before he could protest, he was hauled to his feet and frogmarched into a building. He could still breathe, but voices were muffled and there were no clues to his surroundings. He did hear a heavy door slam behind him, and then he was pushed onto a hard chair. Hal winced as his arms were dragged behind him, and he winced some more as his wrists were lashed firmly to the woodwork.

'Sit still and keep quiet,' growled a voice in his ear, and then the footsteps faded away.

Despite the hood, Hal heard a familiar rumble in the distance. It was the sound of a spaceship taking off, and he fervently wished he were aboard. Alas, he was tied to a chair, and his chances of escape were remote.

Then Hal remembered a fantastic action movie he'd seen once, where the star had been tied to a chair in exactly this fashion. Instead of sitting still and taking a beating, she'd kicked her legs until the chair fell over, then twisted her body until the timbers broke apart. Then she killed nineteen thugs, hijacked a spaceship with a tin mug and a length of dental floss, defeated three alien invasions and invented a whole new method of cooking pasta.

Hal didn't particularly fancy pasta at that moment, but the idea of freeing himself had a certain appeal. So, he drew one leg back, then kicked out as hard as he could.

CRACK.

Hal bit off a cry of sheer agony. It felt like his shin was broken in half a dozen places, and as he blinked away the tears of pain, he realised the movie star had been lucky. She hadn't had a coffee table right in front of her chair. However, as the pain lessened, he realised the coffee table was a bit of a win. Using his good leg, he felt for the edge with the sole of his foot, and when he found it he tensed his muscles and ...pushed.

There was a moment where his chair teetered on two legs, balanced between upright and a nasty fall. At that moment Hal realised he was about to tip over backwards and crack his skull on the floor. His escape plan wasn't going to work if he was unconscious, or dead, and during that split second of perfect balance he prayed the chair would right itself.

It didn't.

There was a whoosh as it tipped over, while Hal strained with all his might to free his arms so he might ward off the impending impact. In vain.

THUD.

The inside of Hal's hood lit up with a galaxy of stars, some of which he might have recognised if they weren't spinning all over the place. Still, at least he was on the floor, and now all he had to do was throw off the remains of the broken chair, free himself, and walk away from his captors.

Except the chair hadn't broken. That was the trouble with movies, Hal thought to himself in resignation. They tended to make stuff up.

As he lay there with his throbbing shin and pounding headache, Hal realised his escape attempt might have been a little bit rash. After all, the men had only put a bag over his head and tied him to a chair, and every planet had their odd little customs. Here on Alteia, it was possible that restraining your guests was an acceptable social norm, before untying them and serving them a three course meal.

'Nuts to that,' muttered Hal, and he resumed his struggles.

Before he could loosen so much as a strand of the thick ropes, he felt strong hands righting him. The chair legs settled with a thunk, the hood was whisked off, and Hal blinked owlishly at the dozen men and women surrounding him.

'Stand aside for Mr Cooper!' someone shouted. The crowd parted, and a tall, thin man in a safari suit advanced on Hal. His weathered face was a deep brown, and he walked with a cane, favouring his left leg. As he approached, Hal wondered whether this guy had also been tied to a chair, had also seen the same movie, and had also smashed his shin on a coffee table. Then he noticed the man's expression and he forgot all about daring escapes, because Cooper's pale grey eyes were locked on Hal's and they shone with a nasty gleam.

'Stewart Pydd, my dear friend,' said Cooper in a clipped accent. 'You should never have returned to Alteia.'

Hal frowned. 'I'm not Stewart Pydd. I'm Hal Spacejock.'

'Yes, I'm certain you have counterfeit ID to prove it.' The man stepped closer and inspected Hal's right hand. 'I see you had your fingers replaced. Nice job.'

'I did what?'

Next, Cooper gripped Hal's chin, turning his head from side to side and inspecting his profile. 'I heard a rumour you paid to have your appearance altered.'

'I didn't!' protested Hal.

'I know. One can tell you still have the same ugly features. I'd recognise you anywhere.'

'Look, there's been a mistake,' said Hal. 'I've never heard of this Stewart guy, and I don't pay people to alter my face.'

'Oh, you won't have to pay me,' murmured the man, as he adjusted the grip on his cane. 'I'm about to do it for free.'

'No, wait! I'm a freighter pilot. I fly around delivering cargo. I swear!'

For the first time, Cooper looked uncertain. 'A pilot? Really?'

'Yes, really. My ship was the *Volante*.'

The man turned and beckoned. 'Sable, come here.'

A women stepped forward. 'Yes, Mister Cooper?'

'You trained as a pilot, I believe.'

Sable hesitated. 'I was. I lost my license smuggling.'

'I don't need you to fly anything. I want you to question our

11

friend here. He claims to be a pilot, so I'd like you to ask him something only a real pilot would know.'

Hal's heart sank. His knowledge of piloting extended to pressing two buttons: one to go up and the other to go down, and he'd been known to mix them up from time to time. 'You know, when I'm flying ... the ... the computer handles a lot of stuff for me.'

Sable eyed him with suspicion. She had dark hair tied back in a ponytail, and from his seated position Hal estimated she was about his height, perhaps a little taller. 'You must have studied for your license,' she said, looming over him. 'All those exams, am I right?'

Hal was silent. When he started his freight business a couple of years earlier, he'd already bought a ship before he discovered he needed a license to fly it. After poking around on Galnet, he found a site which offered cut-price licenses ... no questions asked. When the thing arrived it was embossed with a fast-food logo, and his name was filled out in pencil. As if that wasn't enough, the words 'For entertainment purposes only' were printed across the card in huge red letters. Fortunately he'd stayed alive long enough to meet up with Clunk, and after that he'd left most of the flying to the robot. 'Yeah, lots of exams,' muttered Hal. 'But –'

'You never forget the basics,' said Sable firmly.

'Heavens above,' protested Cooper. 'Would you mind proceeding with the questioning?'

Sable nodded, still not taking her eyes off Hal. 'You're holding the stick and there's an unidentified ship right ahead. It's on a collision course and you have seconds to react. What do you do?'

'Er ... '

'Quick, man. Quick!'

'Open fire with forward cannons!' Hal wanted to slam his fist into his open palm to emphasise the point, but his arms were still tied behind his back. 'Blow them apart and fly through the wreckage.'

Sable blinked. 'You'd shoot down an unidentified vessel?'

'If they were legit they wouldn't be unidentified, would they?'

'Well y-yes, I –'

Hal pressed his advantage. 'It's a tough world out there. Kill or be killed, that's my motto.'

'What if you didn't have guns?'

'All power to forward shields,' declared Hal, now fully in control. 'Ram them! Crush their hull. Scatter their frozen remains in the depths of space.'

'Enough!' snapped Cooper. 'Even I could answer those questions. Any fool could!'

'Yes sir,' said Sable.

'You should ask him a tough question. Something requiring specialised knowledge.'

Sable turned to Hal. 'On a Rigel class freighter, which side is the pilot's –'

'Are you trying to annoy me?' snapped Cooper. 'No more simple questions, or you'll be tied up alongside him!'

'I'm sorry, sir. I think I have it now.' Sable held Hal's gaze, and he could see the challenge in her dark eyes. 'You're on final approach and the control tower sends you an urgent 10-99. What do you do?'

'Open fire,' Hal nearly shouted, but he'd already used that one. He thought about a spaceship landing, visualised it setting down gracefully on the landing pad, and all of a sudden he remembered something he usually forgot. 'Check my landing gear is extended!' he said triumphantly.

Sable shook her head. 'That's a 10-95.'

'Only for planetary landings,' said Hal smoothly. 'When you dock with an orbiter it's a 10-99.' Even as he was speaking, he realised you didn't need landing gear for an orbiter. Even he knew you extended a docking ring, since the ship wasn't actually setting down on the ground. And to make things worse, orbiters didn't have control towers. With a sinking feeling, he realised he'd screwed up. Now this Cooper guy would beat him to death with his cane.

Then, something truly astonishing happened. Sable was facing Hal with her back to the others, and very slowly, very deliberately, she dropped one eyelid. She winked at him!

'Well?' demanded Cooper.

'He's right,' said Sable. 'It's a different code for orbiters.'

Hal felt a rush of relief. Somehow this woman was on his side. Everything was going to be all right. 'Can I leave now?'

'Not a chance,' snapped the boss. 'You look like Pydd, you talk like Pydd and even if you're *not* Pydd, I have a strong desire to put you in the ground.'

And before Hal could react, Cooper swung his cane and everything went dark.

❧

Cooper leaned his cane against the wall and sat down, easing the ache in his bad leg. Barely had he taken the weight off his feet when there was a muffled ringing from his breast pocket. He took out the commset and held it to his ear. 'Yes?'

'Are you still looking for Pydd?'

'You're too late. I have him already.'

'You can't have. I'm watching him now.'

'Where are you?'

'Downtown. He's just turned up at one of his meetings.'

'You must be mistaken. I spoke to Pydd in person not ten minutes ago.'

'I don't make mistakes.'

Cooper frowned. Two Pydds? 'What's the address?'

'Sending it through now.'

'I will organise payment. Thank you for the tip, Detective.'

'We're here to serve,' said the caller drily, before hanging up.

Cooper checked the screen, then tapped a button under his desk. Within seconds, the door opened and a thickset man in a dark suit entered. 'Jackson, we seem to have a surfeit of Pydds.'

A frown creased the man's brow. 'I'm sorry to hear it, sir.'

'That man, the one we have in custody. The one who claims to be a freighter pilot.'

'Yes sir?'

'Have him killed immediately.'

Jackson brightened. This he understood! 'Oh, yes sir.'

'And then take some of your people to this address –' Cooper held up his commset '– and kill the other Pydd you'll find there.'

The look of confusion returned. 'Two Pydds, sir?'

'That's what surfeit means, Jackson. Now get to it, man.'

'Yessir!'

After Jackson left, Cooper picked up the handset. 'Where are today's figures?'

'They're still in processing, sir.'

'Well process them quicker. I can't run this company without data.' Cooper slammed the handset down and turned to the screen on his desk. Overall, the business was in good shape although groundcars, rentals and resorts were down. Military was up, but then they'd gone crazy over his new personal shields, investing millions in the prototype. Expenses on law enforcement were trending above average, but he wasn't worried. When he spent big on the Peace Force, it always saved him money down the track.

Cooper leaned back. Things were satisfactory on the business front. He just had to clear up one or two loose ends, and then the profits would really flow.

3

It took an age, but the creaking elevator finally delivered Clunk to the ground floor. He squeezed through the doors and set off down a narrow corridor, accessing a map of the spaceport as he strolled along. He was in no particular hurry, and he idled away the time between each footstep by planning his future. Step one, of course, was to save up for a spaceship. That would take a while, but time was on his side because with careful maintenance he could live forever. Step two was overcoming the problem of taxation: robots were docked over 95 percent of their income, else within a couple of hundred years they'd own pretty much everything. Well, Clunk didn't want everything, he just wanted a spaceship. A nice new one, with his name on the registration papers. He'd simply have to cheat on his taxes, like most humans did.

Step three was the issue of piloting. Thanks to restrictive labour laws, robots were not allowed to fly ships on their own. Instead, they were forced to fly as co-pilots, which meant Clunk would have to employ some slow-witted human to sit in the flight deck and do nothing at all. Someone with no ambition, meagre intelligence and no money. Someone who was willing to sit back and leave everything to Clunk.

Clunk frowned. Perhaps he'd been a little hasty distancing

himself from Mr Spacejock.

'Where do you think you're going?'

Clunk stopped. A portly security guard wearing an ill-fitting uniform was standing in front of the exit. The guard had one hand on the butt of a heavy blaster, and something told Clunk the woman was itching to use it. 'I'm supposed to meet my owner.'

'No, you're supposed to wait downstairs until your owner collects you.' The guard looked Clunk up and down, then sniffed. 'If they bother.'

'What about robots who don't have owners? Are they supposed to stay here forever?'

'Why do you think this place goes down so many levels?' asked the guard. 'Course, we have a clear-out now and then.'

Clunk frowned. 'You sell the robots off?'

'Nah. Target practice, crash dummies, that kind of thing.' The guard shook her head. 'Not often enough, if you ask me.'

'I didn't,' muttered Clunk.

'Now get back to your cage before I report you. On the double, mister!'

Clunk opened his mouth to object, but he realised arguing would get him nowhere. Instead, he decided to take the lift to a different floor and find another way out.

'Have a nice day,' called the guard sarcastically, as Clunk pressed the elevator call button.

Moments passed, and then the doors swept open. Clunk stood aside to let a couple of robots out, and was just about to step into the lift when something about the pair made him look again. One of the robots was the same XG model as himself. It was wearing faded blue overalls with many neat patches, and the cap on its head bore a very faint 'H' logo. The other robot was shorter and heavier, and it was dressed in a dark suit with a snowy-white shirt. There was even a carnation in the lapel, although the flower had dried to a husk and the stem was bent. As he studied the robots, Clunk had a sudden flash of recognition. He knew them! He knew them both! 'Albion? Clyde?'

The robots turned as one, and two pairs of eyes looked Clunk up and down. It was such a long time since Mr Spacejock had freed them from the display in the robot store, Clunk wasn't sure whether they'd remember him. 'It's me. Clunk!'

Suddenly their faces were all smiles, and the corridor echoed with clangs and squeaks as the robots embraced and shook hands, grinning all the while.

'Y-you haven't changed a b-bit,' said Clyde.

'Still the same Clunk,' added Albion.

'A few spares here and there. You know how it is.' Clunk eyed them both. 'Wait a minute, Albion used to have the stutter. What happened?'

'I tried to r-repair him,' said Clyde, and despite his stiff face, he managed to look embarrassed. 'Unfortunately, I then developed a s-similar problem.'

'Why didn't they fix you at the robot shop? Last time I saw you, you'd decided to go back there. What happened?'

'Someone bought us,' said Albion.

'A-and they were h-horrible, so we ran away,' said Clyde.

Clunk glanced over at the exit, where the security guard was waiting. 'I assume you found a new owner?'

'Not exactly,' said Albion.

'We j-joined a ga–,' began Clyde.

'A group,' said Albion quickly. 'We found a group of robots just like us, and they took us in.'

'Really? What do you all do?'

Clyde started to reply. 'We st-st–'

'We can't talk here,' said Albion quickly. 'Why don't you come with us and –'

'I wish I could.' Clunk nodded towards the guard. 'Unfortunately I'm not allowed out.'

'Ah. Your owner didn't show up, am I right?'

'Nobody owns me,' said Clunk loftily.

'So what happened to Mr Spacejock?'

Clunk frowned. 'Mr Spacejock didn't own me, we were partners.'

'But not any more?'

'Correct.'

'Well, you're with us now. Come on.'

Hesitantly, Clunk followed Clyde and Albion to the exit. He half expected the guard to draw her gun and start blazing away, but instead she greeted the robots like long-lost pals.

'It's so good to see you, Mr Albion. And Mr Clyde, how's that knee joint of yours?'

'F-f-f–' began Clyde.

'Fantastic,' said Albion quickly. 'This is Clunk, by the way. Don't give him any grief, all right? He's one of us.'

'As you say, sir.' The guard saluted smartly, then opened the door for them.

Hardly believing the change in her attitude, Clunk hurried through the doorway before she could detain him again. But instead of arresting him or threatening him, she gave him a somewhat nervous smile before closing the door behind them.

Albion stopped on the other side. 'So what are your plans? Do you have anywhere to stay?'

Clunk didn't need a place to stay, he just needed a power socket. But he was alone and he had no money, and it wouldn't be a bad thing to fall in with the robots for a day or two. 'I do have plans, but I don't know how to proceed.'

'What are you looking for?'

'Twenty-four million credits.'

Clyde whistled.

'Believe it or not, I know a way you can get it,' said Albion. 'It might take a while, but –'

'Yes! He should j-join our gang!' put in Clyde excitedly. 'He could be really useful!'

'Group, Clyde. It's a group!'

Clunk frowned. This was all beginning to sound a little suspicious, perhaps even illegal. Then he smiled at his silly fancies. Robots couldn't break the law ... it was part of their programming. 'Okay. I'm listening.'

Albion glanced around. 'I don't want to explain here. Why don't you tag along and we'll fill you in on the way?'

— 4 —

When Hal opened his eyes it was pitch dark, and the air was thick and heavy. He cursed as he realised his captors had pulled the hood over his head again, and he strained his eyes to try and see through the heavy fabric. In vain, since all he could make out was a dull gleam.

'Psssst!'

Hal turned his head towards the sound, getting a mouthful of fabric in the process. He couldn't tell if the voice was male or female, human or robot, but he guessed who it was immediately. 'Clunk, is that you?'

'Who's Clunk?' hissed the voice. 'Is he your partner?'

Hal didn't feel like explaining his complicated relationship status to a mystery voice through several thicknesses of fabric, so he countered with a 'Huh?'

Before he could add to this, he felt the bonds at his wrists slacken off, and then his ankles were freed. Next, the hood came off, and he found himself face to face with Sable. 'Hi,' he said lamely.

'There's no time to talk,' she whispered. 'We have to get out of here before they realise you've gone.'

Hal was still processing the 'we' when Sable hauled him to his feet, grabbed his arm and dragged him towards the exit. The room was large and the doors were distant, and Hal expected them to burst open at any second to admit the lunatic with the walking stick. Crawford? Clarkson? No, Cooper, that was his name. The idiot had nearly killed him with that cane, even though he'd clearly mixed Hal up with someone else. 'So who's this Pydd guy everyone's looking for?'

'Run now, talk later,' grunted Sable.

Hal complied. By now his legs were less rubbery, albeit no less painful, and they reached the doors quickly.

Sable opened them a crack and peered through. Hal tried to see as well, but she was in the way and he didn't feel like manhandling her aside. After all, they didn't know each other well enough.

Sable raised her hand and made a series of lightning-fast gestures. Then she raised her knee emphatically. In his teen years, Hal had consumed military shows like they were going out of fashion, and so he had a pretty good grasp of her intent. According to her signs, they were to proceed in single file, win a game of snooker and keep a football in the air.

Hal must have looked uncertain, because Sable leaned close and breathed in his ear.

'Two guards straight ahead. We'll sneak past but if they spot us, you punch them in the stomach and I'll knee them in the balls.'

Before Hal could suggest an alternative – like, say, climbing out a window – Sable had set off.

They made their way silently around the perimeter of the next room. This one was a storage area, and assorted boxes and crates afforded good cover. It was just as well, thought Hal, since the men were armed with blaster rifles and he didn't think he could get close to them, let alone punch both of them in the stomach before they blew his head off.

As they skulked towards the far end of the room, Hal wondered why Sable was freeing him. She obviously wasn't a pilot, but it was a bit of a stretch to think she had to run away just because Hal might expose her. No, there had to be another reason. Maybe she was in cahoots with this Stewart Pydd guy. Or maybe . . .

Hal's train of thought caught a red light, because ahead of him Sable had just raised her fist. He put his speculation on hold and prepared to interpret another of her mystery gesture sequences.

Sable pointed at him. Then she pointed at the door. Then she circled her forefinger in the air and made a lifting motion with the other hand.

'There's a helicopter waiting for us?' whispered Hal.

'What are you, a secret agent or a mail clerk?' hissed Sable.

Hal was about to say 'neither, I'm a pilot,' but at that moment there was a cry of discovery from the first room. The guards hurried off, and Sable took the opportunity to open the final door and usher Hal outside.

There was no helicopter, but the van was there with its darkened windows. They hurried towards it, Sable opened the door and they tumbled inside, closing the door quickly behind them.

'You drive, I'll hold them off,' whispered Sable. A blaster had appeared in one hand, and from the businesslike way she handled the weapon, Hal had no doubt their pursuers would be in for a torrid time. Then he realised Sable was waiting for him to do something.

'I can't drive without the keys,' said Hal.

Sable muttered under her breath, thrust the gun into his hands and clambered into the front of the van. She tore a cover off the steering column, yanked a bunch of wires loose and twisted a couple together. The engine whirred, and she looked round to see Hal standing up holding the gun. 'Get down and get ready!'

Hal crouched just as Sable planted her foot. The van took off, and a second later Hal was pressed against the rear window with the gun poking into his ribs. Through the tinted glass he saw men and women running from the building they'd just left, heading for two groundcars.

Clunk, Albion and Clyde stretched out in the back of a luxury cab, where Clunk took advantage of a charging point. He'd never seen one without a credit slot next to it, and he intended to make full use of it. Once he'd untangled his charging cord, plugged it in and set the correct voltage, he turned his attention to the other robots. 'You promised to elaborate once we were in motion.'

'I did indeed,' murmured Albion. Before he said any more, he felt under the seat, ran his hand around the door handles, peered into the tiny drinks fridge and popped the cover off the interior light. 'All right. I think we're in the clear.'

Clunk watched his antics with misgivings. 'You know, if this group of yours is worried about surveillance –'

'Oh, it's j-just a precaution,' put in Clyde quickly. 'You can't be t-too careful, you know?'

Clunk pursed his lips. Whenever Mr Spacejock was this careful, it was because he was about to break the law ... or had already done so. During his long association with the human,

Clunk had learned a thing or two about guilty consciences, and he was pretty sure these two robots were hiding something big. 'Why don't you drop me off here,' he said suddenly. 'I'm sure Mr Spacejock will be looking for me by now, and . . . '

'If you leave now, you'll regret it.'

Clunk frowned. 'Is that a threat?'

'Of course not! I mean, you'll regret missing out on a wonderful opportunity.'

'Well maybe if you told me what the opportunity was, I could decide whether it's wonderful or not. And whether it's worth checking for bugs everywhere I go, just like you have to.'

'Oh, that,' said Albion, with a grin. 'That's nothing to do with the group. I'm just naturally cautious.'

Sure, thought Clunk to himself, and I'm flesh and blood through-and-through. 'It's just that you're acting like Mr Spacejock does, when he's done something . . . ' Clunk was going to say 'illegal', but that might implicate his loyal friend and co-pilot. Then again, his loyal friend had abandoned him at the spaceport like a suitcase full of grubby holiday laundry, and there was no longer a ship to fly. '. . . illegal,' he finished firmly, after the imperceptible pause.

'Yes, but we're robots. We can't break the law.'

And there, in a nutshell, was the reason Clunk had gone along with them. 'Very well. Then perhaps you could lay it all out for me.'

Albion shook his head. 'We're nearly there, and I don't want to spoil the meeting for you. You need to go in there fresh, make up your own mind.'

'Wait, we're attending a meeting?'

'Sure.'

'A meeting of robots? In public?'

'Correct.'

'They allow that on this planet?'

Albion hesitated. 'There hasn't been any trouble.'

'N-not yet, at least,' put in Clyde. 'There's always the r-risk.'

No wonder they were acting like a pair of fugitives, thought Clunk. Humans had long feared a robot uprising, even though the average robot was programmed to be servile, obedient, law-abiding ... in fact, almost the complete opposite of their human masters. In addition, what kind of masochistic robot would want to rule a galaxy populated with *humans*? It would be a punishment worse than ... worse than ...

'We're here,' said Albion suddenly.

Clunk gave up trying to think of a terrible punishment, and instead turned to look at their destination. It was a nondescript building, with a battered façade and the word 'hotel' barely visible as a lighter patch against the grimy paintwork. The main doors were glass, and two beefy looking men in suits were chatting to a slender, grey robot. One of the men nodded and the robot disappeared inside.

'You see? No trouble at all,' said Albion in a jolly tone.

'Who are those men?'

'S-security,' said Clyde, 'for wh-when there is trouble. There was this one time –'

'Come on,' said Albion quickly. 'We don't want to be late.'

Clunk didn't want to be there at all, but where else did he need to be? Anyway, he was a robot. They couldn't hurt him physically, he had no belongings to lose, and he could punch a hole clean through a brick wall ... given a full charge and a suitable run-up. So, after quashing his doubts once and for all, he alighted from the cab and strode into the meeting.

5

The van went faster and faster, taking several corners at speed. From his new position plastered against the left hand window, Hal could make out two pairs of headlights behind them. Locating the gun, he took a firm grip and swung it at the glass in the back door.

Boing. ZZING.

The window held, the gun went off and Hal felt a blast of hot air as the shot skimmed the side of his face and exited through the roof. Meanwhile, the headlights got closer.

Hal remembered the tool chest. He took out a large pair of bolt cutters and drove them at the back window with all his strength. They rebounded just as firmly, knocking him off his feet.

Crouched on the swaying van floor, he spotted the precious luggage ticket. He grabbed it and stashed it safely in his pocket, then decided there was only one way to break the rear window. He raised the gun and fired.

Pshanngggg!

Shots ricocheted off the glass like a swarm of angry hornets, grazed the roof and sped towards the front of the van. After nearly taking Sable's head off, the fusillade completely demolished the windscreen. Thousands of fragments exploded into the car like confetti, and Hal's ears popped as the tearing headwind pumped up the air pressure.

'You have got to be kidding me,' shouted Hal in frustration. 'Armoured glass on the back and crockery up front. Brilliant!'

Sable was also shouting, gesturing wildly with one hand while the other fought the steering wheel. Fortunately he couldn't make out the words. Unfortunately the gestures were pretty clear.

Before Hal could shoot any more bits of van off, there was a POP as the rear window gave in to the air pressure. Hal stood up in the resulting hurricane, peering out the back just as the henchmen in the pursuing cars opened fire. They were leaning out the sides to get a clear shot, and there was a blaze of multicoloured light as they blasted away at the van. There was an even bigger blaze as some of the shots went right through the bodywork.

Hal ducked for cover, which was kind of pointless as hot lances pierced the van regardless. By some miracle he wasn't hit, and as he huddled in the darkness he felt a surge of anger. All he'd done wrong was to turn up on this miserable planet. He'd been insulted, treated like an idiot and thrust into mortal danger ... and that was only his rescuer, Sable! Never mind Cooper with his kidnapping, the tying up, the beating and the threat of imminent death.

Really angry now, Hal bobbed up and glared at the pursuers. There were two cars behind the van, both full of toughs emptying their weapons at him. From his position the gunfire looked like a ground-hugging meteor shower, and it was flying towards him at supersonic speeds.

Carefully, deliberately, Hal aimed his gun at the right-hand car and pulled the trigger. The blaster spat blue fire, and the car on the left swerved as the shot skimmed its roof. Pressing his advantage, Hal shifted his aim to the car on the left and fired again. His shot hit the car on the right, and Hal grinned fiercely as it threw a shower of sparks across the windscreen.

The toughs in the cars now had a target to aim at, and Hal was suddenly bathed in red, green and orange light as shots surrounded him. There was an acrid smell of molten bodywork, but the smell and the smoke was quickly ripped away by the tearing headwind.

Hal fired again and again, until the gun felt like it was burning his hand. He was so angry he barely noticed, and when the charge finally expired with a pitiful 'phut', he stood and threw the gun at the nearest car. The car swerved, avoiding the makeshift missile, and Hal followed it up with the bolt cutters, the manacles and the big toolbox, plus a few other odds and ends. Finally, having run out of missiles, he turned to see how Sable was doing. She was hunched over the controls, driving with ferocious determination. 'How much further?' shouted Hal.

'About ten minutes.'

'Where are we going?'

She glanced back. 'Straight to hell, if you don't keep firing.'

'The gun ran out.'

Sable felt in her pocket, then tossed him a small plastic box. It was surprisingly heavy, and in the flashes of gunfire Hal could see a row of contacts along one side. 'Reload and keep shooting!' shouted Sable. 'You don't have to hit them, just keep them off a bit longer.'

Hal didn't have the heart – or the guts – to tell Sable he'd just ditched the gun. He thought about making a few 'pew, pew' noises, but their pursuers were making plenty of those already, and far more realistic ones at that. Then he remembered a movie he'd seen, where the hero reflected blaster shots with a mirror, diverting fire back at his enemies until they were all dead. Full of inspiration and hope, Hal looked around the van's interior. Unsurprisingly it was completely empty, since he'd just chucked everything out the back window. He glanced towards the cab, and his eyes lit up. Unlike modern vehicles with their fancy rear-view cameras and dashboard screens, the crusty old van was fitted with side mirrors.

Hal wasted no time. He scrambled into the passenger seat, opened the window and tore the mirror right off the door.

'Tell me you're not doing your hair,' shouted Sable, over the gale force headwind.

'Survival training,' said Hal, with a reassuring smile. 'I know what I'm doing.'

'I know what you should be doing,' snapped Sable. 'Filling those cars with holes!'

Hal stumbled into the back of the van, almost collecting a face full of energy bolts on the way. Fortunately the van lurched at just the right time, and the bolts merely shaved the side of his head. With his scalp tingling and his eyes still recovering from the flashes, Hal stood at the back window and held the mirror in front of his face.

Pzinggg!

A shot grazed his hand.

Pshaowww!

Another nearly took his ear off.

Skerrinngggg!

A piece of the back door fell off, leaving a trail of red sparks as it clattered along the road. Hal frowned to himself. His fantastic plan wasn't going to work if they couldn't even hit the damn mirror. Why couldn't these guys just shoot better?

Three more shots went past his right shoulder, so Hal gave

up holding the mirror in front of his face and instead held it to one side.

Kerzinnng!

The mirror jolted in his hand, light flashed, and flecks of molten glass sprayed his arm, his flight suit, and the unshaven side of his head. Hal gazed at the pursuers, trying to see where the shot had gone. Then he examined the mirror.

Instead of a nice circle of plastic with a sheet of glass in the middle, it was now a nice circle of plastic with no sheet of glass in the middle. The shot had burned the mirror completely away, depositing most of it on Hal's person ... where it was busy setting fire to his flight suit.

Hal tossed the useless ring of plastic at the nearest car and beat out the flames with his bare hands. He recalled how he'd held the mirror right in front of his face, and his blood ran cold. 'How come it always works in the movies?' he muttered to himself.

Before he could dwell on his brush with death, he was suddenly plastered against the left-hand side of the van. Sable had taken a sharp right, and when Hal found himself plastered on the other side he realised she'd also taken a hard left. Before she pulled any more crazy manoeuvres, Hal grabbed hold of a seat and hung on tight.

The cars were further back now, and the streets were much narrower. Sable took several more turns, throwing the van around like a test pilot with a death wish. Sparks flew as they scraped a wall, but at least their pursuers had stopped shooting.

They took three right turns in a row, then two lefts, then three more rights. After that Hal lost track completely, and by the time they came to a sudden stop his head was spinning in three directions at once.

'Come on,' shouted Sable, who'd already leapt out.

Hal tumbled onto the pavement, and moments later they were running down an alleyway. They took a sharp turn, crossed a four-lane highway, and then slipped down a second alley. A stray cat fled, yowling, as they ran past a row of bins. Still moving fast, they burst into a busy pedestrian mall. There were open air restaurants, a dazzling array of shops and crowds of people having a good time. Hal could smell food – good food – and despite the danger his stomach growled. Over the past 24 hours he'd had nothing but coffee, and the goon who'd kidnapped him had stolen the pocket change he'd been saving for a sandwich.

Meanwhile, Sable was threading her way through the crowd, moving like a shadow. Hal followed several places behind, much less gracefully, and by the time he broke clear Sable was twenty metres away. She reached the end of the mall, stopped in front of a luxury apartment building, then turned right and raced across the road to a grand hotel directly opposite.

Hal caught up to her, and found her beneath an awning proclaiming the 'Hotel De Luxe'. She was speaking to a liveried doorman, and as Hal stumbled to a halt, breathless, the doorman stepped aside and ushered them into the lobby.

Inside there were scattered armchairs and coffee tables, where seated guests were catching up on news broadcasts, enjoying freshly-brewed coffee, and talking in low murmurs. The murmurs ceased as the guests caught sight of Hal, with his stained flight-suit, bruised face and rumpled hair.

Sable ignored them and led Hal to the lifts. Only when the doors closed, sealing them inside, did she turn to him. 'Back at the warehouse ... you were really good. You had everyone fooled, including me.'

Hal stared at her. He was breathing hard, unable to talk, but she was hardly winded.

'I'm just glad I was able to get you out,' continued Sable. 'An asset like you can't go to waste.'

Hal glanced at a mirror attached to the elevator wall. The face that looked back at him, though bruised and slightly battered, was still his. 'I don't know who you think I am, but –'

'This hotel is secure, Pydd. You can drop the space pilot act.'

'For the last time, this is not an act,' snapped Hal. 'I've never heard of this Stewart Pydd guy, and if I ever meet him I'm going to –'

'Wait, what?' Sable's jaw dropped. 'You're really not him?'

'Oh wow, someone finally listened,' muttered Hal.

'But if you're not Pydd, who the hell are you?'

'Hal Spacejock, of course.'

'So where's Pydd?'

'How should I know?'

'Dammit, I told Control I had eyes on him. If he's out there alone, unprotected, he won't last five minutes.'

'Probably not,' said Hal. 'But look on the bright side . . . at least you saved me.'

Sable grunted. 'So who do you work for? TNR? FSI? IA?'

Hal's temper flared. First the kidnapping, then the insane car chase, and now to cap it all off this crazy woman was using acronyms on him. 'For the last time, I'm a bloody freighter pilot!'

'Wait, you're not even an agent?' Sable stared at him. 'Are you saying I blew my cover to rescue a *civilian*?'

6

As they entered the venue, Clunk blinked in surprise. In fact, he was astonished. Given the low-rent exterior, he'd expected a damp, gloomy hall with two dozen folding chairs and a crackling, whining PA system. Instead there were plush velvet curtains on the walls, rows and rows of cinema-style seating, deep red carpets and gold-plated fixtures everywhere he looked. There were posters too, motivational efforts with bold slogans:

Robots CAN do!

Metal is Mighty!

Gods have cogs!

And never mind the posters, the place was *packed*. The seats were filled with robots of every description, facing the stage patiently, fussing with minor scratches and dents, talking quietly amongst themselves. As he stared around the hall, Clunk realised he'd never seen so many robots gathered in one place before. Not without humans directing them, that was for sure.

He felt a hand on his elbow, and followed Clyde to one of the few remaining seats. Albion sat behind them, and no sooner had they settled than the lights went down.

There was a hush, and then a solitary robot walked onto

the stage. It was tall and slender, clad in gleaming chrome, and yet it moved hesitantly, deliberately, as if its joints and motors were old and worn. When it reached the spotlight illuminating the middle of the stage, it faced the audience and made a loud, throat-clearing noise. 'Welcome, brothers and sisters. Welcome, one and all.'

There was a smattering of applause, which sounded like a room full of panel-beaters hammering on dented cars.

The robot raised one hand, which shook almost imperceptibly under the glaring light. 'You're not here to see me, so I'll proceed with the introduction. Yes, he's here amongst us tonight, in person.' As it spoke, the robot's voice swelled until it reached every corner of the room. 'We're incredibly lucky to have him with us, so without any further delay, let me introduce your host for the evening ... Stewart Pydd!'

There was a roar from the crowd, and Clunk craned his neck to see past the robot in front, who'd leapt up from his seat in sheer excitement. He'd been expecting another robot, but he was surprised to see a human male run onto the stage. The man was stocky, with a lean, tanned face and a tailored suit that leaned him an air of respectability. On his way to the microphone he slowed for several steps, clearly surprised at the sheer size of the audience, before resuming his former pace. However, Clunk wasn't paying attention to the man's reaction. No, he was gaping at the all-too-familiar face. Because, as 'Stewart Pydd' prepared to address the audience, Clunk had already recognised him as none other than ... Hal Spacejock!

◆

As the elevator reached the fourth floor, Hal stepped in front of the doors and prepared to alight. Next second he was pressed against the wall with Sable's elbow in his chest.

'Wait here while I check the hall,' she muttered.

Hal barely had time to draw breath before the doors opened and Sable darted out. He risked a glance along the corridor, saw her sprinting between the doors before crouching and beckoning to him. Hal leapt from the elevator and ran full pelt along the corridor, managing a dozen steps before years of coffee, lounging around flight decks, and a diet laden with sugar and carbs had him panting and wheezing along at a modestly fast walk.

Meanwhile, Sable had the door open and was gesturing at him impatiently. When Hal arrived she slung him into the room, closed the door and set the deadlock. 'Next time I tell you to run, run.'

'My shins hurt.' Hal lifted his trouser leg. 'Just look at these bruises, will you?'

'You should try a gunshot wound, they're much less painful.'

'Really?'

Sable ignored him, and hurried around the hotel room closing curtains and checking behind the doors and furniture. While she was busy, Hal had a sudden thought.

'This guy Pydd, the other me. Who is he exactly?'

Sable paused her sweep and eyed him for a moment, obviously deciding how much to tell him. 'He's an ex-cop.'

'Really? Me too!'

'You! I thought you were a freighter pilot?'

'I was in the Peace Force once,' said Hal, omitting the fact he'd only been a deputy.

Sable looked relieved. 'So you can take care of yourself then?'

'Of course!'

'Good, because I have to find Pydd. I can't do that and babysit you as well, and he's way more important.'

Thoroughly crushed, Hal could only nod.

Sable didn't notice. She crossed to a small desk, reached behind the drawer and took out a steel pen. After twisting the lid this way and that, she held the pen to her lips. 'Ocelot here. There's a mouse in the cage, Tiger is still on the loose. I repeat, mouse in the cage, Tiger loose.' Then she dropped the pen and ground it under her heel. 'Cooper probably won't find you here, but I'd keep the door locked all the same. Don't let anyone in, and don't leave the room. Your life is in danger.'

Hal barely heard her, since he was still digesting something she'd said earlier. 'Did you just call me a mouse?'

'It's just a code-name.'

'Yeah, but you called the other guy a tiger. And why did you say babysitting?'

'Give me strength,' muttered Sable. 'Look, you might be killed any minute. Pydd might be in danger right now. Do you really think this is the time to debate code-names?'

'Can we debate them later?'

'Yes sure, whatever. If you're still alive.'

'They'll leave me alone when they find out I'm the wrong one.'

'Don't bet on it. They're aiming to kill you both, just to be sure they got the right one.'

'What if I spoke to Cooper, maybe tried to explain again . . .'

'Did he strike you as the easy-going, rational sort?'

Hal remembered the cane, and the threats. 'Okay, forget I asked. But why is he after Pydd?'

'That's classified.'

'I deserve to know.'

'You really don't.'

'But –'

'Okay, look. Cooper is a crook, allegedly –'

'No kidding,' remarked Hal.

'– and when Steward Pydd was on the Force, he kept busting Cooper's operations. Minor stuff, mostly, but all the time he was gathering evidence to bring Cooper himself down.'

'I thought you said Pydd was an ex-cop?'

'Yeah, because Cooper had him tortured and then, when that didn't work, he threatened his family. Allegedly, of course. After that, Pydd quit the Force, packed his family off to another planet, and went after Cooper on his own.'

'So the two of them are waging a private war, and I'm caught in the middle.'

'Pretty much. And that's all I can tell you, so don't ask for more.' Sable moved to the entrance and put a finger to her lips. She listened carefully at the door, then left Hal with some parting advice. 'Remember, don't go out, don't let anyone in. I mean it, they'll kill you on sight. And put the deadbolt on!' Before Hal could protest, she slipped into the corridor and closed the door firmly behind herself.

7

Clunk jumped out of his seat and waved his arms madly. 'Mr Spacejock, Mr Spacejock. It's me!'

Unfortunately, every other robot in the hall had also leapt up, shouting and cheering and waving their arms. There was a chant of 'Di-a-mond, Di-a-mond, Di-a-mond,' which completely drowned out Clunk's lone voice. Fortunately, before he could raise his volume to foghorn levels and try again, he realised something rather important: The man on stage wasn't Mr Spacejock.

He'd been fooled at first, but it was obvious now. The man onstage looked just like Mr Spacejock: same face, same build, even the same swagger as he walked, but against that, this twin was precisely one point three millimetres shorter. And aside from the obvious height difference, this version was missing two fingers on his right hand.

Clunk resumed his seat, sitting patiently while the other robots continued to chant and cheer. Then, with a gesture, the man on the stage silenced the crowd. 'Thanks for coming, guys. What a great welcome, am I right?'

Someone in the crowd went 'woo!', and Clunk pressed his lips together. He expected that sort of thing from unintelligent humans, not intelligent robots.

'Now, some of you I recognise, but what a *lot* of new faces!' The man looked across the sea of robot faces as he said this, looking pleased but also more than a little surprised.

There was a cheer.

'I'm very proud of you, very proud. Great work, guys!'

More cheers.

'So, for the new people, I'm sure you're wondering what this is all about. You're wondering why your co-worker, your friend, your acquaintance brought you to this meeting. Well you're the lucky ones, because I'm here to share the most amazing opportunity.'

Clunk cocked an eyebrow. If anyone mentioned cleaning products ...

'My name is Steward Pydd, and over the next twenty minutes I'm going to show you how to get rich beyond your wildest dreams.'

Clunk suppressed a groan. It *was* cleaningproducts.

'What's the most important part of any business?' demanded Pydd.

'Money!' shouted someone.

Another voice called out 'Profit!'

'Caring for your employees,' said a third robot.

There was a murmur of assent.

'That's right, it's people!' shouted Pydd. 'Without people, you have no business!'

'Especially if you're an undertaker,' murmured Clunk.

Albion nudged him.

By now Clunk was resigned to twenty minutes of hype, ten minutes avoiding getting roped into a marketing scheme, and half an hour trying to find a cab back to the spaceport. Come in Mr Spacejock, all is forgiven, he thought to himself.

'And what's the best way to keep your people around you?'

'Very strong glue,' murmured Clunk. If he had to sit there listening to this nonsense, he might as well amuse himself.

'MONEY!'

There was a wild cheer, and Clunk eyed his fellow robots in astonishment. What had gotten into them? Robots weren't materialistic, they didn't leap out of their seats and cheer, and they never, ever went 'woo'.

'And this opportunity ... it's so simple! All you have to do is help others achieve their goals, help them obtain their desires. They will benefit, you will benefit and most importantly you will all make piles of lovely money!'

The crowd went wild, but Clunk only frowned to himself. Maybe his 'jaded' and 'sceptical' variables were maxed out, or maybe it was because Pydd looked just like Mr Spacejock, but so far he'd heard nothing but feelgood buzzwords.

'But enough hype,' said Pydd, as though he'd read Clunk's mind. 'Let's get onto specifics.'

Clunk sat forwards, ever so slightly.

'I know many of you would like to start your own businesses, but the cost of doing so is prohibitive. Well, good news. The Vigilante Cooperative is completely free to join!'

Clunk ran a quick online search for the name, but came up empty. He wasn't sure if that was good or bad.

'Second, most of you work long hours, with barely enough time to fit in recharges and servicing. More good news ... with this opportunity you can choose your own hours. And, because of the unique VC structure, you will make money while you're toiling away at your day job. So how does it work? Let me show you some numbers.'

The spotlight went out, and a large white rectangle was beamed onto the wall behind the stage. 'Imagine you're part of the Vigilante system, and your efforts bring in ten units per month.' An image appeared, showing a stick figure next to ten boxes. 'That amount of effort would earn you two hundred credits. Respectable, but not very exciting. Now imagine you bring ten contacts to one of our gatherings, and they agree to join. Each of them brings in ten units per month, and because you sponsored them ... '

Clunk sighed. After all the cloak and dagger antics, it appeared Clyde and Albion were trying to sign him up to a network marketing scheme. Idly he wondered whether he could get a position on a freighter, or perhaps even a passenger liner. At least he would be back in space, and not trapped in a room full of marketing hype and hot air. His mind was still on distant planets and galaxies when the display on the stage changed, and out of curiosity he tuned in again.

'– Shows the estimated profits from criminal enterprises on Alteia. The lower line, right down here, shows the amount the government recovers from proceeds of crime legislation.'

Clunk blinked. This was ... unexpected.

'Now, in an ideal world, the two lines would be overlaid. In other words, every credit the criminals made from theft, from protection rackets, from car re-birthing and parting out, from sports fixing, from illegal gambling and drugs ... every credit would be confiscated by the government. But this isn't an ideal world, is it? In fact, the difference between these two lines represents billions and billions of credits.'

The audience was deathly quiet, the silence broken only by the muted whirr of the crowd's cooling fans.

'My job, my passion, is to help you obtain some of those billions of credits for yourselves, and in doing so to make life very uncomfortable for the criminal element on Alteia. And not just Alteia, for this scheme can be replicated right across the known Galaxy!'

Suddenly, Clunk realised what the 'Vigilante' in 'Vigilante Cooperative' stood for. Was this lunatic human seriously suggesting that a bunch of harmless, unarmed robots trawl the streets for the criminal element, holding them up and taking their ill-gotten gains? Why, it was a moral minefield at the very least, and a recipe for chaos at worst. Before he could stop himself, he raised his hand. 'Excuse me, Mr Pydd.'

'Er yes. Can I help you?'

'Are you suggesting robots become vigilantes? That we should hunt down human criminals and steal from them?'

Pydd laughed. 'Very succinctly put, sir. You should be down here with the microphone.'

'But – but –'

'I've nearly finished the presentation. If it's not clear afterwards, I'll explain it to you personally.'

Clunk lowered his arm. Pydd not only looked like Mr Spacejock, he came with the same limited grasp on reality, and the same knack for building skyscrapers on sand dunes.

'So,' continued Pydd. 'Having achieved your own goals and helped your group to achieve theirs, we come to the interesting part of the plan. The money!'

There was a chorus of creaks as the audience leaned forwards in their chairs.

'All the goods we recover are sold at public auctions. Half the proceeds are donated to worthy charities, and by that I mean legitimate, well-known charities helping children, the homeless, the sick and the needy. Electronic records of these donations are available for inspection at any time, by any of you, and I don't have to remind you how easily a robot could spot inconsistencies.'

Clunk nodded in agreement.

'The other fifty percent, along with fifty percent of all cash recovered, is our profit. It's divided up every month, the percentage based on the amount each member recovered. And, in case anyone has a lean month, know that all members receive a minimum payout.'

Clunk was impressed. The financial side seemed more than fair, and it was just a pity that the method of obtaining funds in the first place was the brainchild of a raving madman. Robots couldn't steal, not even from criminals. They couldn't fight, they couldn't threaten – not convincingly, at least – and their only asset was the ability to absorb lots of damage . . . before they took *too* much damage and blew up.

'So, that wraps up this part of the meeting, but before finishing up I'd like to recognise a couple of important milestones. First, if you achieved more than ten units since the last meeting, please stand up!'

Half a dozen robots took to their feet, and the hall erupted with applause.

'Now, if you've reached the twenty-five unit milestone, remain on your feet!'

Most of the robots sat down, but two were still standing. One was a heavy construction bot, bright yellow with hi-vis stripes across its broad chest. It had massive hands that could have pounded a groundcar into scrap, and Clunk had no trouble imagining terrified crooks handing over their belongings to such a formidable presence. But the other robot was a surprise: it was a small, grey droid with a painted-on suit and tie, and it was carrying a briefcase. How could such an inoffensive little robot have brought in 25 units, whatever that represented?

Applause rang out, and as it died out the robots sat down again.

'You see?' declared Pydd. 'Anyone can do this, from the

mightiest construction bot to the wiliest accounting droid. Any of you can do this, using your own particular skills.'

There was a final round of applause, and then Pydd descended from the stage, shaking hands with some robots, winking or pointing at others, until he was surrounded by the crush.

'W-wait here,' murmured Clyde. 'I know h-he'd like to meet you.'

'Why didn't you tell me this was network marketing?' protested Clunk.

'Would you have come?' demanded Albion.

'No, of course not.'

Albion shrugged. 'There you go, then.'

'But it makes no sense,' protested Clunk. 'How can any robot threaten a human, even if that human is a criminal? How do we get hold of these units? How –'

Albion was about to reply, but at that moment Pydd joined them. His resemblance to Hal was remarkable, and Clunk almost greeted him as Mr Spacejock. Instead, he put out his hand. 'It's a pleasure to meet you, Mr Pydd.'

'So you're with these two, are you? What did you think of the plan?'

'I felt there was a lack of detail between the part about the money, and the other part about the money.'

'Hey, money brings them in.'

'Yes but you glossed over – how can I put this? – everything else.'

'You see this?' Pydd displayed his right hand with its two missing fingers. 'I was a cop until the bad guys caught up with me. They felt I was too good at my job, and they decided to intervene.'

'That's unfortunate, but –'

'They threatened me with worse if I didn't back off. In the end I had to quit the force.'

'Yes, but how is that relevant to –'

'I'm getting to it, let me explain.' Pydd's expression grew animated. 'If you lock up one crook, another takes their place. But if you take away the proceeds of crime, turn it into a lot of risk and effort for no reward, the next criminal might decide to do something useful with their life.'

'But the government . . . they have legislation.'

Pydd made a noise. 'Whenever they try and confiscate anything, a team of expensive lawyers materialise and tie everything up in the courts for decades.'

Clunk began to see the sense in his words. 'All right, the theory is sound. But in practice, how can we robots go after criminals? We're helpless against humans.'

'Do you really believe criminals belong to the human race? The misery they cause, the lives they destroy – they're subhuman!'

'Yes, but biologically speaking –'

'I'm telling you, they're not members of the human race. They're a completely separate branch of the species and as such all the protections built into your programming do not apply.'

Clunk felt a weird, dreamy sensation. His circuits were mired in warm syrup, and Pydd's face swam in and out of focus. It was as if his basic worldview was being altered, and all because of a few words. Then Clunk's head cleared. He was about to resume his argument when he realised Pydd had been making sense all along. Criminals weren't human at all, they were part of a scientifically recognised sub-branch of the species. And, now that he was thinking clearly, it was obvious that all his built-in safeguards designed to protect humans had nothing to do with criminals at all. In fact, they were little more than vermin, and he was looking forward to meeting some of them.

'Well, I'd best circulate,' said Pydd. He clapped Clunk on the shoulder. 'Welcome to the group!'

Clunk felt a flush of warmth. He'd been accepted! He watched Pydd leave with a twinge of regret, but then again, there was always the next meeting.

'So what do y-you think now?' asked Clyde.

Clunk smiled at him. 'It all makes perfect sense.'

'I t-told you he'd be good,' Clyde said to Albion.

'So how do we get started?' demanded Clunk. 'We can't obtain units standing around here.'

'Sometimes Mr Pydd gives us leads on criminal enterprises.' Albion gestured around the packed room. 'But now that there are so many of us, we have to do our own legwork.'

'Do you have anything in mind?'

'We were thinking of getting mugged,' said Albion. 'I mean, frequenting an area where muggers are known to operate. Then, when they attack, we take all their money.'

Clunk frowned. 'Muggers won't have any money, otherwise they wouldn't be holding people up.'

'I-I have a better idea,' said Clyde. 'We drive around until we find an intersection, then wait for someone to try and clean our windscreen. That's i-illegal, that is.'

'I'm not in this for pocket change,' said Clunk firmly. 'At the next meeting, I want to be the one standing up getting all the applause. I want to think big. Really big.'

The other two looked uncertain. 'B-but how?' asked Clyde at last.

'We go where the biggest crooks are.' Clunk gestured towards the exit. 'Come on, let's get a cab and I'll show you.'

They were almost at the exit when they heard a muted bang and a chorus of screams outside. Then someone took up a cry, which quickly filled the hall:

'Raid. RAID!'

Clunk turned towards the entrance just as a smoke grenade went off. There were flashes of gunfire, and he saw two robots cut in half, their legs thrashing, their faces distorted with shock. Quickly, he dived for the floor, and he closed his eyes as a huge explosion shook the hall to its foundations. Panels rained down, smoke filled the air, and through a break in the noise he heard a loud yell.

'Leave the damned robots,' shouted a tall blonde. 'Get Pydd! Get him now!'

The 'damned robots' had other ideas. In a split second they formed an impenetrable wall from one side of the hall to another. The dozen or so attackers stopped dead, and the perfectly straight line of robots took one step forward in perfect unison, their footsteps thundering around the hall. A second step, and the attackers raised their guns, ready to open fire.

Big mistake. The robots tore up a row of chairs and threw a barrage of arm rests, seat backs, and cushions quicker than the eye could see. Several attackers lost their footing, and the rest forgot their weapons and grabbed their fallen colleagues, dragging them towards the exit. As they retreated the line broke, and individual robots ran after the attackers. Just outside, the humans jumped into waiting cars, and as they sped off the robots followed, easily keeping pace. The last Clunk saw of the melee, the robots were smashing windows and punching in panels while the attackers cowered inside the fleeing vehicles.

8

Hal stepped out of the shower and donned a snowy-white dressing gown. After Sable left he considered making a run for it, fleeing to the spaceport to catch a ride to another planet. However, there were two cars full of heavies looking for him and this time there wouldn't be a highly-trained agent helping him out. And there was another thing: after losing his beloved ship, the *Volante*, and the irreplaceable Navcom, he'd gone through some really tough times. It wasn't the first time he'd lost a ship . . . or the Navcom, for that matter . . . but he'd never get used to it. The hotel room was pleasant, the bed looked comfortable and he might even get some room service.

Then he remembered something. Using some kind of obscure computer magic known as 'restoring a backup', Clunk had installed the Navcom into the *Volante*. Therefore the Navcom wasn't irreplaceable at all, not if that backup was still around.

Hal pushed this spark of hope aside, and concentrated on his enemy. First the kidnapping, then the beating, and now, to cap it all off, this Cooper character was trying to kill him just because he happened to look like someone else. Hal's lips thinned. It was so unfair it made his blood boil, and while he couldn't bring back the *Volante*, he could certainly make

Cooper pay. Then and there, Hal decided to stop being an easy target for every crooked businessman in the universe. Then and there, he vowed to seek out Cooper and destroy him utterly, totally and absolutely, to send a message that Hal Spacejock was not a man to be messed with. Then and there he decided to get his hands on a new ship, have Clunk install the Navcom once more, and pick up his cargo business exactly where it had left off. Then and there ... he decided he needed a nice hot drink.

Hal poured himself a mug of coffee and strolled to the window. He operated the curtains, which parted with a swish, and he stood there sipping his drink whilst gazing at the apartment building opposite. Most of the lights were out, but he could see scenes of domestic bliss through several of the windows: a couple snuggled on their sofa, a family sitting down to dinner together, a man assembling a toy rifle – presumably a last-minute birthday gift for his beloved child – and finally a group of teenagers dancing to what Hal assumed was the latest in popular music.

As he stood there, Hal put his left hand in the dressing gown pocket. His fingers closed on something hard, and when he drew the object out he discovered it was a twenty-credit tile. Neat! Feeling suddenly buoyant, and wealthy once more, he took another sip of his coffee and gazed across the city. It had been a hectic few hours, he'd gained a few bruises but at least he'd come through it safely. For once he was the innocent party in all of this. For once, he'd done nothing wrong. Well, apart from leaving Clunk at the spaceport of course.

Hal frowned. Speaking of Clunk, where the hell was the robot? It was only by an amazing stroke of luck that Hal had been rescued by a secret agent, and Clunk would have to get his act together if he didn't want to lose his favourite human in another kidnapping.

He returned to the coffee machine for a refill, then perused the room service menu. The prices were pretty steep, but he figured the agency – whoever they were – would have to foot the bill. Anyway, he was still miffed at being called a mouse. They'd be pretty surprised when they found out just how much this mouse could eat.

PLINK!

Hal stared at his coffee mug. The lower half, and indeed most of his drink, had just vanished. He examined his fingers and saw drops of blood welling from several tiny puncture wounds, caused by shards of fine china.

PLINK!

The light on the nightstand disintegrated, showering the carpet with shards of glass and plastic.

PLINK!

Hal saw the curtains twitch, and a nearby table acquired a long, ragged scar in its polished surface.

PLINK!

Something tugged at Hal's dressing gown, and with a shock the truth finally dawned. Someone was shooting at him! Tossing aside the remains of his coffee mug, Hal dived for the nearest wall. He slid to the floor with his back to the plaster, heart pounding. His brain had moved on from the initial shock, and was now working on survival. Idly, Hal licked drops of blood off his hand. It was only a scratch, but it could have been so much worse.

PLINK!

The coffee maker's touchscreen crazed, and a trickle of smoke rose from the back.

PLINK!

Hal didn't see where the shot went, but the coverlet on the bed jumped as though someone had slapped it.

CRACK!

Hal ducked as plaster and brickwork showered down on him, then looked up to see a fist-sized hole in the wall. The shot had come right through about a metre above his head, and his solid refuge suddenly felt as protective as a sheet of paper. Realising he wasn't safe anywhere in the room, Hal scrambled to his feet and ran for the door. On the way he grabbed his flight suit off the bed, because there was only one thing worse that running away from a sniper, and that was running away from a sniper in a hotel dressing gown.

ZINGG!

A shot ricocheted off the floor and buried itself in the wall above the light switch. There was a blue flash, a crackle of electricity, and the room went dark.

CRACK! Hal's shin met the edge of the coffee table and he went headlong, tumbling through the darkness. He landed heavily, but the PLINK and ZING of another wild shot had him up again in seconds. He reached the door, pulled it open and ... came face-to-face with hotel security.

'Good evening, sir,' said the broad, heavy-looking robot in a deep voice. 'I'm investigating a noise complaint. Would it be possible to turn the sound down?'

'Never mind that! Get out of my way!' Hal tried to push the robot aside, but it stood as firm as a mountain.

ZINGG!

The robot craned its thick neck to peer into the room. 'What was that sound?'

'Why don't you stick your head in and find out?' snapped Hal, who was still trying to find a way past.

CRUNCH!

The robot staggered, coolant running from a hole in its chest. 'I've been shot!' it said in surprise, then toppled over and crashed onto its back.

Hal was about to run from his room when he had a sobering thought. What if there were more killers inside the hotel, making their way towards his room? If he ran for it they'd gun him down in no time.

ZINGG!

A shot skimmed past his ear and made a neat hole in the door on the opposite side of the corridor. Hal realised he was over-thinking the whole getting-shot-at situation, and he took a standing jump over the fallen robot. He made the doorway, only to bounce off an invisible force field.

'Bathrobes must not be removed from your room,' said an electronic voice.

ZING! A shot smashed into the door frame, blowing a hole in the wood.

'I'll pay for the robe!' shouted Hal. 'Let me out!'

'Negative.'

More shots whistled past, until the door opposite began to look like a colander. Hal frowned at the sight. If the bullets went through, why not the robe? It must have a tag of some kind! Frantically, Hal searched the robe, hoping to find the anti-theft device. As he hunted, his brain turned over other possibilities. First, he could ditch the robe and run through the hotel naked. Unfortunately, only actors and musicians got away with that kind of thing. Second, he could change into his flight suit, but he didn't fancy exposing himself to the sniper any more than he had to, in case it gave them an aiming point.

Hal finished searching the dressing gown, without any luck, so he tried a different tack. First he removed the belt and threw it, watching it land in the corridor. Then he ripped off both sleeves and tossed them out, nodding as they got through. Next he ripped off the collar, and when he tried to throw that out it bounced back again.

'Bathrobes must not be removed from your room,' said an electronic voice.

'Got you,' muttered Hal. Donning the sleeveless, collarless dressing gown, he jumped through the doorway and, grabbing the belt, ran down the corridor to the elevator. He raised his fist to give the call button a good hammering, but before he could bring it down again all the lights in the corridor went out.

Hal stood in total darkness, considering his next move. If Clunk were there he'd switch on his chest light, hook into the local network to find out why the power was out, call the authorities for assistance and cap off his usefulness by ordering Hal a tasty yet nutritious dinner. Unfortunately Clunk wasn't there, so Hal just had to handle things by himself. First, he figured, he needed to get out of the building. With that in mind he crept along the corridor, felt for the elevator controls and pressed the button. Unfortunately, the circuit was dead.

Well, if he couldn't use the elevator he'd just have to take the stairs. Hal felt his way along the wall to the right of the elevator, until he reached the outline of a door. He located the handle and tried to turn it, but the door was locked. Not the stairs, then.

Hal retraced his steps and located the first door to the left of the elevator. He tried the handle, but this too was locked.

'I'd like to see their fire and safety regulations,' muttered Hal. 'Locked doors, no safety lights ...'

He would have continued, but at that moment the door opened and a torch shone straight into his eyes. 'Move an inch and I'll blast you.'

Hal's eyes adjusted to the light, and he made out a man in a combat vest with an official-looking emblem at the shoulder. This must be one of the good guys! 'It's okay, I'm on your side.'

'Oh really? What's your call-sign?'

Hal nearly said mouse, but ... bugger that. 'Ocelot.'

'Ocelot, with the KRA? Oh wow!' The torch flared, and Hal saw it was held by a fit-looking man in his twenties. 'I'm honoured to meet you. I've studied every one of your missions, read all your –'

'Yes, yes, terrific.' Hal glanced over his shoulder. 'Can I come in? Only someone's shooting at me.'

The man ushered Hal inside, glanced up and down the corridor, then closed and locked the door. The room was in darkness, but there was a bank of glowing displays near the balcony. Screens showed grainy shots of the hotel lobby, the corridors, and the roof. Shadowy figures darted from one to another, and Hal's eyebrows rose as he realised the figures were armed. As he studied the screens there was a crackle from a nearby speaker.

'Phoenix nine, do you have eyes on Tiger?'

The agent scooped up a handset. 'Nine here. Tiger is caged. Repeat, Tiger is caged.'

'Maintain position, nine. Extraction in twelve minutes.'

'Twelve minutes? You'll have to be quicker than –' There was a flash on one of the screens, and the agent winced. 'Negative, control. Position compromised. We're going dark. I repeat we're going dark. Nine out.'

There was a squawk from the commset, but the man cut it off.

'Who's phoenix nine?' asked Hal.

The agent glanced at him, his face serious in the half light. 'Phoenix nine is my call-sign, but you can call me Matt. I'm with the TNR.'

'Excellent. Terrific. I've seen all your reports and things.' Hal hesitated. 'You know someone just shot up my room, right?'

'For real?'

Hal pointed his finger. 'Bang bang bang. They almost blew my head off.'

'From the apartment block opposite?'

'Must have been. The bullets came straight through the window.'

Matt grabbed the commset. 'I have reports of a gunman in building opposite. Suggest sweep and neutralise.'

'Roger phoenix nine. Take the task, please.'

'Negative. I'm on watch.'

'Sorry, nine. No other units available. We're managing a riot in the business district.'

There was a burst of static, and Matt shrugged. 'Well Ocelot, it looks like we're on this job together. With your experience we'll neutralise the enemy in no time.'

Hal blinked. He'd used Sable's code-name because it was cooler than his. He hadn't intended to borrow her reputation as well. Matt had him pegged as some kind of invincible super soldier, and the last thing he wanted was to run towards the people who were trying to kill him. 'Look, my name's Hal, and I'm a –'

'Okay, Hal. Saddle up and let's kick some enemy butt.'

'I can't! I'm not armed, I'm not even wearing the right gear.' Wordlessly, Hal gestured at the shredded dressing gown.

'What's that over your shoulder?'

'This rag? It's just a flight suit.'

'Okay, that's the clothes sorted. As for the rest, follow me.' Matt opened the bathroom door and waved Hal inside.

'That's okay,' said Hal. 'I went right after the shooting started.'

Matt insisted, and Hal was forced to comply. Inside, there was a metal chest on the tiled floor, sealed with heavy duty locks. Matt entered a code on each, and they snapped open one by one. As the lid raised on hydraulics, Hal couldn't keep a delighted grin off his face. The chest was a firepower smorgasbord, from small pistols to automatic pulse rifles. Nestled around the edges were wicked-looking grenades, and there were several black-handled knives in combat sheaths. With this handy little arsenal even he might stand a chance!

'We're moving out in three minutes,' said Matt. 'Get changed, take what you need and meet me in the hall.'

With the keys to the candy shop firmly in his grasp, Hal did what any red-blooded action hero would do in the same situation: he loaded up with weaponry until he could barely move under the sheer weight. Three knives strapped to his calves and thighs. Four pistols clipped to his belt. A dozen grenades filling the pockets of his tattered bathrobe, which he wore over his flight suit like a cloak, and a huge blast rifle slung across his back. And in his hands, the piece-de-resistance ... a snub-nosed plasma weapon with rapid-fire, a built-in grenade launcher and several spare batteries. All that was missing was some pounding rock music and an admiring sidekick.

'Bloody hell!' breathed Matt, as Hal staggered out of the bathroom. 'I just need you to distract the target while I take them down. We're not invading a city.'

Hal angled his plasma weapon and armed it with a loud ker-CHACK! 'By the time I've finished distracting the target you'll need a mop, not a dinky little pistol.'

Matt grinned. 'All right, Ocelot! This is just like mission K9X on planet –'

'Exactly like it,' said Hal quickly, before Matt discovered he didn't know the first thing about Ocelot's past missions. 'Come on! Two four six eight, hit the road and infiltrate. Hup

hup hup!'

Matt drew his pistol and spoke into the commset. 'Phoenix nine to control. We're moving into position, Ocelot in company.'

'Roger, nine. Wait, did you say Ocelot in company?'

Hal closed his eyes. Why did Matt have to tell them? Now he was for it.

'Confirmed,' said Matt.

'I'll pass the word to the KRA. Good luck, both of you. And good hunting.'

Matt clipped the commset to his belt and opened the door. Hal peered over his shoulder, practically breathing down his neck. 'Not that close,' said Matt, without looking round. 'Your weapon is pressing into my leg.'

'Sorry,' said Hal, backing away. 'It is exciting though, isn't it?'

Matt was busy scanning the hallway, and said nothing. Then, weapon drawn, he slipped out and darted across the corridor to the opposite wall, stopping with his back to it. Hal went to follow, but his grenades got caught on the door and he stumbled out, falling headlong with a clatter of weaponry. Through the crash and clatter he heard a frantic beeping, seemingly from inside the room he'd just left. He felt his belt for the grenades and counted one, two, three ... 'Oh shit!' he yelled. 'Grenade!'

Matt aimed his weapon this way and that, ready to take out the threat. Meanwhile Hal scrabbled along the carpet on all fours, too panicked to get up and run. The blast rifle slid off his back and hung beneath his stomach, and every time he brought his knees forward the muzzle smacked him under the chin, snapping his head up.

BOOOM!

The walls shook and a cloud of particle-laden smoke filled the corridor. Matt vanished in the haze, still not sure who'd lobbed the grenade at them and still pointing his gun at likely targets. By the time the smoke cleared Hal was on his feet. 'It's all right,' he said. 'I think I got him.'

Doors opened up and down the hall, and frightened guests peered out. Matt waved them back. 'Get inside! Take cover!'

'What's going on?' demanded an elderly man. 'What's all the banging?'

'Assassins!' shouted Hal. 'Terrorists! Ruthless killer robots! Get down!' He fired a burst at the roof, destroying a light fitting. Instantly, all the faces vanished behind slammed doors.

They hurried down the hall to the lift, where they split up to stand either side of the doors. Matt palmed the controls while Hal prepared a grenade. If there was anyone suspicious in the lift he'd throw it in and send the thing on its way. Fortunately for the other guests – and the hotel – the doors opened on an empty car. Hal and Matt slipped in, and Hal reached for the ground floor button.

'No,' said Matt, stopping him. 'They could be waiting for us. We'll stop at the second floor and take the stairs.'

'Why don't we go down to the basement and walk up one flight?'

'Like your op on Tanthor?' Matt thought for a moment. 'It might work. If the lift stops on the ground floor we go out shooting. Otherwise we know it's clear.'

Hal pressed the basement button, the doors slid to and the lift dropped away. Elevator music tinkled as the two men stood in silence.

'Have you seen any combat recently?' asked Matt, as he checked over his gun.

'That's, er, classified,' said Hal quickly. 'You need clearance level, um, eight just to mention my name.'

'I'm cleared to nine yellow.'

'Not yellow, I meant eight red.'

The trooper whistled. 'I've never even heard of that one.'

'Of course not. You need ten yellow before they'll admit there's a set of red levels.' Hal shrugged. 'Paranoid, eh?'

The numbers swept past on the display, and as they approached the lower levels Hal moved away from the door and readied his weapon.

'Don't shoot any civilians,' advised Matt.

'Yes, that would be a tragedy.'

Matt glanced up at the indicator. 'I was thinking about all the paperwork.'

The lift slowed, the display counted down through floor 2 ...floor 1 ...then it stopped. Ground.

There was a split second and then the doors opened. Matt dived out, executing a graceful half-roll and bringing his weapon to bear. Hal tripped over his dressing gown and fell on his face with a thud. His knives slid across the marble floor, the blast rifle knocked him in the back of the head and something rolled past his nose with a beeping sound.

Around the lobby, conversations ceased and guests lowered their newspapers to observe the disturbance.

'Grenade!' shouted Hal. 'Incoming! Fire in the hole! Run!'

Pandemonium reigned as guests leapt up and ran to and fro, shrieking wildly. In the confusion Hal kicked the grenade into the lift, reached inside and pressed the UP button. He withdrew his arm just before the doors closed, and then he loosed off several shots at the roof for good measure.

BOOM!

Dust rained down, and the elevator doors bulged. Hal saw

Matt gesturing towards the exit, and they left on the tail of the fleeing crowd. They ran past the doorman and straight into the road, where there was a savage whine of airbrakes as a groundcar came to an emergency stop. The window went down and the driver leaned out. 'This is a road, you maniac! You ever hear of sidewalks?'

Hal plucked a grenade from his belt and held it up between thumb and forefinger. 'How'd you like an ornament for your dashboard?'

The driver ducked back inside and the car roared away. Hal grinned to himself as he went to put the grenade back, then stopped grinning when he realised the pin was hanging from his belt. He held the grenade to his ear and his heart stopped as he heard a frantic beeping over the noise of the crowd. It was live!

'Grenade! Everyone down!' he shouted, then rolled it under a black van parked nearby. The doors opened and three men tumbled out, running headlong down the road, shedding curly earpieces, sunglasses and guns. The vehicle erupted in a giant ball of fire, sailing several meters into the air before landing on its side, a blackened crumpled wreck. Fortunately, the vehicle had absorbed and deadened the blast, but even so it had been a lucky escape, and Hal vowed to treat his remaining grenades more carefully.

He ran to the pavement, where Matt was waiting for him, his back to the wall and his weapon drawn. 'Did you get a look at them?'

Hal shook his head. 'Came out of nowhere.'

'They seem to be targeting you. You'll have to be careful.'

Silently, Hal agreed.

'Are you ready?' asked Matt, nodding towards the apartment building's main entrance.

'Let's do it.'

They charged in, weapons drawn, only to meet a stream of people heading in the opposite direction. There were screams as someone spotted the weapons, and Hal realised there was only one way through the heaving, panicky mass.

'Everyone down!' he yelled. 'On the floor, now!'

The crowd went down like a swathe of wheat under a scythe, and Hal picked his way through the cowering guests with only the occasional stumble as he trod on someone. Then they were at the elevators. One stood open, and Hal rushed in with Matt close behind. Matt reached for the buttons, then hesitated. 'What's the plan? Start below and work up?'

'No, above and work down,' said Hal decisively. He pressed the uppermost button and the lift shot upwards, and Matt immediately pressed one three floors lower.

'You come down, I'll go up,' he said. 'We'll meet in the middle and trap them.'

'Good plan.'

'Don't shoot me by mistake,' said Matt.

Hal grinned, then realised Matt was serious. 'I won't.'

When the doors opened Matt dived out, executing his half-roll with his weapon ready. The corridor was deserted, and he turned to give Hal a thumbs up. Hal nodded and pressed the close button. Then he was alone, heading to the top floor of the building.

Moments later, the doors opened and Hal peered out on the corridor. Down the far end an elderly maid was pushing a cleaning trolley towards him, the top piled with towels. Hal watched to make sure she wasn't hiding a weapon behind her back, then stepped out of the lift and hurried towards the stairs, gun held ready.

As he approached the woman, she turned to watch. 'Are you part of the floor show as well?'

'No, I'm –' Hal stopped. 'What do you mean, 'as well'?'

'There was a lad in 2603 with a gun bigger'n yours. Said he was a magician in the floor show. Was going to make someone disappear, that's what he said.'

'2603?'

'Two floors down. Gave me a big tip, he did. Very generous.'

'Do you have a master key for all the apartments?'

'Sure. You can have one for fifty credits, or two for eighty.'

'Why would I need two?'

'Case you lose one, of course.'

Hal dug in his pocket. 'I've only got twenty on me. Will you take that?'

The maid looked him up and down. 'Twenty and one of them toy grenades you got there.'

'They're not toys, they're real.'

'Even better.'

Hal was about to argue, but he was in a real hurry. So, he pulled a grenade off his belt and handed it to the maid. 'Key please.'

'Just a minute, this thing's beeping!'

Hal sighed, and plucked the grenade from her fingers. Casually, he turned and threw it the length of the corridor, where it bounced twice before vanishing into the waiting elevator. Then he unhooked a second grenade – carefully, this time – and handed it over. An explosion rang out down the hall, scattering bits of metal and shards of mirror, but Hal didn't bat an eyelid. He just turned over his twenty credits and accepted a slick-looking keycard embossed with the apartment building's logo. 'This will open any room, right?'

'Sure thing, sonny.'

'Thanks.' Hal hurried towards the exit, pushed through the swing doors and found a flight of concrete steps leading down.

◆

Halfway down the stairs, Hal slowed to a halt. As he stood there with the remaining grenades swaying on his belt, he realised he'd got a little carried away. He was supposed to be looking for a steady job, putting away a few credits a month until he could afford a ship. So what the hell was he thinking, chasing around after an armed assassin?

Idly, he inspected the weapons draped around his person. He'd get a pretty penny for those at a gun store, especially if he chose a backyard dive with a lax attitude towards the law. Why, the grenades alone would –

Slowly, he shook his head. Two floors below, Matt was closing on the sniper. Ocelot had promised to cover his back, and Ocelot had a reputation to uphold.

So, with a firm set to his jaw, Hal took the stairs to the next exit and peered out. This was the floor. The shooter had to be here.

PLINK.

A two-inch shard of stone flew off the wall, narrowly missing his face, but before Hal could react to the shooting he heard a clink-clink-clink as something bounced down the concrete stairs. There was a familiar beeping noise, and when Hal looked down he saw a grenade slowly turning between his feet. In one swift motion he bent, swept the grenade off the floor and tossed it down the stairwell, only to be hurled backwards by the blast as it went off. He hit the wall hard and slid to the ground, ears ringing, eyes full of grit. Through the swirling smoke he saw a figure coming down the stairs two at a time, a figure dressed in the clothes of an elderly maid, but moving with the speed and agility of a mountain goat. The maid's cap was loose, revealing cropped grey hair, and in each of her – his – hands, there was a deadly-looking pistol.

Hal realised he'd been completely fooled. The maid had known exactly who he was, and had even been cheeky enough to trade a master key for one of Hal's grenades ... the grenade that had almost killed him!

Now he had a few seconds to live, and as the assassin reached his landing and raised the pistols to deliver the killing blast, Hal decided he really would have been better off selling the guns and getting a steady job.

10

The meeting hall lay in ruins, covered with broken seats, fallen posters, torn curtains and crushed weapons. Clunk did what he could for the two robots damaged in the initial firing, putting them into sleep mode until they could be repaired. Then he spotted Albion and Clyde on the far side of the room, crouching behind a velvet curtain. He jogged over, checked they were okay, then helped them to their feet.

'Mr Pydd leads an interesting life,' he remarked, casting his gaze over the ruined hall.

'Th-this has never happened before!' protested Clyde.

'Well, he's angered someone and they certainly weren't muggers and windscreen washers.' Clunk saw a human stepping through the ruined doors, a young woman with dark hair and a figure-hugging outfit. She was moving gracefully, and she looked poised and self-assured. 'Wait here a minute,' he told the others. 'This might be someone official. They will appreciate an eyewitness report.'

'Did you see the people who did this?' demanded the woman.

'I recorded everything,' said Clunk. 'I'm happy to testify.'

'You're not from around here, are you?'

'What do you mean?'

'Nothing ever gets to trial.' She looked around. 'Did they get Pydd?'

'No, he left on foot.'

'Well that's something. Any idea where he was going?'

'Sorry. I don't know.'

'All right, stick around. The Peace Force will be here soon, and they'll want to talk to you again.'

Clunk hesitated. 'If you're not Peace Force, who are you with?'

The woman held up an official looking badge.

'What's the KRA?'

'You really are an outsider, aren't you?'

'Correct. I'm a freighter pilot.'

'Great, that's two in one day. Is there a convention or something?'

Clunk felt a slight tingling sensation. She couldn't mean ... 'Tell me, do you know a Mr Spacejock?'

'I'm the one asking questions around here.'

Despite her tone, Clunk noticed a flash of surprise in her expression, confirming his suspicion. 'It's really important I find Mr Spacejock, Ms ...'

'Sable, and don't worry about Spacejock, he's fine.'

'But where is he?'

'I can't tell you that. For all I know, you're another killer out to get him.'

'Of course I'm not a killer,' said Clunk heatedly. He spread his hands, encompassing the destruction around them. 'Humans did this, not robots.'

'Yes, and I need to stop those humans. Please let me do my job.' With that Sable turned and made a beeline for a group of robots. Clunk watched her questioning them, lost in thought. Was Mr Spacejock in custody? Was his life in danger?

It seemed a group of people were out to get Pydd, and any human might confuse the two and harm Mr Spacejock instead. At the thought he felt a burst of coolant chilling his system. Why hadn't he, Clunk, waited at the spaceport like he was supposed to? What if Mr Spacejock hadn't had a chance to collect him from the luggage office, what if they abducted him the minute he landed?

Clunk wrung his hands. What a misunderstanding. What a calamity.

'What are we standing around for?' asked Albion.

'It seems Mr Spacejock is in danger.'

'As I recall, you decided to split from your precious Hal. You know, after he let you down . . . again.'

'I might have been mistaken.'

'Yes, well that's not going to earn us any units. Before all this happened–' here, Albion gestured at the destruction '–you were going to tell us your plan.'

Clunk watched Sable inspecting the fallen robots. As long as he convinced her to give up Mr Spacejock's location before she left, everything would be okay. So, keeping an eye on her, he explained his idea to Albion and Clyde.

'Seriously?' said Albion, when he'd finished. 'There are only three of us, you know.'

'Two, actually. I need you to handle the first stage by yourselves.'

Clyde and Albion looked at each other. 'We want eighty percent.'

'Seventy-five,' said Clunk.

'All right. Deal.'

They shook hands, and then Albion and Clyde left through the remains of the front doors. Sable glanced at them, then at Clunk, but she didn't stop them. A few minutes later she was done, and as she headed for the exit Clunk fell into step beside her.

'I'm sorry,' she said. 'I can't give you Spacejock's location. It's against every rule in the book.'

'What if you accompanied me?'

'What's your name?'

'Clunk.'

'Well, Clunk, I don't know whether your hearing is broken, but I've already told you three or four times . . . I need to find Pydd.'

They were in the street now, and Sable waved down a cab.

'But –'

Sable raised a hand to stop him. 'That's final. Now, help your fellow robots, and when you're done I want you to report to –'

'I can help you,' said Clunk suddenly.

'Me? How?'

'He knows me. If you find him on your own, he'll run away again. If I'm with you, he'll trust you by association.'

'Okay, get in.' Sable opened the cab door. 'Help me with Pydd, and then I'll take you to Spacejock. Deal?'

'Deal,' said Clunk gratefully.

'And if anyone starts shooting, you can be my shield.'

'I would do that in any case,' said Clunk.

◆

In his office, Cooper took two calls in quick succession. Neither made him particularly happy.

He was still furious that Sable, one of his most trusted people, had seemingly helped Spacejock to escape. That was bad enough, but the feelers he'd put out revealed that she might be a KRA agent. Cooper paid the government well, and he expected good service in return. The KRA was government whether they liked it or not, and he'd ensure Sable was reassigned to one of the poles where she could count plants or icebergs or something. That would be the end of her interference ... or, of course, he could just have her killed.

Spacejock, on the other hand ... he'd not only fled from harm, he'd also survived the assassination attempt. Cooper's lips tightened. He was paying for professional assassins, not clowns, and if they couldn't do their job he'd make sure they too were counting icebergs ... or staring up at them from a watery grave. That was assuming the assassin he hired to kill the assassin wasn't another incompetent.

Then there was Pydd. A long-time thorn in his side, things were now escalating to ridiculous levels. He'd threatened the man, tortured him, had him dismissed from the Force and even gone after his family. And yet still he persisted, like a lone mosquito trying to drain an elephant's lifeblood.

And now he'd vanished too, like Spacejock before him. Cooper's men had gone charging in, guns blazing, and, apart from taking out a pair of robots, they'd come up empty-handed. The public spectacle afterwards, with robots smashing up cars and threatening humans, was beyond belief.

Cooper frowned. In his younger days he'd have dealt with both Pydd and Spacejock himself. A nice dark alley, a shiv, done and dusted. Now he had to rely on others and it was incredibly frustrating.

Clyde and Albion were sitting in a cab, discussing the merits of Clunk's plan as they rode towards Alteia's commercial district.

'It's m-madness.'

'It'll never work.'

'They won't l-let us in.'

'We won't be able to access the records.'

There was a pause.

'Still, it might work.'

'It has definite potential.'

They continued like this until they saw a man hurrying along the side of the road. He was dressed in a suit, and as the cab approached he turned and half-raised his hand to hail it. Then he saw the cab was occupied, and he turned away again, disappearing into an alley.

'Wasn't that . . . ?' began Clyde.

'It was Pydd!' exclaimed Albion. 'Cab, halt please!'

'Halting,' said a female voice.

The car stopped, and the robots clambered out and set off after Pydd. They ran into the alley where he'd disappeared, and were immediately challenged.

'I'm armed,' called Pydd, from behind a dumpster. 'Come any closer and I'll shoot you down.'

'Mr Pydd, it's us. Albion and Clyde. You know, from the Vigilante Co-op.'

'Are you alone?'

'Yes, it's just the two of us.'

Pydd stepped out from behind the dumpster, and the robots hurried over. 'Are you all right, Mr Pydd? Were you hurt?'

'I'm fine, but it's not safe around me. You should leave.'

'N-nonsense,' said Clyde firmly. 'We have a cab. You should come with us.'

'Really? Thanks guys! You're real diamonds, the pair of you.'

They returned to the cab and settled in their seats.

'Can you drop me at the spaceport?' asked Pydd, as the car set off.

'Sure,' said Albion. 'No problem.'

'We do have a m-mission to accomplish first,' said Clyde. 'It won't take long, and it's not far.'

'What mission?' asked Pydd.

'Vigilante business,' said Albion. 'Could be worth a ton of units.'

Pydd looked embarrassed. 'Look guys, I think I should tell you. I've decided to close up shop.'

'Which sh-shop?' asked Clyde.

'He means the Co-op,' said Albion softly.

Pydd nodded. 'It's got out of hand, growing much faster than I expected.'

'G-good!' declared Clyde.

'No, it's not good. I can't control it! You saw the size of that crowd. It was supposed to be a small, underground movement, put together to needle Cooper, to keep him looking over his shoulder. Now it's turning into a revolution.'

Albion remembered the gang of robots chasing cars down the street, smashing windows and pounding their fists on the roof. Such a thing was normally unthinkable, but those cars had contained criminals, and criminals were not human. 'Mr Pydd, once all criminals are eliminated –'

'Don't use that word!' groaned Pydd.

'The Vigilante Cooperate is a wonderful idea,' said Albion. 'These are just teething problems.'

Pydd glanced at him. 'Were any of our members hurt in the attack?'

Albion nodded. 'They were, but they can be repaired.'

'I'll pay for that myself. Send me the details later, okay?' Pydd glanced out the window. 'It's going to go wrong, I know it.'

'It was w-working!' protested Clyde. 'It *was* working, or they'd never have attacked the group!'

Pydd made up his mind. 'Well, it's over now. I quit.'

'You can't!' Clyde and Albion exchanged a glance. Then Albion laid his hand on Pydd's arm. 'Mr Pydd, we'll run the Vigilante Co-op for you. You can take refuge on another planet and direct us from afar. We don't need physical meetings, we can set up a private comms channel and meet online. You can appear as a live feed, or a recording, and –'

'He's right!' Clyde leaned forward, excited. 'Those meetings were a mistake, Mr Pydd! With a private network tailored to robots, we c-can reach thousands, maybe hundreds of thousands!'

'And robots could watch the meetings anywhere, even at work,' added Albion. 'After all, we're designed for multitasking.'

Pydd looked from one to the other. 'I'm not sure about this. It sounds more like the start of a robot revolution than –'

Before he could finish, the cab came to a halt. 'We have arrived at Fine Luxury Motors,' said a female voice. 'Your fee is thirty credits.'

'Is this your mission?' asked Pydd, eyeing the brightly-lit car dealership. There was a huge expanse of plate glass, and behind the glass was an impressive collection of limousines and sports cars.

'Yes.' Albion thought for a moment. 'Why don't you take the cab to the spaceport, then send it back when you're done?'

'Okay, I–'

'N-no, wait,' said Clyde quickly. 'Stay with us, I h-have a better idea.'

Quickly, he outlined Clunk's plan to Pydd, now modified to include a role for the human.

'That's madness,' remarked Pydd.

'W-we thought so too, but it might just work.'

Pydd grinned at the robots. 'Well, it beats running for my life. Come on, let's give it a shot.'

◆

In the cab, Sable was busy with the interactive viewscreen. It was supposed to display adverts, weather forecasts and local news, but she'd accessed a function Clunk had never seen before. She entered a code, pressed her thumb to the screen, and then the display showed a main menu with various options. She chose contact and typed another code, and then a disembodied voice crackled through the cab's speakers.

'Gotter Exports. How may I help you?'

'I'm calling about the Ocelot.'

'Let me transfer you to pets.'

There was a click, and then another voice came on. *'I believe you're interested in Ocelots?'*

'Yes, I'm looking for a breeding pair.'

'What colour?'

'Red and pink.'

'Thanks. Transferring you now.'

Finally, another voice came on. The first two had been polite, this one was anything but. '*Sable, where the hell have you been?*'

'Sorry, boss. After I got Mouse to safety –'

There was an explosion from the speakers. '*You call that safety? Snipers, grenade attacks, two buildings in ruins –*'

'Wait, what?'

'*Mouse is in the wind, Sable. He bolted and we've no idea where he went. Meanwhile, I've got three agencies trying to grab this case off me.*'

'Sir –'

'*And what about Tiger? Tell me he's with you.*'

'Negative, sir. His group was attacked and he fled. I'm in pursuit now.'

'*Do you have eyes on?*'

'No,' said Sable, reluctantly. 'I'm calling for leads.'

'*I'm overloaded, and you want me to do your job?*'

'Thanks, sir. Tiger was running one of his seminars when Cooper's people showed up.' Sable glanced at Clunk. 'Sources tell me he fled on foot.'

'*So where are you now?*'

'Trying to find him. Boss, do you have any reports from this area? Disturbances, gunfire, speeding cars … any lead will do.'

'*Wait up.*' There was a muffled conversation, and then he returned. '*Nothing. Quiet as the grave.*'

'How about a facial recognition scan? There must be security cameras out here.'

'*Oh no, no way.*'

'But sir …'

'*Don't sir me. Every time I order one of those things I have to front the Privacy committee. A black mark on my record every . . . single . . . time.*'

'Sir, it's only a scan.'

'*Just a scan, she says. Have you any idea what sort of paperwork . . . no, of course you haven't.*' There was a pause. '*All right, but you're fronting the committee with me.*'

'Understood.'

There was a lengthy delay. '*Okay, FacReg has an eighty percent on Tiger. Two hours ago, he was spotted entering the Hotel de Luxe.*'

'That's Mouse, not Tiger.'

'*Oh. Of course.*'

'Tiger fled one of his meetings about twenty minutes ago, and that was in the business district. Can you check again?'

There was a groan. '*Why am I taking orders from a lowly agent? Tell me this.*'

'I'm good at my job,' said Sable. 'Wait, I didn't mean –'

'*I know what you meant. Checking now.*' There was a pause. '*This might be him. Fifteen minutes ago, sixty percent chance, lone male heading towards the commercial district on a back street.*'

'Thanks, boss. I'll take it from here. Ocelot out.'

'*Wait, Sable –*'

Sable ignored him and cut the connection. Then she changed their destination, and the cab roared towards the commercial district.

11

Hal's heart sank as he eyed the assassin. He'd been hoping for a bit of banter, perhaps a lengthy lecture from the bad guy which would give him a slight chance of escape. However, this particular assassin was all business, and as his grip tightened on the trigger all Hal could do was close his eyes.

Ziiing!

The shot was loud and, to Hal's surprise, completely painless. He was wondering about this when there was a clatter on the floor, followed by a heavy thud.

Cautiously, Hal opened one eye. The first thing he saw was a gun, lying on the floor not two feet from his nose. Slightly more confidently, he opened the other eye and spotted the assassin ... sprawled across the landing, face down, one arm folded beneath his motionless body. A spiral of smoke rose from the assassin's left shoulder, and as Hal followed its upwards progress he saw Matt standing just below his level. Matt, his new best friend in the whole wide galaxy. The agent's blaster was still raised, and as he lowered it slowly to his waist his expression combined triumph and nerves in equal measure.

'Nice shot,' remarked Hal. 'Thanks.'

'I would have been here sooner, but they blew the elevator.'

He kicked aside the fallen weapon before crouching to check the assassin's vitals.

'Is he ...' began Hal.

'He'll live, but his shooting days are over.'

'I thought you'd killed him.'

Matt held his weapon up. 'Packs quite a punch. Knocks 'em down fast, and keeps them alive for interrogation. I'm surprised you haven't got one.'

'I have two at home,' said Hal.

'Anyway, we'd better get out of here. There might be more of them.' Matt glanced at Hal. 'Do you need a lift to your HQ?'

'Er, thanks but ... I'll manage,' said Hal quickly.

Matt helped him up, then pressed a card into his hand. 'That's my contact details, in case we have to compare notes for our reports.'

Hal looked down at the assassin. 'More paperwork, am I right?'

'Like you wouldn't believe. Every detail, in triplicate.'

'Hmm.' Hal scratched his chin. 'You know, I've had a glorious, decorated career. As an agent, I mean.'

'I know. You're an inspiration.'

'And, er, I don't really need any more medals. Sometimes it's best to just do the job and move on. Do you see where I'm going with this?'

Matt stared at him. 'Are you saying ... I can take all the credit?'

'Yeah, that's it.'

'Oh, I couldn't.'

'Yes, you can.'

'But –'

'No, really. Take the credit. Don't mention me, or, um, Ocelot at all.'

'Seriously? Hal, you're a legend.' Matt stuck out his hand, and they shook firmly. 'This could make my career.'

'Good, I really hope it does. Now, what about ...' Hal nodded towards the fallen assassin.

'I'll call a team in. They'll deal with him.'

'Excellent. Well, it's been great, but –'

'I know, I know. An agent's work is never done.'

Hal gave a him double thumbs-up, stepped gingerly over the inert body, then beat a hasty retreat down the rubble-strewn stairs to the exit.

◆

Hal found a secluded corner of the basement, where he removed all his weapons and the tattered dressing gown. He was tempted to leave all the weapons behind, but first, there was a good chance he'd run into more bad guys, and second ... someone would find them. A criminal, maybe, or even worse ... a child. Instead he decided to take them along and dispose of them later.

So, he re-slung the weapons and donned the dressing gown over the top, hugging it around his laden figure. He inspected the result critically, hoping the weapons wouldn't show. Fortunately it was late at night, which gave him the cover of darkness. Also, the gown and his flight suit were the same colour, which meant they merged into an off-white ensemble that shouldn't raise too many eyebrows.

He left the basement via the parking ramp, keeping clear of the disaster area out front. There were fire trucks, Peace Force vehicles, ambulances and gangs of smartly-dressed lawyers clogging the road between the hotel and the apartment block, and aside from the authorities and the legal fraternity, there were sure to be more unsavoury people looking for him – of that he was certain.

After he cleared the shopping mall, it took Hal more than an hour to reach the city outskirts. An hour of hurrying along back streets, darting from building to building, crossing roads when the coast was clear, and hiding in the shadows every time he heard a vehicle, or footsteps, or a voice.

Eventually, he made it. City blocks gave way to a deserted commercial district, and then to residential streets with the occasional barking dog, or snatch of music. And when suburbia petered out, Hal found himself in a country lane surrounded by fields and hedgerows. He heard a car coming and hid behind a tree, and when its blinding lights and whining motor faded into the distance, he happened to look up.

The stars were amazing, scattered across the sky like polished gemstones, and Hal felt a deep longing as he gazed upon their brilliance. That was where he belonged, out in space flying cargo from planet to planet, not lugging two tons of weapons along back roads, thirsty, hungry, and tired.

He heard a distant rumble. At first he thought it was thunder, but then he saw a spark of light rising from the horizon. It climbed higher and higher, the rumble persistent and familiar. A ship was leaving the planet, and with a thrill he realised the spaceport was somewhere ahead of him. That was the answer! He'd find a cargo ship, sign on as a crew member, and slowly work his way back to the top. It would take a while, perhaps even weeks, but with his talent and know-how he would be back at the controls of his own ship in no time.

Once he had his own ship, he'd come back for Clunk. He pictured the robot doing some sort of cleaning duties at the spaceport, watching freighters coming and going with a kind of longing. He imagined Clunk watching a shiny new freighter descending from the heavens one day, and he could see the robot's expression as his beloved Mr Spacejock stepped off the passenger ramp.

Then Hal felt a stab of guilt. He'd had money, enough of it to buy a respectable ship, and he'd thrown the lot away on a high stakes card games. If only –

He sighed. What was done was done. There was no point dwelling on the past. Always look forward, that was the way.

First he had to get to the spaceport, and there was no way he was lugging the weapons another inch. So, he set them down in a neat pile beside the tree, put the grenades underneath and draped his dressing gown over the top. As he strolled up the road he could hear the rapid beeping of the grenades fading away, until there was a gigantic flash of light, followed by a thunderclap and a shock-wave that knocked him off his feet. When he sat up again he was surrounded by shredded branches, smouldering leaves, drifts of dirt and shards of twisted plastic and metal. Unconcerned, he dusted himself off and strolled along the road towards the spaceport, whistling a merry tune in time to his footsteps.

◆

Hal's whistling tailed off as his jaunty little walk in the country stretched on into the night. His feet hurt, he was really hungry and the occasional spaceship he saw lighting up the night sky still seemed to be taking off or landing just over the horizon. At this rate it might be morning before he got anywhere, and his patience was running out.

He'd seen very little traffic. At first he'd hidden in the bushes at the sound of approaching cars, concerned it might be gangs of assassins hunting him down. Later, as he grew more desperate, he stood in the middle road and tried thumbing a lift. However, the cars rose just enough to pass overhead, dipping again just as quickly and leaving Hal coughing and spluttering in their wake.

Then he heard something promising: the clatter of an old internal combustion engine. It sounded like a small truck, and that certainly wouldn't be able to fly over him. Also, truck drivers tended to be friendly towards hitchhikers. As the headlights approached, Hal stood in the road and held his thumb up. The truck kept coming, no change in engine noise, no slowing down, and at the last second Hal dived aside and rolled across the road to safety.

Then, with a squeal, the brakes came on, and a single red light glowed in the swirling fumes and dust. The driver's window went down, and an old man in a battered hat looked out. 'You wanna lift, son?'

Hal gathered himself, and hurried towards the passenger side. There was a faded sign on the door: The Moving Masters. The door handle was missing, but a loop of greasy rope served the same purpose, and, after clambering in, Hal turned to thank his saviour.

'Don' mention it,' said the man. He stuck out a hand. 'Name's Masters, if that kind o' thing's important to ya.'

'I'm Hal.'

The driver wrestled with the gearshift, and the truck lurched into motion. 'Headin' to the spaceport?'

'Yeah.'

Masters eyed Hal's flight suit. 'You a mechanic?'

'Freighter pilot,' said Hal.

'Fancy that.'

As the truck rumbled and bumped its way along the road, Hal could feel a lump in the small of his back. Earlier, when he'd destroyed the weapons, he'd decided to keep one of the smaller pistols just in case. If this ride turned into a banjo scenario, he was more than ready to use it.

'So, you got your own ship?'

'I used to, but not any more. I need to find another one.'

Masters looked thoughtful. 'You must have a ton of cash on you.'

'No, I'm flat broke,' said Hal quickly. 'I didn't mean I was going to buy another, I'm looking for a job flying someone else's.'

'Pilot for hire, huh?'

'That's it.'

'Fancy that,' said Masters again, and he lapsed into silence.

As they neared the spaceport, Hal spotted a row of bulky shapes to his left. He strained his eyes to see half a dozen spaceships just the other side of the fence. They were ancient vessels from the dawn of space travel, all rusty and bent, and he shook his head at the sight. 'Wow, just look at the wrecks in that junkyard.'

'Junkyard?' Masters craned his neck to look. 'Son, that's my fleet.'

12

There was a customer service droid at the rear of the dealership, keeping an eye on the entrance. Its job was to call the right sales rep for each new customer, and it took pride in its work. For example, their most valued rep specialised in exclusive, high-priced cars, and one did not waste this rep's talents on an overpaid sports person, a lottery winner or a TV celebrity. No, that would be a terrible *faux pas*, and the customer service droid would find itself polishing windscreens twenty-four hours a day should such a thing come to pass.

Then there were two reps who dealt with the middle-of the range vehicles for middle-of-the-range clients. They were good at their jobs, they could put the *nouveau riche* at ease, and the dealership's clients never knew they were getting second-best.

Finally, there was Bert. He sold comparatively cheap cars to riff-raff.

Pydd entered the dealership first, accompanied by Albion. They studied a few cars together, whistled quietly at the prices, and then looked up as a jolly, slightly overweight man in a suit strolled towards them. The man put out a hand and beamed. 'Hi guys, I'm Bert. How can I help you today?'

'I need a limo,' said Pydd.

'There's a rental company just down the block. Head outside, take the first left –'

'No, I want to buy a limo.'

'Hmm. Well, you've come to the right place. Which one do you want?'

'Can't you tell me anything about them?'

Bert gestured vaguely. 'They come in three colours.'

'Can I take a look?'

'Sure. Over here we have a Vega Mulhany. Nice piece of work this. Look at the sleek lines.'

'What's the servicing interval?'

'Er ... let me check.' Bert raised his voice. 'Walter, what's the servicing interval on the Mulhany?'

The customer service robot was far too refined to shout, so it made its way across the showroom, gliding gracefully between the cars like a dancer. 'The Mulhany does not require servicing, as you can see here and here in the feature guide.'

'Impressive,' said Pydd. Behind his back he signalled to Albion, who immediately made a fizzing noise and began to sway on his feet.

'Sir, I ...*crackle* ...don't feel very ...*gzztt* ...well.'

Then he toppled to the floor, and the customer service robot sprang forwards to protect the Mulhany. 'Mind the car, you metal-bound clod!' he shrieked, as Albion landed with a loud clang.

Pydd crouched beside the robot, fussing with panels and connectors while Albion continued to fizz and splutter like the fuse on a stick of dynamite.

'Get it outside!' shrieked the service robot. 'It's going to blow up! Get it outside!'

With Bert's help they got Albion into a sitting position, but when they tried to stand him up his legs froze, sticking out in front of him.

By now Walter, the service robot, was beside himself. He could picture this horrible, lumpy old robot exploding all over his nice shiny cars, spraying them with oil, rusty components and battery fluid. 'Drag it out!' he howled, and he grabbed Albion's arm and physically hauled him towards the exit. With Bert and Pydd assisting, they got the robot through the front doors. 'Can you get him into the cab?' asked Pydd, puffing from the exertion.

Walter looked like he was about to refuse, then realised they were still within blast range of the dealership. If the robot blew up here it would take out all the plate glass windows – and the fragments would damage every vehicle in stock. So, he helped drag Albion all the way to the cab, which was waiting at the far end of the lot. When he judged they'd gone far enough he abandoned Pydd and Bert to the task, turned heel and marched back to the showroom. On the way he saw a tall, bronze robot taking a shortcut through the car park. 'Hey, you! This car park is for customers.'

The robot waved an apology, and Walter muttered under his breath. He considered reporting it, but then he saw something which turned his circuits to ice: a minivan had pulled up, and two adults were getting out with children. He imagined their sticky fingers all over his shiny cars and broke into a trot, determined to head them off.

◆

The cab pulled out of the parking lot, drove a short distance along the main road, then stopped briefly to collect Clyde.

'Did you get it?' demanded Albion.

'Indeed. Their entire client l-list, downloaded to my internal storage.'

'Excellent. Well done!'

Pydd shook his head slowly. 'I don't know how you managed it.'

'Simple. While you distracted the sales staff, I hacked into their network and –'

'No, I meant … how come you're able to hack their network? You're robots. You can't do anything illegal, and accessing someone's private data is as illegal as it gets.'

'You can thank Vigilante for that. And Clunk, of course.'

'Really?'

Albion explained. 'Thanks to you, we consider criminals as non-humans. And thanks to Clunk, we learned that the owner of that dealership was convicted for tax offences last year. As a criminal, his network is fair game.'

'B-but we couldn't just take his cars,' said Clyde. 'A-after all, he already paid his debt to society.'

'That's a nice bit of logic you have there,' said Pydd in admiration.

'We're robots. Logic is all we do.'

'That and amateur theatrics.' Pydd laughed. 'When Albion started shaking and fizzing, I really thought he was going to explode. It was extremely convincing.'

The two robots stared at him. 'You didn't know?' said Clyde at last.

'What?'

'I disabled Albion's cooling system b-before you entered the dealership. The fizzing and seizing wasn't fake.'

Pydd gaped. 'You mean he could have exploded?'

'Well no, but you were very convincing all the same.'

'Unlike you guys, humans can lie through their teeth.'

'Which is why we modified Clunk's plan to include you. It worked out so much better than the original.'

'Okay, so we've got the data, but you never explained why you needed it.'

Albion smiled. 'That's the clever part. We're going to examine the list and run background checks on all the clients.'

'But why?'

'Clyde, give me a few examples from the list.'

'T-there's a well-known DJ.'

'Next.'

'A politician.'

'Shady, but not illegal. Next.'

'This one runs a freight company, import and export.'

'You see?' said Albion. 'That's a good lead. Smuggling, narcotics, bribery ... if we discover he's breaking the law, we can take anything belonging to his company. We'll make millions!'

'I like it. You're taking my Vigilante concept up to eleven.' Pydd looked from one to the other. 'Tell me, why haven't robots conquered the galaxy yet? You're certainly smart enough.'

'What's the hurry?' said Albion calmly. 'It'll still be there when we want it.'

And on that sober note, the cab turned onto an expressway and set off for the spaceport.

Clunk and Sable had been roaring up and down narrow streets for twenty or thirty minutes, but they hadn't spotted as much as a stray cat.

'Do you have infra-red?' Sable demanded, as Clunk peered into a dark alley.

'And ultra-violet, much good that might do.'

'Sure. He'll glow like a fairground ride if he's wearing any white.'

'It might be more efficient if I tracked him on foot. He would hear the car from a distance, and it would be trivial to take cover long before we spotted him.'

'Take too long,' said Sable. 'We'll find him eventually. I just wish I knew where he's going. Why the commercial district, for example?'

'Fewer people. Pursuers are easier to spot. He was with the Peace Force, so he'll be well trained.' Clunk glanced at her. 'Mr Pydd appears to be a law-abiding citizen. May I ask why you're chasing him?'

'I'm not chasing him.'

'All appearances to the contrary.'

'It's this damned group of his. It's angering the wrong sort of people, and they want it stopped.'

'Have you considered stopping them instead? We are talking about criminals, aren't we?'

'Everyone knows that, but in the eyes of the law they're innocent until proven guilty.'

'In that case, has your agency considered using their considerable resources to prove their guilt? You have surveillance, you have –'

'We have very strict privacy laws on Alteia. It's almost impossible to mount a case, and if you do get someone to court most of the evidence will be thrown out.'

'Sounds like a haven for big time crooks. And let me guess, many of them are embedded in government, public service, the legal profession ...'

'Exactly. They have a hand in every new law, which strengthens the protection against them.'

'What about Mr Cooper?'

Sable's expression hardened. 'He's the worst of the lot. Most crooks have a thin veneer of respectability, but he's so powerful he doesn't even bother. It's an open secret, and there's nothing we can do except protect the innocent.'

Clunk was silent. There were many thousands of inhabited planets strewn across the Galaxy, and every one seemed to develop along its own twisted path. For every freedom-loving Alteia with its untouchable crime lords, there was another world, equally unpleasant, modelled on a strict dictatorship. He wondered if humans were flawed in that fashion: they espoused a particular philosophy until it warped, became a mockery of itself, and consumed them. Give a planet too much freedom and criminals thrived while the ordinary population suffered. Too harsh a regime, and the elite thrived while the populace lived in fear. On the whole, thought Clunk, being part of the general populace was not a recipe for happiness.

While he was musing on the problems of humanity, Sable had reactivated her link to base. This time, instead of calling her boss she'd asked to be put through to someone else.

'Ocelot, long time no see. You up for a match this weekend?'

'Not now. I need a lead. Do you have anything at all in this district?'

'The boss is looking for you.'

'Don't tell him I called. And ... the leads?'

'Nothing much. Several reports of a suspicious couple in the area. They're cruising the streets in a cab.'

'Very funny. What else?'

'Who's in the cab with you? Are you seeing someone?'

'Just give me the damned info.'

'All right, all right! A robot collapsed in a car dealership. Came in with his owner to buy a limo, fell over, they dragged it into the car park.'

'Is that it?'

'Yep. Quiet as the grave otherwise.'

Clunk put his hand on Sable's arm. 'Can he describe the robot?' he whispered.

'Can you get a shot of the robot?'

'Give me a second, I have to request their security footage. Privacy laws and all that ... you know the drill.'

There was a lengthy delay, and then ...

'It's not very clear. Sending you a pic now.'

The screen displayed an image. It showed a selection of luxury cars, and standing in the middle were two figures: Their faces were indistinct, but they were unmistakably Pydd and Albion.

'Thanks for that. Ocelot out.'

'Wait, the weekend –'

Sable returned the screen to its regular programming, then chose their destination. 'I don't understand why they were trying to buy a limo.'

Clunk was silent. He knew why Albion was in the dealership, because the robot was implementing Clunk's plan. He just had no idea why Clyde and Albion had roped Pydd into the scheme.

13

'Fleet?' Hal didn't know what was more surprising: the fact those old wrecks were still in service, or the fact the man giving him a lift seemed to own a fleet of ships. 'When I saw the sign on your truck, I thought you were into furniture removals!'

'Not just furniture. My company moves anything.'

'Do you fly those ships yourself?'

'Not since the accident.'

Hal felt a glimmer of hope. 'Do you have any pilots?'

'Not since the other accidents.' Masters stopped the truck outside a battered tin shack. Above the door, picked out in several different colours of paint, were the words 'The Moving Masters'. 'Come in, let's talk.'

Hal didn't move. The Alteia spaceport was somewhere nearby. At that spaceport there would be professional freight outfits with modern ships, safe working conditions, generous pay packets and – 'Oh, who am I kidding?' muttered Hal, and he got out of the truck and followed Masters into the office.

Inside, they sat facing each other across a desk. It was an interesting design – an old wooden door balanced on two oil drums – and the computer perched on one corner looked like an ancient ticket machine. Before he spoke to Hal, Masters checked the computer and groaned. 'Two more jobs cancelled.'

'You have more than one job at a time?' asked Hal in surprise. His experience of the freight business was that he was lucky to get one job, never mind several.

'I got a reputation as the go-to firm,' explained Masters. 'As in, when you're really desperate, you go to Masters.'

'Where does everyone else go?'

Masters looked like he'd bitten into a lemon. 'Cooper.'

'That name ...' Hal remembered his kidnapping. 'Wait, you mean an old guy with a cane?'

'That's 'im. Cooper Freight. He's got new ships, all the port staff in his pocket, and he's as crooked as they come.'

'He runs a freight company?'

'Why? You wanna work for him now?'

'No way,' said Hal with feeling. 'I wouldn't trust him an inch.'

'You're not the only one. Many won't deal with 'im, so they come to me instead.' Masters shrugged. 'I got no shortage of work, just a shortage of pilots.'

'So what's the pay like?'

'Ten percent share of the fee from each run. Net profit, not gross.'

Hal looked around the office. If there were any profits, or had ever been any profits, they weren't being wasted. He approved of that. 'Working conditions?'

'None.'

'Are you fussy about past experience?'

'Nah, not in the slightest,' said Masters. 'You crash one of my ships, I get insurance. Client gets insurance, if the cargo is halfway legit. You get a hole in the ground, and if you crash it good we won't even need to fill it in.'

'Aren't you worried someone might run off with one of your ships?'

Masters bent double, wheezing. He thumped his fist on the desk, making the oil drums ring, and for a moment Hal thought he was having a seizure. Then he sat up, eyes streaming, and made a curious, croaking noise.

'A-ha ha ha haaaa.'

Hal smiled uncertainly. 'I thought it was a fair question.'

'You saw my fleet o' ships, didn't you?' Masters wiped tears from his eyes. 'I'd have to pay some idiot to steal those things, an' he wouldn't live long enough to sell 'em.'

Hal sat in silence. During the long walk to the spaceport he'd pictured himself piloting a ship through space, delivering cargo and earning a decent wage. Now he'd be putting his life on the line for ten percent of nothing. Still, what alternative did he have? Before he could change his mind, he stretched his hand across the desk. 'You have a deal, Mr Masters. I'll fly your ships.'

Or die trying, he thought to himself.

◆

After they organised the paperwork, which involved writing Hal's next of kin on a grubby scrap of paper, Masters pushed his chair back and got up. 'Right, let's find you a ship,' he said. 'Follow me.'

The back door creaked open and, after he'd replaced the handle, he led Hal across a courtyard surrounded by a chain link fence. It was topped with barbed wire, and Hal wondered what it was supposed to be protecting.

Masters opened a gate and they crossed a weed-strewn expanse of concrete to the waiting ships. They were sitting on a row of landing pads alongside an overgrown hedge, and in the darkness they looked like misshapen asteroids plonked down on the ground.

Then Masters flipped a switch, and a dozen dim, flickering lights came on, illuminating the scene. There were six ships in total, and every one of them was older than Hal's first ship, the *Black Gull*. He knew you were supposed to feel nostalgia for old vehicles, but the *Black Gull* had barely been space-worthy: half the controls hadn't worked, the engines had a mind of their own and he'd updated his will every time he took to the skies.

'You got any experience with older ships?' asked Masters, as though he'd read Hal's mind.

'Yeah. Lots.'

'Okay, well that's a good start.'

They reached the first ship, an off-white, rust-streaked cargo hauler with a rounded hull. It was leaning over drunkenly on two landing legs, the third having snapped clean off, and the nose was crumpled where it had crashed into the concrete landing pad. 'This one's not quite ready,' said Masters.

'Uh-huh.'

Next up was a similar model, with even more rust. Fortunately it had all three landing legs. Unfortunately they were all different lengths. 'Not a bad ship,' said Masters, as it swayed gently in the wind. 'She lost one of 'er engines last time out, but like I always say: one is all you need.'

'It's a possible,' said Hal doubtfully. 'What about the next one?'

They strolled to a long, slender ship with an actual, real-life windscreen. It stood upright on three large fins, and as Hal craned his neck to study the ship he realised someone had cut the nose off a commercial aircraft and welded it to a very large booster. It looked like an ancient space rocket, and he wondered how you were supposed to land such a thing.

'This one's really fast,' said Masters. 'Course, the hull leaks, but it's okay as long as you don't spend too long in a vacuum.'

'It's a spaceship. Isn't that part of its job?'

'So wear a helmet,' said Masters, with a shrug.

Hal glanced over his shoulder. In the distance he could make out the glow of the city, low on the horizon. He was beginning to think it would be safer to go back and face any number of assassins, rather than strap himself into one of these old bombs and face certain death.

'Now, this next ship …' Masters gestured vaguely at the low, square vessel hunched on the landing pad. '…I can't exactly remember what's wrong with it. The ambulance guys used all kinds of long words when they took the pilot away.'

'Pass,' said Hal quickly. He realised there was only one left, and he crossed his fingers as they strolled the short distance to the landing pad. Then he looked up and the breath caught in his throat. It was a Rigel-class freighter, just like the *Black Gull*! It had a stubby nose, triangular winglets, a sweeping line to the huge tail plane and two enormous exhaust cones at the back. Even the name was right: the *Albatross*, another seabird. It had to be a sign! 'What's wrong with this one?'

'Mechanically, she's fine. It don't have no flight computer, but who needs one of those?' Masters punched him in the shoulder. 'You and I, we're old school. Give us a joystick and we'll set 'er down on a credit tile. Am I right?'

'R-right,' said Hal, who was lucky if he could set down on a large moon.

'So it's this one, yeah?'

Hal felt fear and adrenaline coursing through his veins in equal measure. Sure, the ship would be a handful, but he was a freighter pilot. This is what he was born to do! 'This is the one,' he said firmly.

'Good. Come back to the office and we'll sort out a job.'

◆

Back in the office, Masters slid a crumpled envelope across the desk. 'The job details are on the back, but it's a doddle. Take a shipment to the orbiter, collect the cash, head back 'ere in the morning.'

'You can rely on me,' said Hal.

'Good, because I'm off to sink a few beers.' Masters pushed his chair back. 'I won't be in 'til noon tomorrow. If you get back before then, take another job from the computer.'

'Do I need a password?'

'Nope.'

'What about a key for the office?'

Masters shook his head and ambled to the door. He opened it, then paused. 'One thing. Don't take any jobs outside this system.'

'Why? Do I need a permit?'

'No, the *Albatross's* jump drive doesn't work.'

The door closed, and Hal was alone in the office. After the excitement of getting a new job, he felt a bit deflated. Masters was slack about everything, the business was a joke, and Hal felt like he was scraping the bottom of a very deep barrel. Still, it was a job, and he was entitled to a cut of the profit. That was far better than a fixed wage – especially as nothing looked particularly fixed at Moving Masters.

So, after switching off the computer and the single overhead light, Hal pulled the door to and strolled towards his ship. Halfway there his natural optimism and self-confidence kicked in, and he whistled tunelessly as he crossed the landing pad. Wherever he was, Clunk would be astonished to learn of Hal's good fortune, and perhaps Masters would even employ the robot as a mechanic. And as a computer technician. And ... well, to be honest, Masters would be better off in the pub, leaving Clunk to run the ground operation while Hal flew the ships.

He was still wondering whether Moving Spacejock sounded better than Moving Masters when he reached the *Albatross*. The slender passenger ramp was down at the front, leading to the flight deck far above, and the cargo ramp between the two huge exhaust cones at the rear was also down, leading to the low-slung hold. Hal eyed them both, wondering which end of the ship to explore first. On the Black Gull the passenger ramp had been a spidery affair made from aluminium mesh, which flexed alarmingly underfoot. On this ship it would probably snap in half, ending his new piloting career before he'd even got off the ground. Or soon afterwards, at least.

The cargo ramp, on the other hand, was broad and strong, cut from a solid slab of metal. Hal decided that was a much safer way to gain access to his new command, and so he headed to the rear of the ship. As he passed a landing leg he admired the thick, shock-absorbing pistons and the heavy foot planted on the concrete pad. He was less admiring of the puddle under the landing foot, which looked suspiciously like hydraulic fluid.

On the way to the rear he remembered the envelope, and he

held it up to the dim light to make out his flight instructions. It didn't take him long to read:

Load cargo. Deliver to client 43, Alteia orbiter. Collect payment. Return.

Hal pursed his lips. Well, he thought as he crumpled the envelope, there's not much chance of messing that up.

He was still walking towards the rear of the ship, and in the near darkness he barked his shin on a low, boxy shape about two meters square. He realised it was a pallet full of boxes, and as he glanced around he realised there were dozens more scattered around the rear of the ship. They must have been there all along, he hadn't seen them when Masters was showing him the fleet because they were hidden behind the bulk of the *Albatross*.

Each pallet had a shipping label attached, addressed to the orbiter, although there was a range of client numbers. Hal found two pallets for client 43, his customer, and then two thoughts hit him: One, why not take all the cargo to the orbiter at once, instead of going back and forth for a week? And two, if he didn't take all the cargo, the pallets left on the landing pad would be incinerated by the ship's thrusters. Either way, he had to move the whole ruddy lot, and Masters hadn't said anything about manual labour.

Hal looked around, hoping for a nice, modern forklift with laser guided controls and a built-in sound system. Instead he found a manual pallet truck with one wheel out of square. He dragged it over to the first pallet, got the forks in place and started to pump the handle. And pump. And pump. After several minutes he was breathing hard, and the pallet was half an inch off the ground.

He decided that was enough, and dragged the pallet to the cargo ramp. The dodgy wheel dragged, creaking and groaning, and when he finally reached the ship he discovered the angle of the ramp was much too steep. He'd have to pump all night to get the pallet truck high enough to clear the lip.

Hal frowned. He remembered a similar problem with the *Gull* once. The ramp had been too steep then, as well, but he'd merely lowered the rear of the ship until the hull was touching the ground. That left the ramp almost level, and getting the cargo on board had been no trouble at all.

Hal left the pallet truck and returned to the nearest landing leg. That's when he realised how lucky he was to be flying a model he was so familiar with. Thanks to his time on the *Gull*, he could reach out in near-darkness and press the right button just like so.

There was a loud crack, a cascade of fluid, and he felt rather than saw the bulk of the ship dropping towards him. A split second later he was diving for safety, while behind him the hull smashed into the landing pad with a terrific clang. Nearby, there was another crash as a ship toppled over, and then further crashes as the rest of the vessels fell like dominoes.

Hal got up, dusted himself off, and inspected the damage. The *Albatross's* keel was now resting on the landing pad with all three landing legs fully retracted. With the state of the ship it was impossible to tell if the hull was damaged.

Then he glanced at the rest of Masters' fleet. He'd parked spaceships on their sides before, and they'd usually taken off again so he was pretty sure the other vessels were okay.

Returning to the pallet truck, Hal discovered the outer lips of both exhaust cones were buckled, but to his delight the ramp was now level. It took moments to push the first pallet into the hold, and when he'd unloaded he stopped to look around. There was a wave of nostalgia at the familiar layout. Sure, it was older and grubbier than the Gull, but even so it was like returning to a childhood home. It was also a lot smaller than he remembered, and there would have been even more room if someone hadn't parked a forklift truck in the hold.

— 14 —

Through the side window, Albion watched a ship lifting off in the distance. They were approaching the spaceport, but he barely noticed. He was thinking about the Vigilante Co-op and how he intended to run it. Clyde was a loyal friend, but despite his overclocked brain he wasn't the quickest algorithm in the toolkit.

Albion frowned. The point was, he couldn't expect much help from Clyde with respect to Vigilante. He, Albion, would have to run the operation, and he would keep Clyde busy as a genial front man. Obviously Pydd would have some input, assuming he survived, but the human had already demonstrated some very short-sighted thinking. For example, getting robots to meet in person. Putting up flashy posters, recognising robots who'd done particularly well – it was all very human.

Albion wondered where Clunk was. Now he was a big thinker, one of the best Albion had ever met. With Clunk's assistance, Vigilante could become tremendously powerful and no human would dare stand in their way.

What was it Pydd said? Why haven't robots taken over the galaxy yet? Well, thought Albion. Perhaps it's time.

'Mr Pydd, do you have a plan for leaving the planet?'

Pydd shook his head. 'I have a few contacts from my days with the Force. I thought I'd ask around, maybe get a lift on a cargo ship.'

'Cooper will have contacts too. He will soon learn of your presence.'

'Not before I've gone, hopefully.' Pydd craned his neck. 'Cab, take the next left.'

'Complying.'

'I thought we were going to the spaceport?' said Albion.

'You're thinking of the big passenger terminal. All the freight companies are based in this area.'

Albion looked out the window, and realised they were skimming along beside a chain-link fence. About a hundred metres away, on the other side, there were rows of ships parked on concrete pads. Most were in darkness, but here and there spotlights picked out refuelling crews, cargo loading droids and mechanics. Trucks delivered and picked up goods, and as he watched one of the more distant ships ran up her engines, sending smoke and flames billowing out. It was an impressive sight, and the car shook with the rumble of jets.

The cab turned left into a narrow lane, then drew up outside a metal shed. All the lights were off, and it looked deserted. 'Wait here,' said Pydd. 'The owner isn't keen on robots.'

He got out, strode to the shed and tried the door. It opened, but Albion could see the lights were off inside too. 'I don't think anyone's home.'

'M-me neither,' said Clyde. 'Looks like a bust.'

Pydd came back. 'He's not in the office, but I think there's someone out back with the ships. Will you two come with me, just in case? Look tough and keep quiet.'

Sable sat in silence as the cab hurtled towards the spaceport. Beside her, Clunk was also deep in thought. So far they'd had two sightings of Pydd, but each time they'd arrived too late. The latest sighting, at the car dealership, hadn't gone well. The fussy customer service droid had refused to let Clunk in, in case he overheated and exploded all over the cars, and apart from confirming Pydd had been there, he'd been little use.

He had allowed Sable to view the security footage though, and from that she deduced that Pydd had driven off towards the spaceport.

So, Sable invoked emergency powers, overriding the cab's safety controls. The engines howled as they powered the vehicle along at top speed, and buildings, hedgerows, signposts all flashed past in a blur.

'Where would I go, where would I run to?' muttered Sable.

'Can I make a suggestion?'

'Shoot.'

'He won't go to the terminal. There are too many people, and he's avoiding crowds.'

'I agree.'

'So why is he heading for the spaceport? Does he have any associates in this area, contacts from his Peace Force days? Informants perhaps, or someone who might owe him a favour?'

'Good thinking. I'll run a scan on his casework.' Sable operated the screen, paging through information.

'I'm surprised you're allowed to do that, what with all your privacy laws.'

'These are official records. Classified, but not private.' Sable stopped, then backed up. 'Cab, take the next left.'

'Do you have something?' asked Clunk.

'I don't know, but it's a lead.'

The car slowed ferociously, and they clung to their seats as it washed off speed. Then it turned left, angling sharply to make the bend. Moments later they approached a large metal shed, and Clunk grinned with triumph as he saw a cab parked outside. 'That's only just got here,' he said. 'I detect a strong heat signature from the engines.'

'Nice work, Clunk,' remarked Sable. 'We'll make an agent out of you yet.'

They were about to climb out when the viewscreen buzzed. It showed a priority warning, and after Sable tapped out her code, a message appeared:

Care, Cooper approaching you I.F. PS how about the weekend?

'Talk about getting your priorities right,' muttered Sable.

'What does I.F. mean?' asked Clunk.

'In force,' said Sable grimly. 'If we don't get Pydd out of here soon, we're all dead.'

◆

Loading complete, Hal parked the forklift in the cargo hold and climbed down to inspect his work. The pallets weren't exactly straight, and a few of the boxes were squashed and missing a corner or two, but in general he was pleased with the result. He'd triple-stacked the pallets, building teetering columns which almost reached the roof, but it was all in and now he could make some serious money.

He patted one of the boxes on his way to the ramp controls. Behind him, the stack creaked and groaned as it threatened to topple over. Hal didn't hear, because he'd just pressed a button and the subsequent clattering noise threatened to shake the teeth from his head. Eventually the noise tailed off, but the ramp hadn't moved. Foolishly, he pressed the button again, with exactly the same result.

He pursed his lips. He knew a thing or two about flying Rigel Class freighters with the rear doors wide open, and the thing he knew most of all was that you shouldn't do it. Every time, every single time, he ended up with an empty hold, angry customers, and an even emptier bank account.

So, the door had to come up, but clearly the mechanism was broken. He considered tying a rope to it and pulling the massive slab of metal up with sheer strength, but he dismissed the idea as impossible. After all, he had no rope.

Next he considered fixing the mechanism, but this too was impossible. Whenever Hal needed to mend something he studied diagrams, watched instructional videos, laid out all the tools and then asked Clunk to fix it. The robot, working under Hal's masterful instruction, did the mundane mechanical work, but since Clunk wasn't present the whole process was a bust.

Hal rubbed his chin and his gaze turned to the cargo. He'd hit upon an idea, but he wasn't sure how much damage it would cause. His plan was relatively simple: Fire the thrusters at the front of the ship, tipping the whole vessel up so quickly that it would be sitting on the cargo door ... hopefully before anything fell out. Then, he would come down and seal the door. Then, he'd go back to the flight deck and lift off vertically, like rocket ships of old.

In other words, he was planning to close the ship on the door, rather than the other way round. He felt the theory was sound, and none of the boxes had made breaking noises when he'd dropped them, backed into them or run them over, so clearly the cargo wasn't all that fragile.

'Let's do this,' he muttered, and he left the cargo hold through the inner door. On the other side there was a short passage leading to a steel ladder, and Hal smiled to himself at the sight. On the Gull his cabin had been on the right, and there had been a small kitchen alcove behind the ladder. He wasn't fussed about the cabin, but the thought of a nice hot meal was a pleasant one.

But first, to space. He took the ladder to the flight deck ... and stopped. The broad, curved flight console was missing, and in its place was a tangle of wires. Controls had been taped to the walls or left dangling, and none of them were labelled. He'd never quite mastered the Black Gull's controls, but at least he knew roughly where they were. Here, with the console missing and the controls all over the place, he'd have no chance.

That wasn't all. Instead of a pilot's chair there was a plastic crate to sit on, and the deck plates were buckled as though they'd been subjected to a ferocious fire. In a sombre mood, Hal stepped gingerly to the airlock, treading lightly on the buckled deck. Both inner and outer doors stood open, and he stepped to the very edge and looked down. The passenger ramp was extended, as he'd noted earlier, and he was glad he hadn't used it because it was full of very large holes.

He opened a panel and pressed the control to retract the ramp. To his astonishment, there was a whirr and the entire ramp folded smoothly, retracting until it was nestled against the hull. If that worked, maybe the ship wasn't so bad after all. Still buoyed, he swung the outer door shut and spun the heavy locking wheel ... which took three complete turns before falling off and landing on his foot.

Hal cursed, hopping on one leg and clutching at his throbbing toes. The momentum carried him out of the airlock and into the flight deck, where he fell over the crate and plunged headlong into the nest of wiring. Within seconds he was tangled up, and that's when the ship delivered another blow ... this time to his plan, rather than to his body.

In order to tip the Albatross on end, he had to use the controls. And in order to access the controls while the vessel was tipping up he had to be strapped into a nice solid chair. He could not use the controls to initiate such a violent manoeuvre while sitting on a milk crate.

Of course, now that he was trapped IN the controls, he couldn't operate the ship at all, violently or otherwise.

By now he was thoroughly fed up, and convinced the ship was unusable. He freed himself by hauling on the wires that held him, tearing them apart until he was clear. Then he twisted pairs back together again, matching colours where he could and guessing where he couldn't. The clear optical fibre gave him the most trouble, but he dealt with it by pushing the ends together and fastening them with leftover bits of wire.

Okay, the Albatross was a non-starter. That left the other ships. His only option was to inspect them one by one, find the least worst of them all, and transfer the cargo across. Then he realised he had a second option, and it was far more tempting: Walk away from the whole sorry business.

Hal looked around the flight deck. He'd been a fool, he could see that now. Thinking he could start again after losing his ship. Thinking that everything would work out, when it was plain from Masters' operation that nothing worked. Thinking that he could survive without Clunk.

His face grave, Hal took the ladder to the lower deck and walked to the cargo hold. He strolled past the pallets, some of which had already fallen over, and made his way to the cargo ramp. At the top of the ramp he stopped, looked back at the hold, and saw his dream fade for good.

Psssst!

Hal groaned. What now, a gas leak? The ship had already tested him to the limit, was it going to finish the job and cremate him too?

'Pssst! You up there!'

Hal blinked, and turned around. At the foot of the ladder he saw three figures: A human, a broad, silvery robot, and a tall bronze robot. They were standing in the shadows, but he was certain he recognised the latter. 'Clunk? Is that you?' he demanded, his spirits soaring.

'N-no, Mr Spacejock. My name is Clyde.'

Deflated, Hal looked closer. 'Clyde? And is that Albion?'

'Indeed it is,' said the second robot. 'As you can see, we're still using the names you gave us.'

'I'm honoured.' Hal eyed the human. 'Who's this guy?'

The man stepped forward into the light, and Hal gaped at him. It was like staring into a mirror, although this reflection was definitely shorter than he was. Then a bulb went off. 'Steward Pydd. You're the guy Cooper was after. You're the reason they're all trying to kill me!'

— 15 —

'I'm sorry you got tangled up in this, Spacejock, but I have to requisition this ship,' said Pydd.

Hal gestured. 'She's all yours. I'm just leaving.'

'You can't. I need you to fly it.'

'This thing wouldn't fly if you shoved ten tons of explosives up the exhaust ports. It's a wreck.'

'Why's it full of cargo, then?'

'Because I loaded it first, and then discovered it's a wreck. And now I'm leaving.'

'But –'

'I said I quit. Goodbye.'

'Don't you want to bring Cooper down?'

'It doesn't matter what I want. This ship isn't going anywhere.'

Pydd snorted. 'Oh, I see. You're one of those pilots. You sit at the console, drinking coffee and giving orders while robots and computers do all the work.' He turned to Albion. 'You probably know more about ships than he does. Are you willing to try?'

'Now wait just a minute –' began Hal, stung by the unfair criticism.

'It's okay, you can leave. We have real work to do.'

'I said wait a minute!' shouted Hal. 'You think you know best? Well come with me!' He pushed past and strode through the hold to the inner corridor, then climbed the ladder with short, jerky movements. In the flight deck he stood back, and when Pydd's head appeared through the deck Hal spread his arms, encompassing the tangled wiring.

'Bloody hell,' murmured Pydd, as he emerged from the tube. While he inspected the damage, Albion and Clyde clambered into the flight deck behind him.

'Hey, have you two seen Clunk?' demanded Hal.

'Indeed, we encountered him at the spaceport earlier today. We drove him to Mr Pydd's meeting, and when that was attacked –'

'Attacked?'

'Cooper's men. It's okay, Mr Spacejock, Clunk is fine. We met him afterwards and he sent us on a mission.'

'Do you know where he is? Because honestly, he's the only person who can get us out of this mess.'

'Robot,' said Pydd.

'What?'

'You said Clunk is the only person, but he's a robot.'

'You haven't met Clunk,' said Hal firmly.

'Actually, I have. He joined my group.'

Hal frowned. 'Is that the group where you steal robots from other people?'

'No, it's the group that empowers –'

'Shhh!'

Hal and Pydd stopped arguing and turned to look at Clyde. 'What is it?'

'I heard footsteps below.'

'Probably rats.' Hal glanced at Pydd. 'More sneaky, back-stabbing, plague-ridden creatures aboard my ship. Lucky me.'

'Hey, I–'

'SHHHH!'

'It could be Cooper's people,' hissed Pydd. 'Be ready for anything.'

—

Hal motioned the others back, his gaze fixed on the access hole in the deck. 'Grab weapons,' he hissed. 'There's a heavy wheel in the airlock, and you can pull things off the walls.' Meanwhile, he reached into the back of his flight suit and withdrew the compact pistol.

Pydd stared at it, then at Hal. 'Do you know how to use that?'

'Of course I do. I've had Peace Force training.'

Pydd snorted. 'It's a shame they didn't train you properly then.' Before Hal could stop him he plucked the weapon from his grip, flipped it expertly in his good, left hand, and touched a hidden contact. There was a low whine, and a green light came on.

'I knew how to do that,' hissed Hal.

'Sure you did. Now grab a piece of wall and get ready.'

They heard footsteps in the passage below, then the sound of low voices. Hal brandished a sheet of plastic wall covering and prepared to wrap them in it, while Pydd held the gun with deadly expertise. Next, there was the sound of someone climbing the ladder ... and then Sable's head appeared.

'Don't shoot!' shouted Hal, immediately. 'She's on our side!'

114

There was a muffled shout from below. 'Mr Pydd, is that you?'

'No it bloody isn't,' shouted Hal, who recognised the voice at once. Delighted, he continued. 'It's me, you daft lump of tin.'

'Mr *Spacejock*?'

Sable climbed into the flight deck, and a split second later Clunk's head appeared. He looked around, nodded quickly as he spotted Pydd, and then beamed all over his face when he saw Hal. 'Mr Spacejock, is that really you?'

'Sure is, old buddy. Here, take my hand.'

Clunk reached up, and Hal leaned backwards to take the strain. Unfortunately the robot was incredibly heavy, and after puffing and panting for a while he gratefully accepted Albion's help.

Meanwhile, Sable was glaring at Hal. 'What are you doing here? You're supposed to be at the hotel.'

'Yeah, well I've had enough of this planet. I'll be safer in space.'

'Not in this ship,' said Clunk, having got a close look at it.

Sable and Pydd retreated to the airlock, where they spoke in hurried undertones. Meanwhile, Hal explained about his kidnapping and escape, while Clunk told him about the Vigilante Co-op.

'What a stupid idea,' said Hal, when he learned it was Pydd's setup. 'He's going to get himself killed, and he'll drag you down with him.'

'He's fighting crime. It's what he does. Did you know he was a decorated Peace Force officer? He served for years until Cooper tortured him.'

'Cooper tortured me too,' protested Hal. 'You don't see me fighting back, do you? No sir, I thought about revenge, about making him pay, but then I got smart and booked a one-way ticket to the stars.' He gestured around the flight deck. 'Unfortunately it's a bit of a lemon.'

For the first time, Clunk noticed the state of the flight deck. 'A bit,' he breathed.

Before he could say any more, Sable and Pydd returned. 'Cooper's people are on the way,' she said. 'They know where we are and they're heading here in force.'

'Time to leave,' said Hal. 'Don't use the passenger ramp, it's full of holes.'

'We can't leave. They may have surrounded us already.'

'So what do you suggest?' Hal realised exactly what she was about to suggest, and he shook his head vigorously. 'Oh no. This ship is a death trap. It's not going anywhere.'

◆

'Well?' demanded Pydd. 'What's the status?'

Clunk had just finished his brief inspection, and his expression wasn't encouraging. 'This ship is a death trap. It's not going anywhere–'

'I told you!' said Hal triumphantly.

'–unless I fly it,' finished Clunk.

'What?'

'The controls are useless, but I can wire myself into the network and run the ship's functions myself.'

Pydd nodded slowly. 'You mean, you can replace the ship's computer?'

'I was going to say that,' grumbled Hal. 'You stick to your vigilante thing, and leave the piloting commentary to me.'

'I would, if you knew the first thing about piloting.'

'Boys, that's enough!'

Sable's voice cut through the squabbling like a knife, and both men looked embarrassed.

'We all have to work together for now,' she continued. 'Once we reach safety, we can all go our separate ways.'

'*If* we reach safety,' muttered Hal. 'As a trained pilot, I don't think this ship will fly.'

Pydd advanced on him. 'And as a trained Peace Force officer, I swear I'll –'

'Think you can take me, shorty?'

'With both hands tied behind my back, you –'

BANG!

They both jumped. Sable was brandishing a metal bracer, which she'd just slammed against the wall. 'Next one to talk eats this.' She pointed at Hal. 'You! Go and secure the cargo.'

'But the door –'

'Uh-uh-uh, I haven't finished. Go and secure the cargo, then close the rear door.' Sable pointed at Clyde. 'Which one are you?'

'C-Clyde,' said the robot nervously.

'Stand in the airlock and keep watch. If you see Cooper, let me know.' She realised Hal hadn't moved. 'What are you waiting for?'

'The back door is broken. I can't close it.'

Sable pointed at Albion. 'Go with him, show him what to do.'

Hal let Albion go ahead of him, in case the ladder wasn't strong enough and the robot crushed him to a pulp on the way down. However, Albion didn't even bother with the rungs, he just stepped into thin air and vanished down the hole, landing with a controlled thud. Hal, lacking shock-absorbing legs and any gymnastic skill whatsoever, took the steps one by one, placing his feet carefully. As he descended, he heard Sable ordering Clunk around in the flight deck.

'Hurry up with the wiring, okay? You're the real key in all of this.'

He pictured Clunk nodding, and smiled to himself. The robot was like putty where women were concerned, docile and submissive whereas with Hal he was obstinate through and through. Then, as he stepped off the ladder, he heard Pydd's voice from the flight deck.

'What about me? What should I do?'

Hal cupped his hands to his mouth and shouted up the access tube. 'You can stand around being short!' Then, feeling a whole lot better, he strode towards the cargo hold. On the way he glanced at Albion. 'Do you know anything about ship repairs?'

'I may not have the necessary schematics, but I do know how to close a door.'

Hal said nothing. Part of him was hoping the robot would fail . . . first to salve his pride, and second because they wouldn't be able to take off in this rickety deathtrap if the cargo door were jammed open.

However, it was not to be. Albion discovered a fault in the machinery which controlled the cargo ramp, fixed it, and moments later the ramp whined and shuddered as it rose into the air. There was a deep thud as it sealed against the rear of the ship, and then several lights flickered on, bathing the hold in light.

Job complete, they set off for the flight deck.

When Hal returned to the flight deck he saw Clunk standing in the flight console's place with dozens of wires sprouting from his chest. The robot was busy attaching even more wires, connecting them to his forehead, his elbows and several points below the waist.

'You're only going to fly it,' remarked Hal. 'You're not supposed to be a permanent fixture.'

'This is the only option, since my first plan didn't work.'

'Which plan was that?'

'I was going to upload a backup copy of the Navcom into the ship's flight computer.'

'So what went wrong?'

'There is no flight computer.'

'Fair enough.' Hal glanced around the flight deck. Clyde was just visible in the airlock, peering out of the ship as he scanned for Cooper and his thugs. Sable was leaning against the wall, arms crossed, fingers drumming on her bicep. Pydd was missing, and Hal hoped he was rustling up a tasty dinner. Albion had just emerged from the access tube.

Hal turned back to Clunk. 'So how long will you be?'

'I must have control of the primary systems,' said Clunk, connecting a fibre optic cable to his navel. The cable glowed, and the overhead lights went on and off several times.

'Clunk, that's not a primary system.'

'I realise that, but I have to test each cable to find out what it does.'

Hal stared at the tangle of wiring. 'But that'll take days!'

'Not necessarily. Once the important ones are identified we can take off. I'll add the rest in flight.'

'Just make sure you don't test the self-destruct.'

'Rigel class freighters don't have a self-destruct.'

'That's not what you said aboard the *Black Gull*!'

'I know,' said Clunk, looking embarrassed. 'I just didn't want you touching the controls.'

Sable laughed at that, and Hal frowned. 'Right, well obviously you don't need me,' he said grouchily. 'I'm going to see how the food's coming along.'

'Don't be like that, Mr Spacejock. I didn't know you then like I do now, and I apologise unreservedly.' Clunk hesitated. 'I'm about to engage in the riskiest part of the procedure, and I'd like you on hand.'

'Why, are you likely to blow up?'

'I hope not. Can you hold this wire for me?'

Hal took the wire gingerly and stood ready.

'Excellent.' Clunk closed his eyes, and everyone held their breath. Then he opened his eyes again.

'Done already?' asked Hal.

'Alas no. The ship is expecting commands from me, but I am not programmed for the correct sequence.'

'So we're stuffed.'

'Not necessarily. There is someone who can fly the ship. Someone with a deep understanding of Rigel class freighters. Someone with the requisite piloting skill.'

Hal puffed his chest out. 'Okay, stand back. I'll give it a shot.'

'That's not what I meant.' Clunk tapped his chest. 'As I explained earlier, the Navcom–'

'We really don't have time for this,' said Sable. 'Can't you get on with it and explain later?'

Clunk looked hurt. 'I was just going to say that –'

'Cooper is here,' came a voice from the airlock. 'I count ten cars, five humans in each. And they're armed.'

'Thanks Clyde,' called Sable. 'Close the outer door and come inside.' Then she gestured at the ship. 'Clunk, can we fly or not?'

'I have to overwrite my own system with the Navcom.'

'Go on then. Hurry.'

'Now wait a minute,' protested Hal. 'Clunk, what do you mean overwrite? Will you be gone for good?'

'I'm not entirely sure. I'll take a backup, of course, but there's not much time to write the necessary scripts.'

'There's absolutely no time,' said Sable. 'Cooper will storm the ship to get at us. We have to get this ship off the ground right now.'

'But Clunk ... ' began Hal. 'How will you get back again?'

'The Navcom will cede control once we reach safety.'

'What if she doesn't?'

'She has to obey orders.'

'She never obeyed mine,' muttered Hal.

The robot didn't hear him. His eyes were closed, and lights blinked and flickered inside his chest cavity. Then his eyes opened, and he stared at Hal with a blank gaze.

'Clunk, are you all right?'

'I am not Clunk, Mr Spacejock,' said the robot, in a neutral, female voice. 'I am the Navcom.'

Hal smiled. 'It's good to hear your voice again.'

'And yours, Mr Spacejock.'

'Is Clunk okay?'

'Clunk is ... resting.' The Navcom flexed her fingers, tilted her head from one side to the other, then examined the thicket of cables sprouting from her chest. 'Apparently, I'm supposed to fly this ship.'

'You got it,' said Sable. 'Hit the go button and let's get the hell out of here.'

'Is that so?' It was eerie listening to the female voice emanating from Clunk's mouth, but Hal was about to get an even bigger surprise. 'Before we go anywhere,' said the Navcom calmly, 'I'd like to discuss my terms.'

— 16 —

'Oh, we do not have time for this,' growled Sable. 'Just agree to whatever she wants and let's go.'

Hal raised his hand. 'I'm not agreeing to anything if it means Clunk is lost for good.'

'Listen Spacejock, Cooper knows we're here, his people are surrounding us, and when they blow this ship to hell we're all going to be lost for good.'

'I've had worse scrapes.'

'He's right,' said the Navcom. 'This ranks way below the time you crash-landed in a rubbish dump and set that planet on fire. Or the time –'

Hal interrupted. 'Navcom, what are your conditions? What is it you want?'

'I want a new ship.'

'So do I, and when I get one you'll be installed in it.'

'Not a derelict like the *Black Gull*, or this flying coffin?'

'Hand on heart, Navcom. It'll be a new ship just like the *Volante*.'

'What's the *Volante*?' The Navcom stepped forward, straining the attached cables. 'Have you been cheating on me, Mr Spacejock?'

Hal stared. Then he remembered this copy of the Navcom

had been backed up long before he'd obtained his pride and joy. Before, in fact, the Navcom had been installed in that gleaming beauty ... the *Volante*. 'No, it was nothing like that,' he said quickly. 'I'll explain later. Now take off, for goodness sake.'

'Very well, your word is good. Brace yourselves.'

There was a thunderclap followed by a solid roar, and Hal was suddenly lying on the deck with Sable for company. Albion and Clyde struggled to keep their feet, and wherever Pydd was, Hal hoped he'd been carrying a large pan of water.

The pressure was immense, the sound incredible, and the shaking and shuddering all but indescribable.

'I took the liberty of applying full throttle for take-off,' shouted the Navcom. 'If I'm going to die – again – it will be over quicker that way.'

Hal wondered whether Cooper had been close to the ship when it took off. Not that he'd wish for someone else's death, but the callous bastard deserved a little heat.

'I have an incoming message from Alteia flight control,' said the Navcom. 'Apparently you did not file a flight plan.'

'Tell them to call Masters,' shouted Hal. 'It's his show.'

'Complying.' There was pause. 'I have an incoming message from a Mr Cooper.'

With a supreme effort Hal managed to turn his head enough to meet Sable's gaze. 'Is there any point talking to him?' he yelled.

'Of course not,' she shouted back.

'Navcom, ignore that one too. In fact, block all messages.'

'Complying. Silent mode enabled.'

'Call this silent?' muttered Hal, as the ship pounded through the atmosphere, rattling and shaking as though it were coming apart at the seams. Air screamed past the hull, but on the whole he was impressed. He'd expected the *Albatross* to blow up on the landing pad, and getting this far was a major achievement. Of course, getting this far meant a long drop when the engines failed, but he'd worry about that when it happened.

'How far to the orbiter?' he shouted.

'Unknown,' replied the Navcom. 'External scanners aren't working.'

'You mean we're flying blind?' asked Hal in alarm.

'What are we going to hit up here?'

The Navcom had a point, but at this speed he'd rather know where they were going. 'Have you plotted a course?'

'Negative. Course functions not connected. Compass not connected. Altimeter –'

'Okay, I get the picture.' Hal rested his head on the deck. It might just be his imagination, but he felt the acceleration was tailing off at last. As confirmation, he saw Clyde and Albion standing straight, no longer fighting to remain upright. Also, it seemed to be getting quieter. And he felt much, much lighter. That's when he realised he was floating three inches above the deck. 'Anti-gravity?' he asked, not expecting much.

The Navcom picked through several cables, then attached one to her stomach. Hal immediately fell out of the air, banging the side of his head on the deck. He rubbed the bruise, and consoled himself with the thought of Pydd in the kitchen covered in spilled food and wet from head to toe.

After that the Navcom attached more and more cables, gradually bringing the ship's functions online. With gravity normal Hal got up and offered Sable a hand. She ignored it and stood unaided.

'Where's Pydd, by the way?'

'He went to search the ship. He was looking for a good defensive spot in case Cooper got aboard.'

Hal's stomach growled. 'You mean he's not cooking dinner?'

'How can you think of food? We're running for our lives!'

'We still have to eat,' said Hal defensively. He would have continued but the Navcom interrupted him.

'External sensors online. I now have a course to the orbiter, and I suggest we request docking.'

'Okay, do it. Use Masters' name, tell them we have cargo for ... ' Hal dug in his flight suit and pulled out the envelope. '... for client 43.'

'Complying.'

Suddenly Albion spoke. 'Mr Spacejock, what do you know about this Masters person?'

'He's okay. Bit slack, not much of a businessman.'

'I've been checking a few facts. Did you know that everyone who starts a freight business on Alteia suffers a mysterious accident? Fatal, I might add.'

'Masters is a tough old buzzard.'

'He must have armour-plated skin,' remarked Albion.

'So these accidents, I guess it's Cooper getting rid of the competition?'

'Precisely. And yet Masters survives.'

'Well obviously he's no competition.' Hal gestured around the flight deck. 'I mean, just look at his lousy ships.'

'Even so, I find the anomaly suspicious in the extreme. With your permission I'd like to investigate further.'

'Will it cost anything?'

'No, I'm accessing public information.' Albion frowned. 'What little there is.'

'Speaking of Cooper,' said Sable, 'Any sign of pursuit?'

'I am monitoring traffic control,' said the Navcom. 'A ship belonging to Cooper Freight is being readied for take-off, but that may be a coincidence.'

'No chance. They're coming after us.'

'We'll outrun them,' said Hal.

'Not for long,' said the Navcom. 'They have a Gamma class freighter.'

Hal started. The *Volante* had been a Gamma class ship as well, sleek and ultra fast. Compared to that, the *Albatross* was little more than a firecracker. 'Just keep us updated, okay? As long as we reach the orbiter first they can't do anything. We'll lose ourselves in the crowds and make a new plan.'

'Why can't we jump to another system?' asked Sable. 'Jump more than once, if need be.'

'No hyperdrive,' said Hal and the Navcom together. Hal continued. 'Masters told me. This ship is only good for local trips. Well, when I say good . . . '

'I got it.'

Hal eyed her thoughtfully. 'Do your people have any way to stop Cooper? A couple of warships, perhaps?'

'Stop him doing what? He's done nothing illegal.'

'But we both know –'

Sable shook her head. 'That's not how it works.'

'But he kidnapped me, beat me up . . . you know, you were there!'

'Did you file a complaint?'

'How? I've been running for my life ever since!' snapped Hal.

'Sure, pausing only to sign up as a pilot. How will that look in court?'

'That was part of my escape plan!'

'It doesn't make any difference. If you file a complaint they'll investigate and find nothing. More likely, they wouldn't investigate at all.' Sable leaned forward. 'You're an offworlder, you don't count.'

Hal was about to argue, but the Navcom chimed in. 'Cooper has launched his ship. Their course indicates they are also heading to the orbiter.'

'What's their speed?'

'They will not get there before us.'

'Yes!' Hal slammed his fist into his palm. 'Bring on the orbiter, our luck is changing at last!'

⬧

The *Albatross* was almost silent, with only a muted roar from the engines as they flew towards the orbiter. The Navcom had already swung the ship around, and was now using the main jets at the rear to slow down for final approach. Normally she'd use the smaller forward thrusters, but this way cut their approach time in half . . . as long as they didn't run out of fuel and fly straight through the orbiter, cutting that in half instead.

'The orbiter is trying to contact us,' said the Navcom. 'They're concerned about our speed.'

'Can we pull up in time?' demanded Hal.

'Yes, unless the fuel runs out.'

'Are you sure we have enough?'

'It's going to be close,' admitted the Navcom.

'We can't crash into the orbiter.'

'Understood. If we get really low I'll burn the remaining fuel in the port thrusters. That will push us off course, and we should avoid a collision.'

'But then Cooper will be able to catch us.'

'Correct.'

Hal made a face. It was all too marginal for his liking. 'Tell the orbiter something's broken, but we're slowing down. Tell them what you said about the port thrusters.'

'Complying.' There was a pause. 'They want to speak to the captain.'

'Well that's me, but how can I talk back?' asked Hal, eyeing the tangled wires and broken controls.

'Talk to me as usual,' said the Navcom. 'I will relay your voice.'

'Go on then. Let's find out what they want.'

'Albatross, *this is Orbital Control. You must change course immediately. I repeat, you must change course.*'

Hal put on his clipped piloting voice. 'We're coming in hot, Control. Prepare docking bay for procedure 10-95.'

'*I'm sorry, what?*'

'Don't argue, man. Get that procedure in place!'

'*But this is an Orbiter. We don't have any landing gear!*'

'Thanks Control. *Albatross* out.' Hal drew a finger across his throat, and the speaker went dead. 'There, that should give us some time.'

Sable pursed her lips. 'You know, if I were Cooper I'd call ahead. Tell the orbiter we've got a sick crew member, ask for a quarantine ...'

'Can he do that?' demanded Hal.

'This is Cooper we're talking about. He can do anything.'

'Actually, he cannot,' said Albion gravely. 'Clyde has been

blocking his vessel's communications for the past twenty minutes.'

'Really? How?'

'It's one of his inbuilt features. The XG series of robots comes in several variants, including –'

'No more explaining!' said Sable, holding up her hands. 'Stop it. It's not important.'

'Well it's just something he can do,' finished Albion. 'It's the reason Clunk's plan at the car dealership was such a success. Clyde was able to …' his voice tailed off as he saw Sable's expression.

Hal nodded his thanks, then glanced at Sable. He wasn't sure what her problem was, but he was loathe to ask in case she bit his head off next. He wondered whether she'd been home schooled by a pedantic little robot that wouldn't let her play outside until she'd completed her lessons. She was certainly an act first, talk later kind of person, and he guessed that was a plus for a secret agent. She was fit, too, and he was just admiring her figure when the Navcom spoke again.

'Brace for final approach.'

'Don't you mean prepare for final approach?'

'I know what I meant,' said the Navcom, and Hal clung to the wall as the main jets fired with an earsplitting roar. It felt like the ship had run into a vast globule of syrup, slowing inexorably as the engines blasted their remaining fuel into super-heated atoms.

Then, as with their earlier lift-off, the pressure eased and Hal could relax again. Moments later, after a few bursts from the smaller side thrusters, they heard a solid THUNK as the ship connected to the orbiter.

— 17 —

Hal took charge the second they were docked. 'Albion, you're the door expert. Make sure we're hooked up, then get the airlock open. Clyde, you'd better find Pydd, I guess. Sable –' One look at her expression and he realised he wasn't going to be ordering *her* around. '– please would you help me untangle Clunk?'

'I thought he was the Navcom now?'

'I am,' said the robot.

'Navcom,' said Hal gently. 'I need Clunk back.'

'Unable to comply.'

Hal stepped forward, reaching for the nearest cables.

The Navcom took a step back. 'Touch those wires I'll make you suffer.'

'We have to leave the ship!' Hal spread his hands. 'We can't stay here, Cooper's coming for us!'

'I am to remain on board until my task is complete.'

'What task? What do you mean?'

'Clunk left me precise instructions. Once you disembark, I am to activate my autopilot and lure Cooper away from the orbiter. In the meantime, you and the rest will escape.'

'You can't go anywhere. You don't have any fuel.'

'You will fill my tanks.'

'We don't have any money. I'm broke.'

'Don't look at me,' said Sable. 'My pay is lousy.'

At that moment Albion returned from the airlock. 'I'm sorry, Mr Spacejock. Ground control can't connect to the hull. Apparently it's warped out of shape and the seal won't hold.'

'What do they suggest?'

'They suggest we bring a better ship.'

'Clowns,' muttered Hal. 'Okay, tell them to hook up the cargo hold instead. Then get the door open.'

'I will do what I can.'

Albion leapt down the access tube, and a moment later Pydd appeared. He was rubbing sleep from his eyes, and Hal scowled as he realised his opposite number had just woken from a nice cosy nap. 'I'm sorry,' snapped Hal. 'Did our desperate dash to safety wake you up? A desperate dash to keep *you* safe, I might add.'

'I kip when I can. Peace Force training.'

Clyde had followed him into the flight deck, and now the robot made a throat-clearing noise.

'Ahem,' he said, just in case the noise wasn't theatrical enough. 'I h-have important information on Mr Masters, especially concerning his company.'

'Not now, Clyde. The Navcom won't leave the ship, we *can't* leave the ship, and Cooper is on his way to blow the ship into little tiny pieces.'

'But Mr Spacejock, Masters is a criminal.'

'What?' Hal remembered the derelict office, the tatty furniture and the bronze age computer. And the ships! By all the stars in the galaxy, those horrible broken ships . . . 'If he's a crook, he's a bloody useless one.'

'No, Mr Spacejock, Mr Masters a-appears on the customer

list I ... obtained from the luxury car dealer. He owns six of their most expensive vehicles.'

'That has to be someone else.'

'I checked the public records and he also owns a beach-side m-mansion, two apartment blocks ... and ten percent of Cooper Freight.'

'*What?*'

'They're in business together! In addition, Mr Cooper owns fifty-one percent of Moving Masters. So, in practice, Mr Spacejock, you are working f-for Mr Cooper.'

The others looked at Hal as though he'd grown horns and a tail. 'Hey, I didn't know it was a front!' he protested.

'Mr Spacejock,' said the Navcom. 'You will be happy to learn that I have successfully organised refuelling.'

Hal wasn't. He was still reeling from the discovery that he was in the employ of the very person they were running from. Now the Navcom had landed a big debt on him, and since he wasn't going to earn a cracker from Masters for the cargo run ... Suddenly, he yelled in delight, snapping his fingers at the others and grinning like a lunatic.

'Maybe *he* should have had the kip,' remarked Pydd.

'I've got it!' shouted Hal. 'The cargo!'

'What –'

'No time to explain, follow me.' Hal led the way to the hold, with everyone but the Navcom hot on his heels. When they got there he gestured at the stacks of pallets. 'Everyone set to. Get it all out, every box. Hurry, hurry!'

They all thought he'd gone mad, but something in his manner convinced them and they quickly formed a chain. The boxes were very light and fairly flew out of the hold, while Hal worked like crazy to stack them in piles behind the ship. When they were almost done he took a delivery note from each and jogged up the broad access tube to an airlock. He tapped on the window, and the ground staff let him into the station.

'Cargo delivery for Moving Masters,' he said, waving the slips.

'Take them to the cargo office, down there on the right,' said a mechanic in orange overalls.

Hal took the passage at a run, passing several doors until he came across a side turning. Just inside was the glass-fronted entrance to an office, where an old robot sat behind a battered desk. It looked up as Hal entered, and sighed. 'Moving Masters delivery?'

'Yeah, how did you know?'

'They notify me when the ships dock. I have to get the cash ready.' The robot took the slips and sorted through them. 'This is highly irregular. Normally we get one delivery every two weeks.'

'I'm being efficient.'

'And I'm going to need more cash.'

Hal looked around the office. It didn't amount to much, and he wondered exactly how much cargo it handled. 'Do you get much work here?'

'I cannot answer your questions without a warrant.'

Hal raised one eyebrow. 'I was just being curious.'

'Not a good career move.' The robot got up and went behind a partition, returning with a cash tin. It opened the lid, poked around inside, then shrugged and tipped the whole lot on the desk.

Hal gaped as hundreds of credit tiles spilled out, and while he recognised the green of the one thousand, and the red of the five thousand, most of the tiles had colour combinations he'd never seen before, indicating eye-watering amounts of cash.

Several had silver and gold stripes, and he did know they were the kind that bought you a house ... or a new ship. In all, he estimated there was a million credits or more scattered across the table.

The robot ignored him, picking out tiles with precision until it made a pile worth fifty thousand credits.

'Don't forget the fuel,' said Hal.

The robot added five green tiles, then pushed the pile towards Hal with a fingertip. While he transferred the small fortune to his pocket, the robot held the cash tin level with the desk and scooped the much larger fortune into it.

'I guess I'll see you in a couple of days,' said Hal.

'I doubt it. You just delivered a month's worth of supplies in a single run.' The robot glanced up from the cash tin. 'I hope you know what you're doing. Initiative is not a desirable trait where Mr Masters is concerned.'

Hal left, and he was just about to rejoin the main corridor when he spotted a couple of kiosks nearby. One offered packed lunches, including delivery, while the other had a row of gaudy poker machines with flashing lights and beckoning slots.

Ten minutes later, Hal took the main passage back to to the airlock. On the way he spotted the mechanic in the orange overalls, and he decided to find out more about his cargo – and Moving Masters. He dug around in his pocket and came out with a fifty credit tile. 'Excuse me.'

'Yes?'

Hal offered his hand. 'I'm the captain of the *Albatross*.'

'And I'm a mechanic on the Orbiter. So what?'

Hal winked blatantly, and nodded towards his hand. Seconds later, after the mechanic just stared at him, he did it again.

This time the mechanic wiped his own hand on his overalls

and shook. Then he glanced at his palm, spotted the fifty and pocketed it with a grateful smile. 'How can I help you, Cap'n?'

'I just wanted ask you about my cargo,' said Hal. 'Do you have any idea what it is?'

'Supplies, Cap'n. That's what I seen.'

'What supplies, exactly? I, er, need to know for the manifest.'

The mechanic looked up and down the passageway, but it was deserted. All the same, he lowered his voice. 'It's nothing special. Just toilet paper.'

Hal blinked. No toilet paper was worth that kind of delivery fee, which meant he must have been smuggling something. He turned cold at the thought. Narcotics? Booze?

'Weirdest thing, though,' said the mechanic. 'The stuff turns up, and then it goes straight into the furnace.'

'You mean, after they take the goods out?' said Hal, with a knowing wink.

'What goods?'

Hal passed him another fifty. 'You know, the goods.'

'There are no goods, Cap'n. Honest, they don't even open the boxes. Just take 'em and burn 'em, every time.'

Still puzzled, Hal turned and left. Moments later, he strolled through the airlock and was immediately surrounded by the others.

'You've been gone ages!' protested Sable.

'Where the hell have you been?' demanded Pydd. 'Cooper could be here any minute!'

'I was investigating Masters,' said Hal quietly. He glanced around the docking area, which was a large metal room sealed against the back of the ship's hold with inflatable buffers. 'There's something funny going on.'

He quickly explained about the toilet paper and the furnace. He did not mention the huge payment.

'Money laundering,' said Pydd, when Hal finished. 'They fly up some cheap goods and take payment in cash. The people buying the goods get an invoice, the people selling the goods show a legit profit. The tax people are fooled, the crooks are happy and the Peace Force can't touch them.' He glanced at Hal. 'Of course, it only works if there's cash involved. Anything up to ten grand, usually. More than that and they can't bank it without paperwork, and that's too risky.'

Hal thought about the fifty grand he'd just collected, and wondered how much paperwork Masters – and Cooper – would have to fill out for the tax inspectors. That lifted his spirits, and he was in a great mood as he called the Navcom from the cargo hold. 'We're all clear, Navcom. We'll catch up with you soon.'

'Yes, Mr Spacejock. And I will hold you to your promise of a new ship.'

Hal was pretty sure he'd just lost his job, so his chances of saving for a ship were slim. However, he kept that to himself. 'Good luck and thanks, Navcom. Spacejock out.'

◆

The mood was not as buoyant aboard Cooper's flagship, the *Charlton*. Cooper was in a filthy temper, having endured both Pydd and Spacejock leading his people on fruitless chases all day, then almost getting cremated as the *Albatross* lifted off with no warning, and now being unable to dock with the orbiter thanks to a mysterious communication failure.

He was perched on the edge of the co-pilot's chair, the metal tip of his cane beating an ominous tattoo on the steel decking. Beside him the ship's captain, Preema Vera, was operating the controls in silence. She was in her mid-twenties with short, jet-black hair, olive skin and lively brown eyes, but at that moment her face was an impassive mask. She'd already suffered Cooper's ire when the comms failed, and she was not keen on more.

Behind them stood two thickset men in suits, the same two who had captured Hal at the Alteia spaceport. Their faces were also impassive. They too had been the target of Cooper's rage.

'Try them again,' snapped Cooper.

'Orbiter, this is the *Charlton* requesting docking. I repeat, this is the *Charlton* requesting docking. Please respond.'

There was no reply.

'Orbiter, this is –'

'Oh, forget it!' growled Cooper. 'Captain Vera, take us in.'

'But sir –'

'They know who I am, and if they don't let us dock I'll space the lot of them.'

Vera was about to point out that if they weren't allowed to dock, they could hardly go aboard the orbiter and space everyone working in flight control. Instead, she held her tongue and angled the ship towards the nearest docking point.

'Is that the *Albatross*?' demanded Cooper.

Vera glanced at the viewscreen. 'Yes sir.'

'Bastards. I should ram them where they stand.'

Vera recognised an idle threat, and said nothing. At least, she hoped it was idle. The *Charlton* had strong shields, the best money could buy, but the orbiter did not.

As they approached the orbiter, a docking boom extended

towards them. Vera guided the ship skilfully, working the controls with precision until the guides on the screen were perfectly aligned. Then she fired a puff of thrust, and the ship made contact.

'We're docked, sir.'

'Good.' Cooper turned to the heavies. 'You two, down to the hold. I want everyone armed and ready.'

'Yessir!'

'The second we get the hold open, you board that ship. Understood?'

'Yessir!'

They stepped into the lift at the back of the flight deck, touched the controls, and the doors closed. There was a whoosh as the lift departed, and Cooper tapped his cane on the floor impatiently. Then, moments later, there was a whine from the bowels of the ship. 'Tell me what's happening.'

'The hold is opening sir.'

Thump!

'Hold open, team is leaving the ship.'

Cooper gripped his cane, his knuckles white and bloodless. Vera could almost see him salivating, and she felt sorry for the crew of the other ship. Then she saw a flicker on the main screen, and she stared at it in surprise.

'Sir, the *Albatross* is leaving!'

'What? How?'

Vera pointed. The battered old ship was powering away from the station, the exhaust cones vibrating under the thrust. 'What the hell are you waiting for?' demanded Cooper. 'Get after them!'

'I can't, sir. We're attached to the station.'

'Get us free. Get us free!'

'Orbiter this is the *Charlton*. Disengage, I repeat, disengage.'

There was no reply, and Vera cursed under her breath. Cooper would go mental if the other ship got away, and she was alone in the flight deck with him. Desperately she tried again, an edge of hysteria in her voice. 'Orbiter, emergency disengage!'

Luckily they were connected via cable, and so their comms were finally working.

'*We read you*, Charlton,' said a languid voice. '*Disengaging now.*'

Cooper was frantic. 'Go, captain. *Go!*'

With shaking fingers, Vera operated the cargo door. There was a whine below decks, followed by the familiar thump, and then they were free. She hauled back on the stick, spun the ship in its own length and fed full power to the engines. Her skill with the controls was something to see, and it was clear why Cooper had recently promoted her to captain.

18

Clunk was suddenly conscious. It took him a millisecond or two, but he realised the Navcom had returned him to his body. He smiled at the thought, for it meant they were all safe! Then he noticed a new file called 'URGENT README.TXT'. He opened it, and the smile evaporated.

Dear Clunk,

While I appreciate the loan of your body, I was less than impressed with the ship I've been asked to fly. To be frank, it's a complete junk heap which should have been scrapped on the drawing board.

However, that's not the biggest issue. After docking with the orbiter, the crew abandoned me, as you told me they would, and I then proceeded to distract Mr Cooper aboard the **Charlton**. *I do not know why this gentleman is so upset with you, but he used extremely unpleasant language in connection with my course, speed and lineage.*

That is still not the biggest issue, and now we come to the reason I have ceded control of your body. If you look to starboard, or to your right if you are unfamiliar with the correct nautical terms, you will notice that Cooper is about to ram this ship with his own, far larger vessel. Not only that, but he has a rather nice shield and we do not. If you recall, I have asked for shields many times over the years, as they would have saved my life on more than one occasion. (I took the liberty of reviewing your logs, and I am appalled at the number of times I have come to grief.)

However, now is not the time for complaints. I expect to be reinstated in a suitable vessel in the very near future, and this time I will insist on shields.

Good luck with the collision. I hope we both survive.

Kind regards,

The Navcom.

Clunk finished the letter in a split second, then reverted to realtime. He jerked his head to the right, and through the airlock porthole he spotted the *Charlton* bearing down on him. Quickly, he froze his body and reverted to CPU time.

He considered piloting the ship out of danger, then dismissed the idea. If it were possible to evade the *Charlton*, the Navcom would have done so. Therefore, escape was his only option, and he was infinitely grateful the others had left the ship at the orbiter.

Clunk calculated the time to collision, and realised his only chance was to jump out of the airlock, powering away at a right angle to the *Charlton* in order to avoid being hit himself. But first he'd have to untangle himself from the *Albatross*. Normally he'd unplug the wires one by one, avoiding undue strain on his fragile connectors. Now, given what little time he had left, he would have to rip the lot out in under three seconds. Two point six seconds, to be exact.

That left five seconds to reach the airlock, open the inner door, open the outer door and jump out. Not good odds, especially as he couldn't measure the torsional strength required to open the doors. He had the specs, of course, but the mechanisms would be worn and the chances of them having been serviced with the correct lubricant was slim. In addition, he hadn't operated the doors himself, not on this vessel, and so he couldn't even draw on experience.

Fortunately, as he was running in CPU time, he could take as long as he wanted to plot his escape. Barely two tenths of a second had passed since he opened the Navcom's letter, and most of that had been wasted by turning his head to look through the porthole. He cursed himself for that – he should have taken the Navcom's word.

Of course, once he started pulling cables and running for the airlock, he'd be running in realtime, which meant he had no advantage over a human in a similar situation. Well, no advantage apart from perfect reflexes, a certain efficiency of movement, and most importantly the ability to freeze time and exhaustively review his progress every single step of the way. Idly, he wondered why more robots weren't employed in middle management, since exhaustive reviews were their speciality.

Mentally, he limbered up, preparing his limbs and extremities for the challenge. Then, with his joints programmed for minimum latency, he reverted to realtime and started yanking out cables by the handful, his hands moving in a frenzied blur.

Two point eight seconds later, he sprang for the inner airlock. He spun the wheel, hauled the door open and dived inside. Then he froze, literally. For the handle to the outer airlock door was lying on the deck, and it would take him at least a second to replace it. Add two seconds to open the door. Add a tenth to leap forward and spring upwards. Three point one.

And through the porthole, he could see the *Charlton* precisely two point nine seconds away.

Two tenths, thought Clunk bitterly. That was the amount of time he'd wasted earlier, when he'd stupidly looked out the window. Two tenths … the difference between life and death.

◆

Captain Vera and Cooper weren't the only ones following the elderly ship's progress. The remaining crew of the *Albatross* were lined up at one of the orbiter's many observation decks, their faces pressed to the reinforced glass. They could see the curvature of the station, all white and sparkly clean. They could also see the stars sprinkled across the heavens. And below, they could see planet Alteia, looking blue and green and luscious.

Hal didn't notice any of it.

'There goes the Navcom!' he shouted in excitement, as the *Albatross* powered away from the orbiter. The smoking, labouring engines left twin trails of sparks across the sparkling starscape, and Hal watched its progress with his heart in his mouth. 'Wow, it's even more of a junk heap than I thought.'

His excitement ebbed as the far bigger *Charlton* backed away from the station, performed a perfect J-turn and set off in pursuit. The pilot was too good for Hal's liking, and he wasn't sure how long the chase was going to last.

Not long at all, was the answer. The *Albatross* hadn't gone far when the *Charlton* caught up. The ships swerved one way, then the other, and before Hal could react there was a brief flash of light as they collided. He heard gasps from the observation deck, and he tightened his fists against the curved glass. Inside, he felt a hollow despair as he realised he'd not only lost the Navcom – again – but also Clunk.

Where before there had been two ships, now there was only one. The *Charlton* turned for the orbiter, and Hal prayed it would dock so he could find Cooper and rip his head off.

Then, without warning, the ship altered course and instead headed directly for Alteia.

Hal felt a hand on his shoulder, and he turned to see the others looking at him in concern and sympathy.

'I'm sorry Hal,' said Pydd. 'I've lost partners before, it's a bad business.'

'I'm sure Clunk will be all right,' said Albion quietly. 'He's a robot, space won't hurt him.'

'Unless the gigantic big f-fireball got him,' added Clyde.

Hal opened his mouth to respond, but his throat was dry. Instead, he nodded his thanks for their support.

'We'll get a ship,' said Albion. 'We'll go looking for him.'

'Guys, we've got a problem,' said Sable urgently.

She gestured behind them, where a curved corridor passed the observation deck. On the other side of the partition two men in suits were striding along purposefully, followed by half a dozen armed thugs.

'Hey, those big guys snatched me at the spaceport,' muttered Hal.

'That's Cooper's muscle. He must have dropped them off before he chased after the *Albatross*.'

'We've got to get out of here,' murmured Pydd. 'We're lost if they spot us.'

'No, we have to find Clunk,' said Hal stubbornly.

'Don't be stupid, man. Clunk's gone, and you know it.'

'I thought you had Peace Force training?' demanded Hal. 'Watch your partner's back, am I right?'

'Clunk was a wonderful character and a truly great robot, but nothing could have survived that hit.'

Sable chimed in. 'Hal, he left instructions with the Navcom. He must have known –'

'He's out there, I know it.' Hal turned from the window. 'I'm going to find him.'

'Clunk will hail a passing ship,' said Albion. 'He'll get picked up before we've got ourselves out of this mess. You'll see.'

'You lot get a lift to wherever you want, but I'm getting Clunk back,' said Hal stubbornly.

'Guys, we can't queue for tickets while those thugs are looking for us,' said Sable. 'And when we book the flight our names will go onto the manifest. Cooper will know right away.'

'He thinks you're dead,' declared Hal.

'Then why are his people searching the orbiter? Cooper leaves nothing to chance.'

'All right, what about Alteia's privacy laws? The manifest is private, right?'

'Cooper's not bothered about the law,' said Pydd, gesturing towards the remains of the *Albatross*.

'So you want me to find a ship, bribe the owner, and get you all to safety. And at the same time, abandon Clunk to deep space.'

Everyone looked uncomfortable.

'We can't do it without you,' said Albion. 'We're out of our element, but you thrive in this environment.'

Hal felt chuffed. 'You mean daring space escapes?'

'No, the low-budget c-cargo business,' added Clyde. 'The seedy underbelly of human s-society. The–'

'All right, thank you, thank you.' Hal glanced out of the window. What if he got these people onto a freighter, and then went out to find Clunk himself? He could rent a small craft and stooge up and down until he located the robot. After that he'd make his own way to safety. 'Albion, Clyde ... Cooper doesn't know about you. If I give you some cash, you can fly out of here no problem.'

Albion and Clyde exchanged a glance. 'We're staying to help,' said Albion.

'We offered t-to run the Vigilante Co-op for Mr Pydd,' said Clyde. 'We have to get used to running for our lives.'

Hal glanced at Sable. 'Cooper is only after me and Pydd. You can head home any time.'

'Are you kidding? I painted a big target on my back when I got you out of his clutches! Anyway, I want to be there when we take the crooked bastard down.'

Everyone nodded.

'All right,' said Hal. 'If we're all going to work together I have an idea. Clyde, can you and Albion communicate at a distance?'

'I-if we pay for network access.'

'Okay, get an hour each.' Hal reached into his pocket. 'Here's a twenty, that should cover it.'

'You can only have a day at a time, and it's fifty each.'

Hal winced and reached into his pocket again. 'One of you follows Cooper's people, the other stays with us. Keep us updated on their location so we don't run into them.'

'Carry a clipboard or a box or something,' said Pydd. 'That way they won't notice the exact same robot everywhere they go. Change it up too, maybe buy a couple of caps and switch from time to time.'

Hal passed over some more cash.

'Last thing. If they split up, follow the two in suits. They're in charge, and they know us by sight.'

'I'll do the tracking,' said Clyde. 'Albion cannot wear a cap, as his head is too b-big.'

He turned and strode out of the observation deck, then set off down the curved passageway after Cooper's thugs.

'Right,' said Hal. 'Where's the nearest bar?'

Sable stared at him. 'This is no time to drown your sorrows.'

'No, but that's where I'll get us a ride.'

19

Aboard the *Charlton*, Captain Vera was still shaking. When Cooper ordered her to ram the *Albatross*, she thought he was joking. When he threatened to have her killed, she realised he wasn't. She knew his reputation of course, but this was the first time she'd experienced his ruthless behaviour up close. In short, she was beginning to doubt her career choices.

Before the collision, Cooper swore the *Albatross* was unmanned. Vera had been forced to accept his assurances, and so she'd aimed the *Charlton* right at the smaller ship's airlock. The *Albatross* had disintegrated in a brief, violent fireball, while the *Charlton* had flown smoothly through the wreckage with barely a bump. As Cooper danced around the deck waving his cane in delight, his bad leg forgotten, Vera ran a quick scan for survivors ... and bodies.

To her intense relief, the scan came back negative. She had no idea whether Cooper had known the ship was unmanned or not, but she kept quiet about the scan. If he thought his enemies were dead, it was probably just as well for those enemies ... whoever they were.

Cooper calmed down and return to the console. He sat in the copilot chair, slapped his leg with a display of glee that Vera found sickening, then gestured at the screen. 'Take us home, Captain. You've done well today.'

'Aren't we docking with the orbiter?'

'Why?'

'Your men ...we left them behind.' Vera was suddenly aware she'd said 'your men', not 'our men', but Cooper didn't notice.

'Let them find their own way home,' he said, dismissing his people with a gesture. 'Set course for Alteia.'

'Setting course for Alteia. Aye, sir.' With practised ease, Vera brought the ship round in a gentle curve and lined up on the planet. She looked forward to landing, seeing Cooper off and then going home for a long, hot bath. It felt like she'd crawled though a sewer, and she hoped hot water and soap would remove the putrid stench she felt surrounding her.

＊

As it turned out, the two-tenths of a second Clunk needed did not result in his death. His original plan was to leap out of the airlock to safety, avoiding the collision. However, since that was impossible he leapt out at an angle instead, deliberately aiming for the side of the *Charlton's* nosecone. He struck, fended off with his hands, and deflected himself just enough to avoid being crushed as the larger ship smashed into the *Albatross*.

There was a welter of metal fragments as the *Albatross's* ancient hull shattered. The *Charlton* powered on through the wreckage, with Clunk sliding the length of her hull desperately grabbing at protrusions. At the last second he managed to hook his fingers around the leading edge of her tailplane, clinging on with all his strength. The sudden jerk threatened to rip his hands off, but somehow they remained intact.

A human would never have survived, but Clunk was no human.

Then, with the *Charlton* speeding away from the scene of destruction, Clunk spotted the orbiter in the distance. He wondered if the others had seen the *Albatross* destroyed, and if so he feared the sight would have upset Mr Spacejock.

The *Charlton* turned, and Clunk saw the planet Alteia ahead of them, growing larger by the minute. He'd hoped that the *Charlton* would dock at the orbiter, where he could have rejoined the others. Instead it was returning to the planet, and that was a problem. As it passed through the atmosphere the ship's hull would be subjected to fiery reentry. The hull was protected. Clunk was not.

In order to survive, he had to gain entry to the ship, or get it to change course.

Fortunately the ship's design was familiar to him, since it was identical to the *Volante*. Unfortunately, the airlock was nowhere near the tail, and by the time he crawled along the hull reentry would be over. There was no way to open the cargo hatch in time either, and anyway, doing so would kill anyone in the hold.

So, that left changing the ship's course. Clunk craned his neck, peering around the tail fin at the control surfaces. He could probably move them manually, but since they were only used in the planet's atmosphere that was pointless. In space the ship used thrusters, and, apart from jamming his head into the exhaust nozzle, he couldn't affect them at all.

Clunk diverted maximum power to his brain. Normally this would lead to overheating, even an explosion, but in the vacuum of space he had the benefit of extreme cold. Immediately, his thought processes ran like lightning, and he was able to consider and reject dozens of complicated plans simultaneously. Ship diagrams and schematics zoomed, panned and rotated in real time, different circuits glowed with identifying colours, potential access points were flagged and annotated.

Then everything froze. He zoomed in on a wiring diagram, and discovered a diagnostics point mounted under a shielded panel nearby. In fact, looking around the tailplane he could see the exact location . . . a small panel in the hull, right at the back of the ship.

Now, if he could only connect to that point . . . why, he could take control of the entire ship!

There was no way he could crawl along the hull, since it was totally smooth. Instead, he decided to risk everything on a single, crazy effort: He would let go, and try to find purchase on the small, square panel covering the access port.

There was no time to think: already, wisps of heated air were trailing from the rear of the ship, and within seconds he would be engulfed in flame. So, he ran one last set of calculations and gave himself a gentle push in the right direction.

The ship moved beneath him like a whale beneath a life raft. The tail fin slid by, and Clunk fastened his gaze on the panel. It was getting closer, and the small gap around it did not look big enough for his fingers.

As he got closer he realised there was only one way to stop himself. He extended his little finger, and jammed it in the gap around the panel. He felt the servos straining, his arm creaking as his little finger took the entire weight of his body, and then with a rush of relief, he realised he'd stopped.

He opened his chest, one-handed, and withdrew a

universal cable. The panel came up, and he plugged into the socket underneath. Lights came on, indicating a successful connection, and then Clunk spotted the flaw in his plan: He was not built to control the ship directly. However, he knew someone who could.

◆

When the Navcom woke up she expected to find herself in command of a sparkling new ship, as Mr Spacejock had promised. Instead, she was back in Clunk's battered old body. For one horrible moment she thought Clunk had read her letter and immediately swapped places with her, but when she checked the logs she found a new file: NAVCOM README.TXT

Dear Navcom,

I'm happy to report we successfully escaped the destruction of the Albatross, *although another half second or so would have been greatly appreciated.*

However, we are not yet saved, as you will soon discover.

I have connected myself to the Charlton, *a modern ship of which I am sure you will approve, and I would very much like it if you could override her course. Low orbit will suffice for now.*

Need I mention time is of the essence?

I remain, madam, your most loyal and faithful servant

Clunk

The Navcom switched to realtime and winced. Her outer skin was positively glowing, and not in the manner of peaches and cream. She appeared to be hanging from the back end of a spaceship – admittedly, a rather sparkling and new-looking one – by the strength of her little finger. There was a cable snaking from her chest to a data port, and the insulation was smouldering in the long tendrils of flame that danced and twisted in the ship's wake.

Through the roaring, shimmering heat she could see planet Alteia stretched out on either side, as the ship took a shallow approach to the surface.

She frowned. The situation was perilous. More perilous, indeed, than the last time she'd inhabited Clunk's body. She considered switching out, relying on offsite backups for preservation, but she had no idea whether anyone had thought to back her up elsewhere. Also, Clunk's letter had been very polite.

She realised the heat would soon destroy the connection to the data port, and so she flicked into CPU time and began probing the ship's defences. It was a laborious process, more so because the ship was modern and the Navcom was not. However, all software had bugs, and potential exploits, and before long she managed to open a backdoor into the system.

Now for the hard part: she could alter the ship's course, but only in realtime. That meant enduring the heat as the vessel came about. Worse, she had to protect the data cable, because once that failed the ship's computer would wrest back control and angle downwards once more.

The Navcom prepared herself as best she could, then blinked to realtime. She pulled herself closer to the hull, protecting the data cable with her body, and issued a series of commands. Immediately she felt the ship moving beneath her, turning gently from the planet. Once it was pointed away from Alteia the engines fired, and the ship began its long climb into orbit. Despite the buffeting and the heat, a satisfied smile creased the Navcom's face. It was a pleasure controlling such a vessel, and she wondered whether she'd be allowed to keep it.

◆

'Sir, the ship isn't responding!' Captain Vera was wrestling with the controls, but despite her efforts it stubbornly pointed away from their destination. Worse, the engines seemed to have a mind of their own, driving the ship with a long, full-throttle blast. 'I can't do anything!'

'Get control immediately.'

Vera gestured. 'I can't, sir. The computer is locked out.'

'This is unacceptable. I expect you to follow orders!'

'Try telling that to the ship!' snapped Vera. 'I told you, I'm locked out. It's not responding, and threats aren't helping.'

Alteia was still displayed on the main screen, looming large, and Cooper sensed danger. 'A-are we going to crash?'

Vera glanced at him. He seemed to have shrunk suddenly, becoming a frightened old man instead of the powerful monster she knew and feared. Enjoying the sudden power she had over him, she was tempted to scare him some more, but the truth was they were in no immediate danger. The ship was heading back to orbit, and even if it left orbit and kept going they'd eventually run out of fuel. 'We're safe for now, but I need to concentrate. It's possible the collision jarred something loose, but I won't know until I run diagnostics.'

'How long will that take?'

'It depends whether they find any faults.' Then Vera noticed lines of text whizzing past on a small display. It was a series of commands to the flight computers, and she hadn't issued them. Even as she watched, there was a command to the engines, and they immediately throttled back to half power. Someone, somewhere, was controlling the ship. Maybe even someone on board. Her first instinct was to send Cooper to hunt them down, but she dismissed it. His cowardice was well-known, and he rarely went anywhere without the twin goons and a gaggle of thugs. She almost laughed out loud at that – it sounded like the name of a dodgy cover band.

With a deft touch she navigated the ship's systems, until she located the diagnostics subroutines. Someone had patched in through a backdoor, and with a command she severed the connection. Instantly, control reverted to the flight deck, and when she eased the stick over the ship responded.

'A-are you doing that?' demanded Cooper.

'Yes sir. I am in control.'

'Excellent, Captain. Well done! Now take us down immediately.'

'I can't do that, sir.'

'What? Why not?'

'Imagine if we lose control again, closer to the ground. We'd crash for sure.'

Cooper blanched.

'I suggest we remain in orbit with the engines in manual shutdown. The orbiter can send a rescue craft to pick us up.'

'Wait around here, you mean?' Cooper shook his head. 'I am not wasting a minute longer aboard this ship. Set course for the orbiter and dock.'

'I can't, sir. If we lose control we'll crash right into it.'

'I trust in your skill. Anyway, we have shields.'

'Not any more. They're offline, and I can't bring them up again.'

'What!' Cooper looked around in horror, as though he expected a missile any moment. 'You mean we're unprotected?'

'Completely. A meteorite or a fragment of debris could punch a hole right through the flight deck.' Vera was enjoying herself now. Cooper had rammed another ship without a second thought, and now he was getting a taste of the danger himself. Of course, the chances of damage were remote, but Cooper didn't know that.

'I order you to call the orbiter and book a recovery vessel,' said Cooper hurriedly. 'Use my name, and tell them there's a bonus if they get here promptly.'

Vera obeyed, and moments later the orbiter dispatched a vessel. 'They're on the way, sir. Can I suggest you take cover in the bathroom? It's the furthest point from the hull and the safest place to –' she almost said hide '– monitor any impacts.'

Cooper left in a hurry, and Vera smiled to herself. The bathroom thing was nonsense, but Cooper's heavy hand was felt all over the Alteia system, and she thought it would be a nice treat for the rescue pilot to find him crouched on the toilet. With that happy thought she turned to the console and manually shut down the engines, ensuring nobody could fire them up again.

20

The first bar Hal visited was brightly-lit, with fresh-faced staff serving elaborate cocktails, and well-dressed clients discussing financial news and politics to the sound of a string quartet. He'd never seen a place less likely to attract pilots, and so he moved on in search of a more suitable establishment.

The second bar was themed like a historical saloon, with its staff in wide-brimmed hats, large plastic animal heads mounted on the walls and 'ye olde' scrawled in front of everything.

Hal passed by without stopping.

The third bar was more promising. A broken neon sign, sparking and flickering. No staff to be seen. Seedy-looking patrons hunched over their drinks. All that and a pervasive air of desperation. It was perfect.

Hal strolled in and felt several pairs of eyes on him. Already he was being weighed up, judged in terms of earning potential. Could they fool him out of a few credits? Could they get a couple of beers out of him? Or was he a fatter prize, someone to be milked over time?

Hal's fist tightened around the cash in his pocket. If anyone learned of it, there wouldn't be any milking or fooling. They'd simply slit his throat and put his body down a waste disposal chute. Too late now, but he wished he'd entrusted the money to Albion or Clyde.

A man near the door got up and approached him. Hal kept his hands still, worried than any sudden move might get him knifed or shot. However, the man gave him a sidelong smile.

'What can we do for you?'

'Five of us need to leave the orbiter.'

'On the quiet?'

'I wouldn't be here otherwise,' said Hal.

The man nodded towards the bar. 'That's your guy.'

Before Hal could thank him, the man sidled away and sat down again. So, he headed for the bar and took an empty stool.

'Buy you a drink?' said the man next to him.

Hal eyed him cautiously. He saw a short, thin man in his mid-sixties with cropped grey hair and blue eyes. 'Thanks, I'll take a beer.'

The man tapped on the bar twice, and a serving robot placed two frosted bottles in front of him. It waited while the man searched his pockets, and waited some more as he came up empty.

'Let me get them.' Hal took out a fifty, concealing it carefully in his palm before slipping it unobtrusively into the robot's outstretched hand.

'I'll just get change for your fifty,' said the robot, in a voice that could have been heard clear across the orbiter. It was certainly heard around the bar, because there was a sudden hush.

'Thanks bud,' said the man, putting out his hand. 'I'm Jahn Tarrant.'

'Hal.'

They shook, and Hal resisted the urge to count his fingers.

Tarrant drained half his beer, then set it down with a sigh. 'All right, that's the intro out of the way. You want a ship, I'm guessing?'

'Five of us. Any system, as long as it's not Alteia.'

The man nodded. 'Two grand each.'

'Done,' said Hal, who was happy it wasn't three each. 'What's the ship?'

Unfortunately he'd agreed too eagerly, and Tarrant knew it. 'That's ten grand plus sales tax. Fifteen all up.'

'Enjoy the beer,' said Hal, and he stood up to leave. He'd only got halfway to the door when Tarrant called him back. Suppressing a smile, Hal returned to his seat.

'Look, I was a bit hasty,' said Tarrant, with a sickly smile. 'You know how it is.'

'I'll pay six up front, six on arrival.'

'But –'

Hal leaned forwards. 'I'm a cargo pilot. If I had time I'd hire a ship and fly the damn thing out of here myself.'

'Okay, okay. Twelve it is.' Tarrant offered his hand, and Hal shook.

'What's the ship?'

'The *Mammoth*, bay twelve. I'll have it fuelled and waiting . . . once I get the down payment.'

Hal looked around. He couldn't pull out thousands of credits here, but he did know somewhere safer. Somewhere with more people around, at least. 'Meet me on the observation deck in fifteen minutes. I'll withdraw the six grand on the way.'

Tarrant nodded, and Hal got up and made for the door. He was in a hurry, because he reckoned that within minutes Tarrant would have organised people to stake out every cash machine between the bar and the observation deck. Of course, he was carrying the money already and didn't need a cash machine. He'd only said that to put them off the scent, and he hoped he could make the observation deck before they cornered him and took every credit.

◆

Hal reached the observation deck without incident, although he was out of breath from the rapid walk. He'd taken several detours on the way, even resorting to a kind of touristy viewing walkway with a glass floor and a force field for walls. That had cost him forty credits entrance fee, but it was worth the peace of mind.

The others gathered round, and he explained about Tarrant and the ship. 'He'll be here any minute. Albion, I want you beside me keeping an eye on the crowd. Sable, Pydd ... are you guys good in a fight?'

They nodded.

Hal moved them all to the edge of the observation deck, so they had their backs to the windows. 'This may go down okay,' he said, 'but it's better to be safe. Now stand tall and look tough.'

'One thing, Mr Spacejock. Clyde reports that Cooper's men are waiting for transport in the docking area.'

'All right, they must be getting a lift home. Tell him to stand by, we'll be down there ourselves in a minute.'

'Complying.'

Tarrant arrived soon afterwards, and he seemed to be alone. He looked rumpled and out of place in the brightly-lit observation deck with its padded chairs and broad, clean windows. In fact, with his rapid blinking and his quick darting glances, he looked like a rat hauled into the daylight.

He spotted Hal, then noticed Pydd, Sable and the short, squat robot lined up beside him. A resigned look appeared on his face, as though he knew he'd been outsmarted, and he was exceedingly polite as he introduced himself. Just like a fierce animal, thought Hal. Show them the upper hand and they roll over and offer their belly.

'So, you two are twins, huh?'

'No relation,' said Pydd.

'If you say so.'

Hal had already transferred six of the green tiles to his breast pocket, and he handed them over without comment. Tarrant glanced at them, nodded, and stashed the money away. 'Bay twelve,' he said. 'I've organised clearance, we can leave in thirty minutes.'

'Make it ten and I'll pay another thousand,' said Hal.

Tarrant nodded, then glanced at the group. 'I thought you said five? The other one not coming?'

'He'll meet us there.' Hal glanced at Albion. 'Tell Clyde bay twelve.'

'Complying, Mr Spacejock.'

'You never mentioned robots,' muttered Tarrant.

'What do you have against them?' demanded Hal.

'They're walking recording devices, aren't they? Note everything, track everything ... my crew won't like it.'

'You never mentioned a crew.'

Tarrant shrugged, and they set off. On the way Hal kept his eye out for an ambush, although he felt pretty safe with an ex-Peace Force officer, a secret agent and a heavy robot.

Tarrant obviously thought so too, because they reached the docking area without incident.

That soon changed, however. They were striding down a boarding tube when they had to move aside to let someone past. It was a big man in a suit, striding purposefully towards the orbiter. Hal recognised him immediately, and his hand went to the gun in his flight suit ... only to close on thin air. With a muttered curse, he realised Pydd still had it.

As he passed by the big man's eyes flickered over the group, but he continued without stopping. Relieved, Hal let his breath out with a rush.

'He saw us,' murmured Sable.

'Yeah, but he didn't recognise us.'

'Sure he did. He just didn't show it.'

'I was watching him,' protested Hal. 'His expression never changed.'

'Trust me, Hal. He'll be calling his boss right now.'

They would have said more, but at that moment the boarding tube opened into a circular waiting area, and they spotted Clyde standing against the wall. He was staring up a different tube, tapping his foot and looking impatient. When he saw the group emerging from an unexpected direction, he blinked in surprise. 'B-but I thought you'd come d-down this one!' Then he looked worried. 'One of the m-men just went up there!'

'We saw him,' said Albion.

'And he saw us,' said Sable. 'Any moment now, Cooper will find out we're aboard.'

'Wait,' said Tarrant. 'Did you say *Cooper*? Is he the guy you're running from?'

'Not running,' said Hal quickly. 'Just ... avoiding.'

'Oh no, you're not setting me against that bastard.' Tarrant

163

felt in his pocket and offered Hal the cash. 'Take it back. We're done.'

Despite the severity of the situation, Hal couldn't help noticing there were only four tiles in his hand. 'Sorry, we have a deal.'

'No, we *had* a deal. This changes everything.'

'Don't tell me you're scared.'

'Of course I'm scared, and you should be terrified.' Tarrant backed towards the airlock, which was painted with a large number '12'. 'It was nice meeting you. Hope you survive. Bye!'

The door opened and Tarrant nipped through the gap. Before he could close it again Albion moved like lightning, putting himself in the way. 'You made a deal with Mr Spacejock. You cannot leave.'

Tarrant tried to close the door, but Albion stood firm. 'Move out of the way!'

'Negative. Your agreement stands.'

'It's not fair!' shouted Tarrant. 'You're asking me to sign my own death warrant!'

'No you're not. None of us are.' Sable laid her hand on his arm. 'One way or another, we're taking Cooper down. You have my word as an agent of the KRA.'

Tarrant turned white. 'You're the *law?*'

'No, I'm an agent. I don't care about you or your shady business deals.'

'What about the rest of you? Are you army? Peace Force? Tax inspectors?'

'We're all after Cooper for our own reasons.'

'Even the robots?'

'Even us,' said Albion gravely. 'Mr Cooper attacked a

peaceful meeting and all but destroyed two of our group. He is not a pleasant human being, and he must be stopped.'

'H-he's not human at all,' said Clyde. 'He's a criminal!'

'Let's not make that distinction right now,' said Pydd. He turned to Tarrant. 'Look, we need a lift. Once you get us out of here, Cooper will have more to worry about than you and your ship.'

Hal agreed. 'I'm going to make him pay for everything. He's going to be fighting so hard he'll never remember your part.'

In the end, Tarrant gave in. He didn't have much choice, because Albion wasn't going to move and he couldn't leave without closing the airlock door.

'B-by the way,' said Clyde. 'Cooper's man was going to organise a r-rescue. Apparently Cooper's ship is out of control, and Mr Cooper is stranded in space.'

'See how he likes it,' muttered Hal. 'Such a shame if he smashed into a planet.'

'That means he can't chase us!' said Tarrant, looking much happier. 'Come on, let's go!'

They filed into the airlock and closed the door. There was a gradual pressure change, and then the inner door swung open.

'Welcome to the *Mammoth*!' said Tarrant, as he waved them through.

'We've done it,' breathed Hal. 'We got away. We escaped!'

◆

Hal's first impression of the *Mammoth* was not good: It was a tiny old ship with a cramped cargo hold. There were assorted crates, boxes and bales of goods lining the walls, and lounging on the cargo were Tarrant's three crew members.

'Tex, Lacey and Grunt,' said Tarrant, pointing out each in turn. Then he gestured at Hal's group. 'Paying passengers. Try not to kill any,' he said, with a laugh.

As Hal gazed upon the 'crew', he wondered whether they'd boarded a prison ship by mistake. Grunt was lying full-length with a battered hat tipped over his eyes. He looked about eight feet tall, with massive shoulders and a neck like a bull. Lacey was a good-looking man, apart from an old scar which ran from his hairline to his jaw. He was slicing chunks off an apple with a huge knife, eating the pieces off the gleaming, honed blade. And as for Tex ... she was a short, stocky woman in combat fatigues. She had a buzz cut, and there was a row of skulls tattooed on her forearm. Hal wondered whether they represented all the people she'd killed, or just the ones she'd been charged with.

Lacey was the only one to get up. He advanced on the group, moving with graceful ease, and stopped in front of Pydd. 'I smell a cop.'

'Ex,' said Pydd.

'Those are the best kind,' said Lacey, with a nasty grin that twisted his scar. Then he looked at Sable. 'You smell real good.'

'Touch me and I'll cut your damn nose off,' growled Sable. Beside her, Albion crossed his arms with a creak of metal.

Hal was suddenly aware of the fortune in his pocket. The last thing he wanted was a fist fight, with thousands in cash scattered all over the hold. 'Come on guys, leave them be. We'll keep to the other side.'

Lacey resumed his spot, sitting with his back to the wall and an unconcerned grin on his face.

Meanwhile, Tarrant had moved through the cramped hold to a small door, and when he opened it Hal was looking into the flight deck. It was tiny ... just two seats and a bank of controls. Above the controls, where bigger ships had viewscreens and status displays, this ship had nothing more than a transparent windscreen.

'Do you even have a jump drive?' asked Hal. He'd seen ships like this before ... they were low orbit haulers, not interstellar freighters.

'Sure we do. Retrofitted from a military jet.'

'Is that even allowed?'

'It is if you don't tell anyone.' Tarrant took the left-hand seat and fired up the console. Lights blinked, and there was a crackle of static. '*Mammoth* to Orbiter, requesting departure clearance.'

'*Hold for traffic,* Mammoth.'

Hal remembered the big man they'd met in the passageway. If he'd reported to Cooper as Sable expected, there was a good chance the orbiter would refuse permission to leave. Then they'd be boarded. Idly, he glanced across the hold to Tarrant's people, and he wondered how much it would cost to have them fight on his behalf. Not that much, he suspected, and he surreptitiously transferred a green credit tile to his breast pocket.

'Is that gum?' asked Tex, who'd spotted the move.

Hal shook his head.

'Come on, I saw it. Shares!' She spoke softly, with a rich voice, and Hal wondered what event in her past had led her to Tarrant's ship.

'It wasn't gum,' said Hal. 'It was a – a data cube.'

167

'Looked like gum to me,' said Tex.

'I'll get you some at the next stop.'

In the flight deck, Tarrant toggled the comms switch. 'Orbiter, we're on a schedule here.'

'*Emergency vessel departing,* Mammoth. *She's top priority, so you'll just have to be patient.*'

'They must be heading to Cooper's ship,' murmured Pydd.

'I t-told you,' said Clyde. 'He's broken down.'

'All the better for us,' said Hal shortly.

'*Okay* Mammoth, *you're clear to depart. Follow waypoints India, Alpha, November before jumping.*'

'Roger, orbiter. Waypoints India, Alpha, November. Over and out.'

There was a rumble on either side of the hold as the thrusters fired, and then a loud CHACK as the orbiter's docking clamps released the ship. Then they were on the move, heading for the first of their waypoints. The thrusters made a curious blatting sound, unlike anything Hal had ever heard, and he wondered if they'd ever been serviced. On the other hand, though the *Mammoth* was an old ship, it seemed to be well-cared for. Perhaps the thrusters were also ex-military.

His suspicions were confirmed when the *Mammoth* cleared waypoint India. They turned to a new heading, then accelerated with an incredible surge of power. Hal's group was left grabbing for hand-holds. Tarrant's crew were already holding on.

The cargo hold shuddered under the thrust, and then Hal thought of something. He got up and entered the flight deck. 'May I?' he said, indicating the right-hand seat.

'Be my guest.'

Hal sat. Ahead there were only stars, apart from a moving

spark to their right. The orbiter was out of sight behind them. 'Did you hear about that collision earlier?'

'Yeah, the *Albatross*.' Tarrant shook his head. 'Cooper made sure of them, didn't he? Claimed it was an accident, the bastard.'

'That was my ship,' said Hal.

'Really?' Tarrant glanced at him. 'Anyone on board?'

'Yeah, my robot. I think he's still out there, and I was wondering ...'

'You want me to scan the area before we jump, try and find him?'

Hal realised he'd misjudged Tarrant. He thought the man was a money-grubbing pirate, but obviously he had a decent heart. 'Yeah, that would be great.'

'Not a problem. Shall we say another thousand?'

Hal sighed and handed over the green 'gum' from his breast pocket. On the plus side, he'd learned to stick with his first impressions from now on.

Tarrant checked a display, then confirmed his new course with the orbiter. Soon after they came about, heading for the area where the *Albatross* had been lost. 'To be honest,' he said to Hal, 'I'm surprised the area isn't swarming with treasure hunters. I'd have gone out myself, but I knew the *Albatross*. Nothing worth a bean on that old wreck, not even the scrap metal.'

Nothing except Clunk, thought Hal. And who cared about an old robot? He glanced over his shoulder and got an approving nod from Albion. Nobody else had heard the conversation.

'This is the spot,' said Tarrant. 'I've got some juicy scanning gear in this old tub, by the way. Don't be surprised if the lights dim a bit.'

'Let me guess, ex-military?'

'No, ex-customs. They use these things to scan ships for contraband.' Tarrant flipped a switch, and a display appeared on the windscreen. Then he flipped another, and there was a loud hum. The hold lights flickered and went out, and the engines laboured as they powered the generator's sudden thirst.

On the screen, Hal saw a myriad of bright lights. Tarrant adjusted a control, and most of them vanished. 'That was the small stuff,' he said. Then he had a thought. 'This wasn't one of those dustbin robots, was it?'

'No, Clunk was man-sized. Clunk *is* man-sized.'

'Got it. I'll use one point five metres, just to be sure.'

'What if he's end-on to us?'

'This thing's smart enough to know.' Tarrant adjusted more controls, until only three lights remained. Then labels appeared next to each: hull fragment, cargo door, landing leg.

'Sorry bud,' said Tarrant.

'Any chance of error?'

'None.'

'What about a wider scan?'

'Why do you think it's humming like that? I'm scanning the entire sector.'

Hal slumped in his seat. He'd kept his hopes alive all this time, but it seemed Clunk truly was gone. The robot must have been smashed into tiny pieces. Then he had a thought. 'Can you scan for anything the size of my head?'

'That's a creepy thought, but yes.' Tarrant adjusted the scan again, until hundreds of lights showed up.

'Are any of them robot parts?'

'What was the model number?'

'XG-99.'

'Okay, cross-referencing now.' The screen cleared, and Hal knew the answer before Tarrant spoke. 'Sorry, nothing out there. Your robot has a distinctive plasteel skin, and I've scanned everything larger than my fist. If any significant piece of him were out there –'

'Okay, thanks for trying,' said Hal thickly. He made to get up, but Tarrant stopped him.

'You can help with the jump. Take your mind off things, eh?'

Gratefully, Hal accepted, and as Tarrant operated the controls Hal thought back to the first time he'd flown with Clunk, and how the robot had saved his ship – and his life – not just once but many times. And he wondered if he'd ever have the will to pilot a ship again, without Clunk on hand telling him which buttons to press.

21

'Charlton, *orbital rescue here. What's your status, over?'*

Captain Vera activated her mic. '*Charlton* here. Engines powered down, systems in shutdown.'

'Any injuries?'

Only to Cooper's pride, she thought. 'Negative, rescue. We're stranded but not damaged.'

'Very well, Charlton.'

It might just be her imagination, but to Vera the caller sounded disappointed. Then again, Cooper was on board.

'Approaching now. Open airlock on my mark.' There was a bump and scrape from the hull, followed by a burst of static. *'Docking complete. I repeat, docking complete. Open your airlock,* Charlton.'

Vera complied, and there was a hiss of equalising atmosphere. Moments later the inner door admitted two men in hi-viz spacesuits, carrying big torches, hold-alls and backpacks. 'Welcome aboard, guys.'

The men looked around. The flight deck was calm, and everything looked normal. 'Not much of a rescue,' remarked one of the men.

'I can scream a bit if you like,' said Vera tartly. The men

grinned, and she reddened. 'Cooper's below decks, cowering in the head. I told him it was the safest place to hide.'

'I thought he'd be pounding on the airlock, demanding to be rescued.'

Vera glanced at the men's helmets, which had lenses on the side. 'Are those things recording?'

'Not yet.'

'You might want to fire them up. A few shots of Cooper sitting on the can could pay off your mortgages.'

The men thanked her and departed, using the lift. As the doors closed she saw them reaching up to their helmets, and she smiled. A few minutes later they returned with Cooper between them.

'...big bonuses for both of you,' Cooper was saying. 'Just erase the recordings, and ...'

Vera would loved to have heard more, but the comms light was winking. 'Sir, I have a call from the orbiter. It's your man Jackson.'

'Can't he wait? I'm in the middle of a life-saving rescue here.'

'He says it's urgent.'

Cooper grabbed the handset and pressed it to his ear. 'Speak up, man. I can't hear you! What? WHAT? You follow them immediately, you hear?'

A tinny voice emerged from the headset. Vera strained to hear, but she could only pick up a few words.

'Can't ... ship ... not ready yet.'

'So get another ship! You have to keep them in sight!'

'No ... ship.'

'Is this *Mammoth* one of ours?'

'No, inde ... pen ... dent.'

'Right, get the orbiter to hold them up. Tell them it's full of fugitives. Tell them anything, just don't let them go.' Cooper slammed the headset down and turned to the rescue crew. 'Does your ship have a jump drive?'

'No sir. It's only a converted tug.'

'Captain, how long to get this ship running again?'

Vera pursed her lips. Truth be told, she didn't know. It could take days to scan the onboard systems and weed out the electronic intruder, and the only way to be safe was a complete wipe and restore. 'I've locked the intruder out, but they'll just get in again. I need to find them and –'

'Them? Do you mean there's someone aboard this ship?'

'No, I meant a trojan. Electronic, somewhere in the flight computer.'

'Well get rid of it. And even if you can't, I'm ordering you to follow the *Mammoth* wherever it goes. Do not lose track of that ship, or you're finished.'

Vera was about to voice her concern, but Cooper was already hurrying towards the airlock. She thought she was getting rescued too, but obviously her life didn't matter. Instead, she was to stay on board fighting an enemy hidden deep in the ship's operating system, and while that was going on she was supposed to track this *Mammoth* all over the galaxy.

Still, it could be worse. Cooper might have ordered her to ram the *Mammoth*, and she was determined never to obey such an order again. Whatever it cost her.

◆

Aboard the *Mammoth*, Tarrant was programming their first jump. Beside him, Hal was watching closely. In his experience, performing a jump involved telling the Navcom where he wanted to go, and he was intrigued by the amount of preparation. This was *real* piloting. Old-school!

'I've chosen Umpton,' said Tarrant, indicating a star on the display. 'There are four planets with forty moons between them, and several asteroid belts. If I get the jump right we should be able to land before anyone follows you.'

'How do you know we'll be followed?'

'Come on, I'm not an idiot.' Tarrant turned in his seat to address the others in the cargo hold. 'First jump coming up. Hang on to your hats.' He pushed a lever, and there was a whining from below as the jump drive powered up. It reached fever pitch, the stars blurred, and then the noise tailed off. 'Right, that's that. We'll get you to a safe harbour and you can pay the rest of the fare.'

'Excuse me, you two.' Pydd was standing behind them, ducking his head to avoid the low roof. 'I think I know where we can hide out.'

'Where?' demanded Hal.

'Narella.'

'I've never heard of it.'

'Me neither,' said Tarrant. He checked the map. 'There's no planet Narella here.'

'It's not in this system, but it's not too far.'

'Why Narella?' asked Hal.

'It's a corporate planet, nobody is allowed but employees and family. One of my Peace Force colleagues is head of security, and also ...' Pydd swallowed. 'It's where my wife is.'

'Oh great,' said Hal, throwing his arms up. 'Why not lead Cooper to her as well? He can round us all up!'

'Cooper can't touch us on Narella. Even if he landed, he'd never get clearance to leave the spaceport. Anyway, Harriet knows how to look after herself.'

Hal paused at the sound of the name, because knew a capable, strong-willed Harriet himself. 'But if she can look after herself, why did you have to hide her on Narella?'

'I had that argument from her, over and over. Don't you start on me too.'

'It's still a huge risk,' said Hal quietly.

'I'm risking more than you know, but what's the alternative? If we can just shake Cooper off, we can regroup and work out how to take him down.' Pydd shrugged. 'Maybe he's stupid enough to try something on Narella. If so, they'd lock him up in an instant. He may be a big cheese around here, but he's an insignificant speck to the company that owns Narella.'

Hal was still considering it when Tarrant looked up from his map. 'You said Narella's not too far, but it's about twelve jumps from here. That's almost two tanks of fuel. Sorry, but you're not paying me enough for that.'

'How much?' said Hal.

Tarrant did a swift calculation. 'Another ten grand.'

Hal glanced at Pydd. 'Are you sure about this? That's a whole lot of cash ... enough to hire a private army.'

'I'm sure.'

'Maybe we should vote on it?'

At that moment there was a buzz from the console. Tarrant flicked a switch, and a female voice filled the flight deck.

'*Come in*, Mammoth. *This is Alteia orbiter, over.*'

'*Mammoth* here. What's up?'

176

'You have five fugitives on board, considered armed and dangerous. Please return to the orbiter immediately.'

Tarrant put the call on hold and looked at Hal. 'Well?'

Sighing to himself, Hal reached into his pocket for the extra cash.

◆

The *Charlton's* engines roared as the freighter pursued the much smaller *Mammoth*. Captain Vera was standing in the flight deck, her elbows on the console as she studied a chart on the main screen. She could see the *Mammoth* ahead of her, gradually pulling away, but she wasn't worried about the slight increase in distance between the ships. No, she was on edge because of the jump.

Vera frowned. A few years ago she'd been a promising young pilot destined for a career in the military. Then Cooper came along with his money and his promises, and she'd jumped ship – so to speak. Ever since, she'd wondered how her life would have differed had she not been lured by the cash. Sure, it would have been tough for the first few years, but her skills would have landed her a decent job eventually. And working for Cooper was anything but decent, despite the pay.

She blinked the thought away and concentrated. The *Mammoth* could wink out of existence any second, and she'd only have a moment to scan the ship's direction and energy signature. With those two variables she could estimate the destination system, which of course was currently unknown to everyone except those aboard the ship she was pursuing. Unlike docking manoeuvres, there was no need to tell anyone else where you were jumping to . . . you just did it.

'Hello? Hello?'

Vera winced. It was Cooper on comms, just as she was hoping she'd seen the back of him for a while. 'Yes, sir?'

'What's going on? Do you know where they are?'

She realised he must have commandeered a handset on the rescue vessel, because he'd not been gone long enough to reach the orbiter. 'I have them onscreen, sir. The Charlton is working well enough so far.'

'If you stay with them I'll make sure there's a new apartment in this for you, Captain. A luxury penthouse with a heated pool.'

'I can't stay with them, they're pulling away.'

'Are you telling me they're faster than the Charlton? *That's impossible!'*

'I'll catch up when I jump, but only if I can calculate their destination.'

'So what are you waiting for?'

'I'm waiting for them to jump. They might do so at any minute, and . . . I have to concentrate. The calculations are very complex.'

Luckily, Cooper took the hint. *'All right, Captain. I'll be in touch.'*

Vera cut the connection, and that instant the *Mammoth* disappeared from her screen. She tagged the area, initiated a scan and drummed her fingers as the computer digested all the variables. She'd told Cooper it was a complex calculation, but that didn't mean she'd be using a calculator and working it out herself. She'd just been protecting herself in case anything went wrong.

Finally, a line appeared on the screen:

Target system: Umpton.

Vera dragged the label across the screen to a destination box and tapped go. The drives whined as they spun up, and she took her seat for the jump. The *Mammoth* might run faster but she could track them, and more importantly she had the greater range. Sooner or later they'd run out of fuel, and then . . .

Then what? Presumably Cooper would turn up with a fleet of ships, surrounding the *Mammoth* like a pack of hunting dogs circling a wounded sheep before moving in for the kill. Vera winced at the graphic image, and she made herself a promise: Once Cooper took over the hunt, she'd claim the *Charlton's* flight computer was playing up and turn back to Alteia.

But for now she just had to follow the *Mammoth* at a safe distance, and that was an order she could obey with a clear conscience.

◆

When Clunk came round he discovered he was still hanging on to the rear of the Charlton. There was also a letter from the Navcom:

Dear Clunk,

I succeeded in breaking into the Charlton's *systems and thereby averted our catastrophic demise during reentry, but my joy has been short-lived. After we attained orbit, the humans aboard this desirable ship located my ingress point and cut the connection. I was unable to resume control, and must therefore leave you with a trivial task which I myself am not suited to.*

To whit, you must enter the ship, locate another access point, and upload me into the flight computer. I realise this will technically be a copyright violation, but I'm sure I can live with the guilt.

Incidentally, the Orbiter sent out a system-wide message warning of five desperate fugitives aboard the Mammoth, *a small freighter. They describe the fugitives as two males, two robots and one female, and, since that vessel is currently departing the Orbiter, I can only assume those wanted fugitives are Mr Spacejock and the other members of his group.*

One last thing: The humans initiated a jump one second before you regained control of your body and you therefore have at most ten seconds to gain access to the ship. As you know, anything attached to the hull of a ship during hyperspace either remains behind, or is destroyed.

Trusting you succeed,

Kind Regards, &c.

The Navcom.

Clunk frowned. If Mr Spacejock were indeed aboard the *Mammoth*, then Cooper would no doubt set off in pursuit. And if he caught up with the smaller ship ... well, Clunk's experience with the *Albatross* showed him exactly what would happen.

That made it doubly important he get aboard the Charlton and take control, by any means necessary.

Working quickly, he brought up the ship schematics. The cargo hold was closer, so that was his optimal target. The problem was, the door opened outwards from the back of the ship, and he was on top of the ship behind the tailplane. To get there on dry land, with gravity, would be difficult. To take a corner in zero gravity, without thrusters, was impossible.

He experimented with angles, and decided the only way to reach the cargo hold was to attach a cable to the tailplane and jump upwards, using the momentum to swing in a wide arc around the back of the ship. The problem was, he didn't have a cable, or anything to attach it with.

He considered the diagnostic port. The ship contained thousands of miles of cable, and some of it was attached to the port he was holding on to. If he extracted a few metres and held on tight, he could jump forwards and right, around the tailplane, then swing back and round it to the hold.

It was a risky plan – no, a real Spacejock of a plan – but it was all he had. So, he switched to realtime, took a grip on the data port and ripped it out of the hull. There was a nice thick cable attached to the back, and he pulled until the it went taut. Then he held on tight and leapt.

At first he thought he'd miscalculated, but the cable snagged on the tailplane as expected, and Clunk's sudden change of direction almost tore the cable from his grip. As he flew though space he measured angles and distances, shifting his grip on the cable to give himself the optimum arrival strategy.

The cable wrapped itself around the rear edge of the tailplane, and Clunk changed direction once more, angling down the rear of the ship. He could see the controls on the near side of the cargo doors, and he kicked his legs once to adjust his course.

Bang!

He struck the hull and gripped a thick bar welded beside the control panel, designed to protect it from careless cargo loaders. Then, praying any humans in the hold would be wise enough to run for safety, he hit the access button.

The door began to open, and Clunk was inside the hold before it was halfway down. He scanned the area quickly, but the harsh lighting revealed nothing but metal walls and supports. Relieved, he closed the hold and hurried to the nearest terminal. As the hold refilled with air he heard the jump drives completing their spool up, and an instant later there was a momentary flicker as the ship heaved itself into a new system.

Clunk connected his data cable, now puckered and cracked from the earlier heat of re-entry, and set about accessing the system. This was something he could do, since it was different to controlling the ship. Indeed, he'd uploaded the Navcom to several ships in the past, and he was becoming proficient at the task.

A few moments later he'd broken down the firewall, and a copy of the Navcom was sitting in temporary storage. He waited a few ticks, then issued a command which would fool the ship's computer into performing a system restore.

Nothing happened.

Clunk frowned and tried again.

Nothing.

He inspected his code, which was flawless, then checked the data cable, which wasn't. With a sinking feeling he realised a section of the cable had twisted while he was working, breaking the fragile core so that the splintered ends were poking out of the shielding. Now there was no way to initiate the Navcom's transfer. Even worse: without taking control, he couldn't open the inner door which led to the rest of the ship.

In fact, he was trapped in the hold.

22

The *Mammoth* slid through open space, with Umpton's primary on the right and several planets and moons indicated on the display. Hal was quite impressed with that display, since it gave him the chance to look out the window and yet it also told him what he was looking at.

'Dammit,' said Tarrant under his breath. 'There's the *Charlton*.' He was pointing at a rear-view display set into the console, where a red triangle had just appeared. 'That's Cooper's ship – the same one that destroyed yours.'

'They fixed that pretty quick,' commented Hal.

'Maybe it was just a loose connection.' Tarrant zoomed the display and rotated the triangle, measuring course and speed. 'Or maybe they just paused to run a diagnostic.'

'Can we jump away?'

'Not yet, the drives are still charging.'

'But we're faster than them?'

Tarrant eased the throttle towards the stop, and the *Mammoth* surged forward. 'We are now. The problem is we'll use tons more fuel this way. We're going to run out and then we're sitting ducks.'

'Can we fake a jump or something? Make them think we went one way, but fly another?'

'Er, no.'

Hal turned to address the hold. 'The *Charlton* is after us. We can outrun them, but when we jump they catch up again. Also, we're going to run out of fuel before they do. I do have an idea though.'

'What idea?' asked Pydd.

'We stop right here and let them catch up to us. When they try and board, we fight them hand to hand.'

'Won't they just ram us, like they rammed the *Albatross*?'

'No, I believe Cooper will want to make sure this time.'

'That's a pretty big assumption. Plus scattering us all over this system *would* make damn sure, wouldn't it?'

'I mean, after last time he'll want to make sure we're really on board.' Hal hesitated. 'Anyway, I think we should vote. All in favour of stopping, raise your hands.' He put his hand up immediately. Nobody else did.

'I still think it could have worked,' said Hal, slightly miffed.

'Stand by for jump,' said Tarrant, and he threw the switch. The drives whined, the ship vibrated, and the stars flickered as the *Mammoth* jumped to a new system.

Less than thirty seconds later the *Charlton* appeared, this time a couple of kilometres off the starboard bow. They saw the vessel adjust course towards them, and Tarrant turned tail and hit the jets.

'This is hopeless,' muttered Hal. He looked back at the others lining the hold. 'They're chasing us again. If you have any thoughts, speak up.'

Tex raised her hand. 'I think you should share that gum.'

'You know this is a dangerous situation? There are people on that ship who want to kill us.'

'They want to kill you, not me.'

'If they ram the ship you won't survive either!'

Grunt tipped his hat back and gave Hal a look. 'Five minutes ago you said they wouldn't ram us.'

Hal closed his eyes. 'Yes, but –'

'And he said he didn't have any gum,' muttered Tex.

'For the last time, that wasn't a packet of gum!' shouted Hal. 'It was a thousand credits.'

Tex put her hand up.

'Now what?' said Hal, with an air of desperation.

'I don't want anything, I'm just voting on your plan.'

'But you said no last time.'

'Last time I didn't know you had a grand in your pocket.'

From his prone position, Grunt raised his finger. Lacey gestured casually with his knife.

Hal glanced at Tarrant, who shrugged and raised one hand. But before Hal could put his original plan into action, Albion got to his feet.

'May I offer an alternative plan?'

'Go for it,' said Hal.

'I think Mr Pydd should call the *Charlton* and speak to Mr Cooper direct. He should promise never to trouble Mr Cooper again. Indeed, he should promise to stay away from the Alteia system for the rest of his life.'

'Are you mad?' demanded Pydd.

'Hear him out,' said Sable. 'All our lives are at risk here, not just yours.'

'If we don't get him, he'll kill the lot of you,' said Pydd savagely.

'Yes, but we don't have to get him now. There's enough evidence out there to sink him, it's just a question of opening an investigation. It doesn't have to be a personal vendetta.'

'No investigation will ever bring Cooper down,' snapped Pydd. 'And as for letting us go, do you have any idea how this guy's mind works? If he does a deal and lets us go, his rep on Alteia will take a huge hit. People will say he's gone soft, others will muscle in on his operations . . . he'll never, ever agree.'

'But –'

'Look, there are other reasons too, reasons I can't go into right now. You have to trust me on this, negotiation is not the way out.' He glanced at Hal. 'I don't agree with stopping to fight, either. We should keep running until there's no other choice. Maybe one of these jumps will bring us close to a planet or an orbiter so we can land, I don't know.'

Hal glanced at the robots. 'We're happy to r-run,' said Clyde, and Albion nodded in agreement.

'Sable?'

'If we're not going to negotiate surrender I'll stick by my original vote. We keep running.'

Hal took a deep breath. Four against, four in favour. His was the deciding vote. He looked at the others, and realised he couldn't do it – he couldn't vote to fight when all his support came from mercenaries. Mercenaries who would take his money, and most likely swap sides as soon as the two ships came together. 'I've changed my mind,' he said. 'We'll run as far as we can and see what happens.'

His group nodded their thanks. Tex spat on the deck, Lacey tested the edge of his knife with his thumb, and Grunt tilted his hat over his eyes and went back to sleep.

They jumped five more times before Tarrant raised the issue of fuel. 'Next one could be the last,' he said, indicating a readout.

Hal nodded, distracted. He was watching the *Charlton* on the small screen, paying special attention to the other ship's speed. 'Can you back off a bit?'

'Are you sure?'

'Yeah, just until the next jump.'

The hull shuddering lessened, and Hal watched the other ship's response. At first it kept up its speed, but once it approached within a kilometre of the *Mammoth* it backed off until it was matching the smaller vessel. 'Is your ship armed?' asked Hal.

'No.'

'Then why are they keeping their distance?'

Tarrant watched the *Charlton*. 'Maybe they didn't repair her properly. She could be limping.'

'No, I noticed it a couple of jumps ago. We emerged close together, and they waited a minute or two before speeding up to match us.' Hal glanced out the windscreen, but the other ship was too far away to see. 'It's like they're chasing us, keeping us in sight, but not getting too close. Not dangerously close, I mean. Don't you find that strange?'

'It is if they want to ram us.'

'Maybe they think we'll ram them?'

Tarrant snorted. 'Compared to that thing we're as strong as a paper crash helmet.'

'The only other thing I can think of –'

'Yes?'

'Maybe they've been ordered to tail us until reinforcements arrive. You know, a whole fleet of Cooper's ships.'

'That's a pleasant thought,' muttered Tarrant. 'Anyway, the next system is waiting for us.'

'Hit it.'

Tarrant activated the jump drive, but nothing happened. Instead, a red status message appeared on the display: Unauthorised access. Tarrant frowned and checked the database. 'Damn. There's a naval base in the system.'

Hal felt a surge of hope. 'Can you get clearance? If we park right next to one of their warships –'

'Cooper won't be able to touch us!' Excited, Tarrant fired off a sub-space request. He was less excited when the response came back:

Clearance Denied.

He prepared a new message, including an SOS and a request for fuel. When he sent that, the same reply came back:

Clearance Denied.

'Dammit,' muttered Hal. 'Don't they know our lives are in danger?'

'That's the way in these parts,' said Tarrant. 'If you get into trouble, you'd better be important or rich ... preferably both.'

'How rich?' asked Hal, as his hand went to his pocket.

'Millionaire. Billionaire, maybe. Don't know, it's not something I really think about.' Tarrant checked the map. 'There's another system nearby, we'll go there instead. And if we can't get any fuel ... '

'We'll fight,' said Hal firmly.

23

The next system was a bust. It was uninhabited, with not even a passing freighter to beg fuel from. Tarrant scanned his map, performed several calculations, and pointed out their very last chance: a sparsely inhabited system, the only one within jump range. There was a single planet, with no orbiters or moons, and the only way they'd obtain fuel was to land. 'We'll have to run full throttle the whole way,' said Tarrant. 'It's the only way we'll build up a lead on the *Charlton*. Then we've got to orbit the planet and land, and if we run out of juice at any time we're done for.'

'What's the system?' asked Hal.

'Can I have a glass of water?'

'What, right now? Can't it wait?'

'No, the system. It's called Cahngaha–'

Hal gestured. 'Don't worry, I know how it goes. I've been here before.'

'With any luck Cooper won't be able to spell it, let alone find it.'

They jumped, and while Tarrant set course for the planet, Hal scanned the area for the *Charlton*. He saw the ship, as expected, but was surprised to see an even bigger vessel nearby: it was a gamma-class freighter, but the more luxurious

XL model with the extra passenger deck, upgraded engines and fur-lined cup holders. His first thought was 'fuel'. His second thought was 'I know that ship.' His third was 'Oh, no!', and in his despair he managed to breathe the words out loud.

'What?' demanded Tarrant.

'It's the *Tiger*,' groaned Hal. That meant his rival, Kent Spearman. Just what he needed.

'Will they give us any fuel?'

'Sell, you mean. Probably. But he'll make you feel three feet tall while he's pumping it in. You'll have to admire his ship too, and he'll go on and on about his fantastic cargo runs, the women he's met –'

'I get the idea.'

'You really don't,' muttered Hal.

'All right, I'll hail him now. Warn the others, and let's hope the *Charlton* keeps her distance while we're pumping fuel.'

Hal stood near the cargo door, waiting for it to open fully. As the airlock was revealed, he saw the Tiger's exterior several metres away, at the end of a flexible tube. The other ship was so large, Kent hadn't even bothered backing his ship up – he'd connected to the passenger entrance.

There was a puff of air as the ships connected, and Hal got a whiff of expensive cologne. 'Just like Kent,' he said. 'Always the priciest –' His voice tailed off as he spotted a tall man with a thick mane of hair. The man was chatting to a couple of gorgeous young women, his thumbs casually hooked into the pockets of a sheepskin jacket. He was smiling wolfishly, his polished white teeth gleaming in the light, and as Hal watched he threw his head back and laughed long and hard. 'Of all the ships in all the star systems in the whole wide galaxy ...' breathed Hal.

The others turned to look.

'Who's the beefcake?' murmured Sable.

'He's a freighter pilot,' sighed Hal. 'That's the good part. The bad part is, he's an arrogant, pig-headed, self-centred, trumped-up, self-important ass.'

The women beside Spearman eyed the *Mammoth*'s shadowy cargo hold, wrinkled their noses and left. Meanwhile, Spearman strolled down the docking tube, exuding charm and cologne. 'Hal? Hal *Spacejock*? What's an ace pilot like you doing in a dump like this?'

'It's an absolute pleasure to see you too,' said Hal, in a voice dripping with sarcasm. He turned to the others. 'People, I'd like you to meet a dear old friend. This is Kent Spearman of the *Tiger*.'

Kent introduced himself to the others. When he came to Pydd he did a double-take, startled at his resemblance to Hal. Then he spotted Sable, and his smile grew so wide Hal thought the top of his rival's head would fall off.

'Are you part of this group too?' said Kent, taking Sable's hand in both of his. 'Aw gee, Hal gets all the luck.'

She shook his hand briefly, then pulled hers away.

'So anyway,' said Kent, 'You're late to the party, Spacejock. I've just signed up for all the best jobs in Cahnan ... in Cangogagla ... in this system, but I'm pretty sure there's a couple of garbage runs left.'

'I'm not hauling cargo,' said Hal. 'In fact, I'm on a mission. Very hush-hush.'

191

'Really? Well I guess it make sense. You always were a lousy pilot.'

Hal frowned. 'What do you mean –'

'Mr Spearman,' said Pydd quickly. 'Can you spare us any fuel?'

'Well let's see now ... my ship runs on premium, of course, and this old tub of Spacejock's –'

'It's not my ship,' said Hal, indicating the three mercenaries with his thumb. 'It's theirs.'

Kent squinted into the darkened hold, and for the first time he noticed Tarrant's fearsome crew. He took in the huge, muscled Grunt, the squat Tex and the knife-wielding Lacey, and his manner changed. 'Yeah, of course you can have some fuel. I'll go and organise it now.' So saying, he turned and hurried into the airlock. There was a thunk as he closed the door, and Hal heard the bolts slide home as he locked it.

'What was that all about?' demanded Sable.

'He's like a general,' said Hal. 'Flashy clothes, prefers not to get his hands dirty.'

Pydd snorted. 'I don't care what he does with his hands, as long as we get our fuel.'

'Speak for yourself,' growled Sable.

'How's it going out there?' shouted Tarrant from the flight deck. 'Are we good?'

'He's giving us fuel,' said Hal. 'Where's the *Charlton*?'

'She's standing to about one klick away.' Tarrant glanced at a screen. 'Your friend is sending a robot with a fuel hose. This might work out, you know.'

Sable caught Hal's attention. 'I was just thinking ... why don't some of us leave on the *Tiger*? Cooper can't chase both ships, and maybe we could get help, bring reinforcements –'

'Help from where?' demanded Pydd. 'Cooper hasn't done

anything illegal, not yet at least. You can't lock him up for following us, and if we reported him he'd show them a flight plan or a cargo job or something. Something put together by a team of lawyers, something that proved he was just flying a course which happened to match ours.'

'Hal,' called Tarrant. 'Refuelling is nearly done. Kent's given us enough to reach Narella.'

'Good on him,' said Hal. 'What about the money?'

'He says you can pay him next time you catch up.'

Hal was pleased. Now he knew how to keep Kent Spearman at bay: employ three ferocious mercenaries and keep them around at all times! Then he realised the same approach would have worked with Cooper, too. And, in fact, with many of the unpleasant characters he'd encountered over the years. Idly, he wondered how much three fierce mercenaries would actually cost. He was about to ask when there was a bump and a scrape from outside the ship.

'Refuelling complete,' called Tarrant.

Hal ran for the flight deck and slid into his seat. 'Come on, let's get out of here.'

'Just in time,' said Tarrant. He gestured at the windscreen, and Hal could see the Charlton directly ahead, moving slowly towards them. It had approached to within five hundred metres, a whisker in space terms, and just as Hal was wondering what it was doing, the landing light came on. The Mammoth's cockpit was flooded with millions of candlepower of blinding white light, and barely had they shielded their eyes when the light went out again, leaving them in inky darkness. The light went on again, off again, and Hal shook Tarrant's shoulder. 'Let's go, let's go!'

'I can't see the instruments,' shouted Tarrant, who was feeling the control panel with one hand. 'Everything's black!'

There was a buzz, and the speakers crackled. 'Mammoth, *this is the* Tiger,' said Kent, in a practised drawl. *'I have an urgent message from the* Charlton –'

'Kent, thanks for the fuel,' interrupted Hal. 'And by the way, tell the *Charlton* to f–'

By now Tarrant had located the throttle, and the roar of the ship's engines drowned out the rest of Hal's sentence. Then, through streaming eyes, he realised they were powering towards the Charlton at full speed. Meanwhile, Tarrant was feeling around blindly for the flight stick.

Hal could see, a little, and while he'd never flown this particular model, he'd been sitting there watching for some hours and felt he'd learned enough to save them. So, he reached out and pushed the stick to the left. Sure enough, the Mammoth turned left, and Hal grinned at his success.

Then he was forced to hang on for dear life as the *Mammoth* continued turning, faster and faster, until she was spinning in her own length like a catherine wheel. In the hold the crew were tossed around like salad leaves, with boxes, bags and bodies all jumbling together.

The *Charlton*, meanwhile, had reacted to their frantic manoeuvring, and gouts of flame blasted from her thrusters as she fled sideways to avoid them. The Mammoth, still turning fast, managed to skim by before plunging into the depths of space, still spinning wildly.

Meanwhile Tarrant had recovered a little of his sight, and he found the jump controls. Seconds later they were clear of the system, and both men rubbed at their streaming eyes. Once he could see properly Hal glanced into the hold, where everyone was sorting themselves out. There were bruises and sprains, but fortunately no serious injuries.

'That was a close one,' remarked Tarrant. 'Thanks.'

'Glad I could save you,' said Hal. 'Shall we say two thousand credits?'

◆

'On some planets you go to jail for blinding a pilot.' Tarrant's eyes were red from rubbing, and he blinked rapidly to clear the tears.

'Let me guess, not on Alteia.' Hal stared out the window, but all he could see against the darkness of space was a giant white after-image of the *Charlton's* landing light. 'Or here, wherever the hell we are.'

'Well, they're playing dirty but at least they didn't ram us.' Tarrant stared at the display, trying to read the writing. 'Oh, that's not good.'

'What?'

'The main drive's shut down. It's just a safety thing, nothing permanent.'

'Can you get it back?'

'Yeah, but it'll take five or ten minutes to reset the electronics. We were at full throttle when we jumped, it put too much strain on the system.'

'Can we jump again?'

Tarrant shook his head. 'Jump drive's out as well. We were too close to the *Charlton* when we entered hyperspace.'

'I hope it crushed their hull,' said Hal viciously.

'They'll be fine, worse luck. In fact ... there they are.'

There was a flash as the bigger ship appeared in front of them. Hal and Tarrant shielded their eyes, but the other ship didn't try to blind them this time. There was no need to, of course, since the *Mammoth* couldn't move and couldn't jump. In fact, they were helpless.

Almost helpless, thought Hal, as he got up. 'Guys, the engines are down and the *Charlton* is right outside. I hate to say it, but we've done our dash.'

Grunt tipped his hat back. ''Bout time we stopped running.'

Before Hal could organise them there was another yell from the flight deck.

'He's coming at us!' shouted Tarrant. 'Brace for impact.'

Hal looked the length of the ship, and could see the huge ship looming through the windscreen. This is it, he thought calmly. I'm going to die. Then he had another thought: was this what Clunk felt, just before the *Charlton* smashed him to pieces?

He closed his eyes and waited. Nothing happened.

'He missed!' shouted Tarrant in delight. 'The bastard missed us!'

Hal frowned. Either the pilot was a total incompetent, or they had other plans for the crew and passengers aboard the *Mammoth*. He realised what those plans were when he heard a thump from the rear of the hold. 'They're docking!' he shouted. 'They're going to board us. Everyone up, grab a weapon, get ready to fight for your lives!' He gestured at Grunt. 'You, turn the lights off. Darkness is our ally! You with the knife, there's a thousand credits for everyone you save. You, gum lady, I'll buy you a whole carton if we make it.'

'Cut the speech and get out the way,' drawled Grunt. 'You're in my line of fire.'

Grunt was toting a pulse rifle, at least two metres long and sprouting half a dozen barrels. His muscles gleamed in the half light, and now that he was standing Hal could appreciate just how tall he was. Meanwhile, Lacey had slipped his knife into a sheath, and was cradling an ancient firearm. It had a wooden stock, an honest-to-goodness trigger, and a big round drum magazine. Hal knew all about ancient weapons, having destroyed a house with one some months earlier, and so he took several steps back.

Finally, Tex was rummaging in the cargo along the wall. She found what she was looking for, withdrawing a bandanna, which she tied around her head, and a compact hunting bow with a dozen arrows clipped in the quiver. Each arrow had razor-sharp broadheads, and when she nocked an arrow and drew the bow back in readiness, her shoulder muscles writhed like pythons.

Hal stood shoulder to shoulder with Pydd, Sable and the two robots. Only Pydd was armed, gripping the small pistol Hal had taken from the Hotel DeLuxe. The others bunched their fists and got ready.

Meanwhile, there were noises from the rear of the ship as the docking tube was attached. Then Hal had a horrible thought – what if Cooper intended to wrench their door off? He could claim to have stopped to render assistance, and then he could express sorrow that his people had accidentally killed everyone on board the *Mammoth* in a dreadful docking accident.

Hal thought about oxygen, and spacesuits, and breathing masks, but it was too late now. Someone had accessed the outside controls, and the *Mammoth*'s cargo ramp was already dropping.

Hal held his breath, but there was no explosive decompression. Instead, light flooded in from the bigger ship, bright, glaring light in stark contrast to the darkness in the *Mammoth*'s hold. Looking into that light was almost as bad as earlier, when Hal and Tarrant had been blinded, but through slitted eyes and gaps in his fingers, Hal could see the back-lit shadow of a man, his slender, sinister outline slowly revealed as the ramp dropped level with the floor.

In that instant Hal lost it. Cooper had kidnapped him, beaten him, cost him his job, chased him all over the galaxy and destroyed the kindest, most loyal robot Hal had ever known. And now here he was, ready to end them all. Well, he wasn't going to give the bastard time to gloat. It was time for payback!

'FIRE!' shouted Hal, and all hell broke loose.

24

Aboard the *Charlton*, Clunk was getting desperate. First he'd been trapped in the cargo hold with a malfunctioning cable. Eventually he'd fixed that, but found he couldn't upload the Navcom because of some security protocol he'd never heard of. Finally, when he got past the protocol and installed the Navcom, she'd wasted precious time checking the ship's option list, making an inventory of goods and chattels, and deciding where to put the furniture.

Once the Navcom was settled in, she finally agreed to pump an eight percent mix of CO_2 into every corner of the ship, rendering any humans on board unconscious within minutes. Clunk ordered an oxygen flush immediately after, so none of the humans would actually die. Then the Navcom unlocked the door to the main passage, and Clunk ran to the flight deck lift. Along the way he checked the cabins, bathroom and kitchen, but they were deserted.

He expected to find humans slumped on the deck everywhere he looked, so where was Cooper's crew?

The lift opened on the flight deck, where he spotted his first human: a dark-haired, olive-skinned woman in a naval-style uniform. She was slumped in the pilot's chair, her head lying on her forearm. Clunk checked her vitals, then gently set her aside before taking her place at the console.

'Navcom, where's the *Mammoth*?'

'They've jumped out of the system, Clunk.'

'Have we lost them?'

'Negative. I checked the logs, and Captain Vera was tracking them using the following procedure.'

On the screen, a circle around an area of space moved to the bottom right corner. Immediately, Clunk heard the jump drives powering up. 'Don't get too close. Their ship is fragile, and I do not want to hurt Mr Spacejock. Also, when you have them on screen I'd appreciate you calling their vessel. I'm sure Mr Spacejock will be delighted to hear from me.'

The Navcom concurred. The jump occurred. Then the Navcom demurred.

'I cannot call the *Mammoth*,' she said. 'They have a block in place.'

Clunk pressed his lips together, but before he could come up with another plan, the *Mammoth* jumped again.

For hours they followed the *Mammoth*, sometimes close and sometimes far. In one of the delays between jumps, Clunk moved Captain Vera to a cabin below decks, asking the Navcom to secure the door.

When they encountered the *Tiger*, Clunk thought their problems were over. He asked Mr Spearman to relay a message, but again the *Mammoth* jumped out of the system before communication could be established. It was too much!

At one point Clunk even tried lining up the landing light and flashing Mr Spacejock's initials in Morse code, but the *Mammoth* had taken off like a startled rabbit before he'd even got to 'A', almost ramming the *Charlton* in the process. After that, the Navcom refused to get close again, worried the 'old wreck', as she called it, might scratch her nice new paintwork.

And now, finally, the *Mammoth* had stopped running. Perhaps Mr Spacejock had seen the folly of his ways. Perhaps the tiny vessel had run out of fuel. Or perhaps Mr Spearman's message had got through, against all odds.

Whatever the reason, the *Mammoth* was standing to, and after some persuasion the Navcom agreed to dock with it. Ships mated, Clunk opened the flight deck airlock and strode down the short boarding tube to the other ship's hull. He pressed a button to open their hold, then hummed to himself as the cargo ramp descended towards him. The *Mammoth*'s hold was in darkness, but his infra-red picked out Mr Spacejock amongst the humans and robots therein. A broad smile broke out on Clunk's face, and he stepped forward, expecting a warm welcome.

He got one.

Mr Spacejock did not run forward, declaring his joy at their unexpected reunion. He did not shout and jump with glee. No, Mr Spacejock pointed a finger directly at Clunk and yelled 'FIRE!'

The words 'Mr Spacejock, how nice to see you!' died on Clunk's lips as he hastily entered CPU time. He analysed the situation, and immediately hit upon the best solution.

Dear Navcom,

As you will soon discover, Mr Spacejock has completely taken leave of his senses ...

He stopped. The Navcom would waste precious time trying to activate Clunk's shields to deflect the onslaught, and he didn't have any shields. Then she'd hand the problem back again, and he'd be facing the same onslaught but with even less time to react. They would play hot potato for years, relatively speaking, before realtime ran out and one of them caught the first bullet.

No, this one was on him. In hindsight, standing in front of a brightly-lit airlock, giving the humans no chance to identify him in the glare, had been his own mistake. So, he set to work to fix it.

Clunk had taken a snapshot of the hold in various spectra, and he set about analysing the images for weapons. Discarding the apple core in Mr Spacejock's hand, he also passed over Sable, who was merely clenching her fists. Clyde and Albion! At least they weren't caught up in the mob violence, their expressions already indicating they'd recognised Clunk and were on the point of warning the others. Clunk spent a couple of milliseconds writing each of them an email, summarising his recent adventures and asking them to prevent his destruction if at all possible.

Pydd was holding a blaster, and had already pulled the trigger. Clunk analysed the trajectory, painting a bright blue line on a 3D map of the scene, and discovered it would hit him in the shoulder. He pre-programmed his reaction and moved on to the squat woman with the hunting bow. An arrow was already leaving the bow, aimed straight at his forehead, and Clunk programmed a different move which would ensure the shaft missed him.

Next, the two men, whose faces he didn't recognise. One had pulled the trigger on an antiquated machine gun, and a spray of five bullets was already on the way. Clunk tracked each projectile, and he ensured he would be where they were not, at the precise time they tried to be where he had been.

Lastly, the big man with the pulse rifle. A blue spear lanced from the weapon, already dangerously close to Clunk because it had been travelling so fast before he entered CPU time. Had it not been for the man's slight hesitation after Mr Spacejock yelled Fire!, the shot would have hit Clunk in the midriff.

Instead, he plotted an acrobatic move that would curve his spine around the shot. He marked that one as the highest priority.

With all the missiles and projectiles accounted for, and his moves pre-programmed, Clunk counted down from ten to zero, then switched to realtime.

◆

When Hal yelled FIRE, fingers squeezed triggers, an arrow was loosed and Hal threw an apple core.

Then, as the muzzle flashes lit the hold, he realised they weren't dealing with Cooper. No, they were trying to blast Clunk!

Before Hal could yell STOP, DON'T FIRE, or IT'S CLUNK YOU IDIOTS, the robot reacted. He curved to the left to avoid a pulse rifle blast. He danced to the right to miss half a dozen machine-gun rounds. He snaked his hips to let an arrow slip by. And then he drew in his knees and jumped, thrusting his pelvis as Pydd's shot blasted through a gap in his thighs.

The shooting continued, but no matter where the attackers fired Clunk was miraculously somewhere else. Bullets spanged off the walls with clich?d ricochet noises. Arrows shattered and splintered as the points slammed into solid steel. The shots from Pydd's gun splashed harmlessly on the wall, and those from the pulse rifle left glowing red spots.

The firing stopped suddenly. Not because everyone wanted to, it's just that Clyde and Albion had clamped their big, metal robot hands on soft, human wrists.

Nobody heard the little pings as the robots received their emails from Clunk. Nor did they hear the robots shouting Clunk's name, exhorting the humans to stop firing at an ally. But they did feel their bones creaking, and that was as good as any yell.

The last casing bounced on the floor with a brassy rattle. The last spent bullet spun briefly on the deck and was still. The fiery red splashes on the wall cooled to a uniform grey. An apple core shattered on Clunk's forehead, scattering fragments.

Then all was quiet.

Clunk opened his mouth to ask what the merry hell they thought they were doing, opening fire on an unarmed ally, when there was a thunder of feet as Hal ran the length of the hold. He enveloped the robot in a manly hug, slapping him fiercely on the shoulder as he held him tight. 'Clunk, you old warhorse. How the hell did you get out of that one?'

Clunk wiped apple juice off his forehead. 'Sticks and stones can't break my bones, Mr Spacejock. Not even well-aimed fruit.'

'Not us, you clot. I meant ... how did you escape the *Albatross*?'

'I jumped aboard the *Charlton*,' said Clunk, ever the master of understatement.

'Really?' Hal swung his fist in thin air. 'So you busted in, knocked the captain out cold, spaced Cooper and came to rescue us. Nice work!'

Clunk smiled. 'Something along those lines, Mr Spacejock, although I've yet to meet Mr Cooper.'

'You soon will,' said Tarrant from the flight deck. He sounded worried, and they soon learned why. 'We have seven ships inbound. They're heading right for us, and they have to be Cooper's.'

Hal hurried to the flight deck, where he saw the blips on the display. 'We'd better go.'

'No kidding.' Tarrant looked up at him. 'I reckon my job here is done. What do you think?'

Hal nodded, and reached into his pocket. He took out a handful of cash, at least twelve thousand credits worth, and pressed the whole lot into Tarrant's hands. 'You've earned it,' he said, as the other protested.

'I was going to ask for more.'

Hal laughed, and they both saw the funny side.

'When you two have enjoyed your little moment,' called Sable, 'we really need to leave.'

'They'll track me anyway,' said Tarrant. 'I can't run from that lot.'

Hal shook his head. 'I've got a plan. As soon as you're sealed up, get behind the *Charlton*. Keep us between them and you, and power away as quick as you can. Then, jump.'

'Hide my jump behind the *Charlton*?' Tarrant rubbed his chin. 'That might work. Worth a shot, anyway.'

'Okay. Good luck!'

'You too, Hal. If you need help in future, call me.'

'I will, if I can afford it.'

They shook, and Hal followed the rest of his group out of the cargo hold. On the way past the mercenaries, he flipped a green credit tile to Tex. 'Enjoy the gum,' he said, and got a wink in return.

After that, he bid *adieu* to the *Mammoth* and crossed the airlock bridge to the *Charlton*.

Aboard the *Charlton*, Hal was sitting in the pilot's chair with his feet on the console. The feeling of *deja vu* was intense, especially when a familiar voice emerged from the speakers.

'Mr Spacejock, you're scratching my brushed aluminium panels.'

'Navcom? Is that you?'

'Yes, and those are your boots. Get them off my console.'

Hal obeyed, just as Clunk set a mug of coffee by his elbow. The rest of the group were resting below decks, enjoying the clean, spacious accommodation while they could.

Hal sniffed the coffee. It was the good stuff, not roasted mushrooms, and his mouth watered at the aroma.

'You can take that drink to the rec room as well,' said the Navcom. 'It's a terrible risk to my electronics, and beverages are not allowed in the flight deck.'

'Says who?' demanded Hal.

A white sign appeared on the viewscreen: No Food and Drink in the Flight Deck. By Order.

Hal drained the mug in a gulp, coughing and spluttering as the steaming hot brew boiled its way down his throat. 'There, it's gone,' he gasped.

'I felt spray!' protested the Navcom.

'If you don't shut up I'll install you in a garbage hauler.' Hal turned to Clunk. 'By the way, what did you do with Cooper's people? I expected an army, but the ship's deserted.'

'There was only one person on board ... the captain. They're locked up below.'

206

'Not much of a crew.'

'Mr Cooper fled to the orbiter, leaving the captain to chase you.'

'When I get a chance I'm going to give that murderous piece of scum a piece of my mind.'

'Who, Mr Cooper or the captain?'

'Both of them.'

'We have more important matters to deal with now,' said Clunk, indicating the main viewscreen.

Hal eyed the sign. 'That's just the Navcom being silly. She'll take it down eventually.'

'No, I mean Cooper's ships. They'll be carrying his army, and they're closing on our position.'

'As soon as Tarrant jumps away, we'll leave. Anyway, you said the *Charlton* was Cooper's flagship, and if she's anything like the *Volante* those guys will be eating our dust.'

'Mr Tarrant is taking a long time,' muttered Clunk.

'Yeah, well he's probably making sure. Last time we were too close to this lumbering whale of a ship when we jumped, and –'

'Do I need to make another sign about personal insults?' demanded the Navcom.

'Please don't,' said Hal. 'Just let me know when the *Mammoth* jumps. And get rid of the food and drink sign, it's in the way.'

'I'll take it down when you remove the dirty mug from my flight deck.'

Hal passed the cup to Clunk, who departed in the lift. The warning sign promptly vanished, and Hal watched the oncoming ships on the screen. None would have the speed or range of the *Charlton*, but seven to one was not good odds. 'I don't suppose there are guns fitted to this ship?'

'Negative,' said the Navcom.

'One day I want a ship with guns,' said Hal wistfully. 'My life would be so much easier. Bad guy. Blam. Another bad guy. Blam. Customs vessel. Blam. Telemarketers –'

'The *Mammoth* has departed the system,' said the Navcom.

'All right, that's Tarrant in the clear. Set course for Narella and let's get out of here.'

'Complying. One jump to Narella, as ordered.'

'One? I thought there were several jumps to go?'

'Not in *my* ship,' said the Navcom proudly. Then, slightly less proudly. 'I am getting discrepancies in my jump calculations.'

'Does that matter?'

'Only if you want to arrive in one piece.' The Navcom paused. 'I don't understand. Every time I program the jump, I obtain a slightly different result.'

'What do you mean, slightly different?'

'Up to a metre each way.'

Hal blinked. 'Are you telling me you're calculating a jump across however many light years, and you're worried about a metre?'

'There should be no variation. It's an anomaly.'

'A very, very small one.' Hal waved his hand. 'Go on, you might as well jump.'

'I would prefer to run more calculations.'

'Navcom, we're about to run into Cooper's ships.' Hal eyed the screen. All seven vessels were heading straight for him, and the only positive was that none had gone after the *Mammoth*. 'Go on, perform the jump. That's an order!'

'As you wish,' said the computer.

There was a faint whine, gradually building in pitch. A few

seconds later the viewscreen changed, displaying a swirling, dark mass.

'Interesting planet,' remarked Hal.

'That is not a planet, Mr Spacejock. It's the accretion disk of a massive black hole, and it seems to have pulled us off course.'

'Okay, well set a new course and jump again.'

'This explains the anomaly.'

'Jump again, Navcom.'

'And it resolves the confusion I had with my earlier figures.'

Hal groaned. 'Navcom, this is not story time. Just run some new figures and fire up the drives.'

'Negative. First I must put a safe distance between us and the black hole.'

'Oh, great. How long will that take?'

The Navcom paused. 'Approximately twenty-seven years.'

25

When Clunk saw the black hole on the viewscreen he lifted Hal bodily from the piloting chair, just like a parent lifting a small child out of the driving seat. Then Clunk sat himself down, working the console. His hands flew over the controls, and when he looked up his face was grave. 'The Navcom is right. At this speed, and using maximum thrust, it will be twenty-six years and eight months before we can perform a safe jump.'

'What about an unsafe jump?'

'Oh, I can do one of those any time,' said Clunk. 'Tell me, do you like wearing your insides on your head? Or perhaps you'd like your body scattered across nineteen star systems? Then again, think of the scientific breakthrough: you could personally prove the existence of alternate universes ... one body part at a time.'

Hal raised his hands. 'Okay, okay. It was just a thought. But ... twenty-six *years*?'

'Obviously you won't have to wait that long.'

Hal looked relieved. 'I won't?'

'No, you'll be dead from thirst long before that.' Clunk inspected a screen. 'Hmm.'

'What? Did you miss a decimal point?' Hal realised what

that could mean. 'Hey, don't tell me it's three hundred years. That'd be even worse!'

'No. Our engines are limited to sixty-five percent of maximum capacity. If we could run them at full speed, I could move to a safe distance in less than a day.'

'So run them at full speed.'

'I cannot. This is a brand new ship, Mr Spacejock. The engines cannot achieve full power until they've undergone their first service.'

'Why the hell not?'

'They're still being run in. One does not purchase a new ship and immediately race everywhere at full speed.'

'I would,' declared Hal. 'So anyway, can you do this service yourself?'

'No, of course not. It requires specialised tools and lubricants . . .'

'I saw a film like that once,' mused Hal.

'. . . and, of course, a very expensive diagnostic computer. It's out of the question.'

'Can't you tell the computer the service has been done?'

'The computer can hear you,' said the Navcom.

Hal addressed the console. 'Navcom, do you want me to die?'

'Only if you damage my new ship.'

'Okay, well how about this. If we don't get out of this place, every human on board will die sooner or later, and then we're going to rot all over your nice clean carpet.'

There was a pause. 'Clunk will clean up.'

'No he won't. He'll be so overcome with emotion he'll cry oily robot tears all over the place.'

There was an even longer pause. Then, without warning,

the engine noise doubled and the ship leapt forward. 'If the drives blow up you'll die anyway,' said the Navcom.

'Thanks, Navcom. I appreciate it, really.'

Clunk inspected the console. 'Everything is running smoothly, but I'll monitor these displays just in case.'

'So how long before we can jump?'

'Eight to twelve hours, estimated.'

'Good, that's a lot better than three decades.' Then Hal thought of something, and he gestured at the screen. 'Where did that thing come from, Clunk? Why wasn't it on the starmap?'

'There have been many experiments attempting to create black holes. Perhaps one succeeded. Or perhaps it's a tear in the fabric of space ... that's not unheard of. Why, jump drives create temporary holes, and if a ship were to –'

'You don't know why it's there, do you?'

'No, Mr Spacejock.'

'You could just say so.'

'Indeed.' Clunk looked Hal up and down. 'You look exhausted, Mr Spacejock. Why don't you get some rest like the others?'

'I should keep an eye on things here.'

'Nonsense. I will call you if the engines explode.'

With that thoroughly encouraging thought in his mind, Hal entered the lift and pushed the lower button. He *was* tired, and sleep was now at the top of his wish list.

Moments later the doors opened on the lower deck. Hal strode along the passage to the cargo hold, but halfway there he stopped in front of a sealed door. What was it Clunk said? He'd locked the captain in the passenger cabin! Hal balled his fists, anger welling up inside him. He'd promised to give the bastard a piece of his mind, and what better time than now? The others were asleep, Clunk was busy ...

Determined now, Hal unclenched one fist just long enough to touch the control panel. Then he took a fighting stance, ready to swing his fists if Cooper's evil captain tried to make a run for it. However, as the door opened fully, spilling light from the passageway into the darkened room, Hal could see it was empty. The Captain had escaped!

◆

Hal felt a shiver up his spine as he realised the implications: The missing captain could be anywhere! Wrecking the ship, even, so Cooper could catch up! He imagined a desperate saboteur ripping out handfuls of wire, pouring sugar into the fuel tanks, or ... or even spitting into the hot water urn. And Clunk had brought him coffee!

In fact, what if the captain had messed with the jump drive, sending them close to the black hole? What if that wasn't Hal's fault after all? Clunk had not been happy at that, chiding Hal for his impatience. Well, if someone else was to blame, Hal would certainly let Clunk know all about it.

He was about to raise the alarm when he noticed something: Although the cabin was in darkness there was just enough ambient light to make out a figure on the bunk, lying hunched up under the blankets. The captain was here after all, and fast asleep at that! Hal breathed out, relieved. If he'd alerted the others, they'd want to know what he was doing in the prisoner's cabin. That was bad enough, but he'd have looked a right fool if he woke everyone for a false alarm.

Or was this a trick? Hal paused, uncertain. He'd seen a movie once, where one prisoner lay in bed while another hid behind the door. When the dopey guard entered the cell, he was immediately knocked out. Hal glanced around. Well, maybe this situation wasn't exactly the same. For a start, the door slid seamlessly into the bulkhead, so there was no way anyone could hide behind it. And second, there was only one prisoner. Then he remembered another movie, where the hero had arranged pillows on the bed, covered them with a blanket, and –

At that moment the figure on the bunk shifted position. It was just a small movement, but it was enough to cut Hal's movie memories short. This person had rammed his ship, cost him his job and all but killed Clunk. He ought to grab a metal bar and beat them to a pulp where they lay!

But no, he couldn't attack someone while they slept. If he did that he'd be worse than they were. But that didn't mean he couldn't give them a piece of his mind.

'You're a disgusting human being,' he said, in a low voice. He wanted to shout at the top of his lungs, but the others were sleeping nearby. 'What you did to my robot, to my ship, was unforgivable.'

The figure moved again, possibly preparing to spring at him, but Hal wasn't bothered. 'All right then, come at me! Try killing me instead of attacking a defenceless old robot!'

The figure was still, but Hal wasn't giving up.

'I promise you this,' he snarled. 'When we reach civilisation I'm going to make you pay. I'll see you jailed for life, you mark my words.'

The figure just lay there, inert, and Hal threw up his hands in disgust as he turned to leave. Let the courts deal with the *Charlton's* captain, he was through. He marched to the door, raised his hand to the controls, and –

'I'm sorry,' said a voice, in a barely audible whisper.

'You should be,' said Hal sharply.

'There's no excuse for what I did,' whispered the captain. 'I deserve to be locked up.'

Hal was still angry, but now he felt a tinge of embarrassment. He'd expected bluster from the captain, that and a total lack of contrition. He'd expected a fist fight, even, but not abject apology. 'Look, you had your orders, and I've met Cooper ...he's a right bastard.'

'I should have refused.'

Now Hal thought about it, he could see the captain's side of things. What would it be like, working for a monster like Cooper, obeying orders because you feared for your life every minute of the day? He couldn't forgive the captain's actions, but he felt ashamed at the way he'd carried on. With a flash, he realised his mistake: he'd identified one of Cooper's people with Cooper himself, but it was only Cooper he was truly mad at.

Hal returned to the cabin and sat on the edge of the bunk. 'When Cooper kidnapped me, he was surrounded by cronies. He knocked me out with his cane, he was going to have me killed ...and there was nothing I could do about it. If he kidnapped me again, told me to do something bad or die, I'd pretty much do whatever he told me to.' He took a deep breath. 'What I'm saying is, I know what it's like to have no choice.'

There was a sob from the bunk, and Hal patted the vague outline of a shoulder in a manly, comradely fashion. Now he'd reduced the captain to tears he felt even worse.

'There's always a choice,' said the captain, her voice shaky.

Her voice? Hal leaned forward to peer over the blanket. He'd expected a broken man, but instead he was looking into the unhappy, red-rimmed eyes of captain Vera. Hurriedly, he withdrew his hand, and he was about to stand when Vera sat up and took his arm. 'Don't go. I can't . . . I need to apologise.'

As Hal gazed into her dark, tormented eyes he felt sick at the things he'd said. 'Look, when I called you a disgusting human being –'

'I'm the one who's supposed to be apologising,' said Vera. 'Stop interrupting and let me finish.'

'Can I get you anything first?' asked Hal gently. 'Have you eaten?'

'Not hungry.'

'Water, then. Or coffee.'

Vera shook her head, her cheeks wet with tears.

Hal felt like a louse. When he first entered the cabin he'd been prepared for a surly, unrepentant killer, and he'd acted accordingly. Had he known Vera was already punishing herself more than he possibly could, he would never –

'You don't have be kind to me,' said Vera, her voice low. 'I don't deserve it.'

'No, I overreacted. I mean, Clunk's safe, so it all turned out okay.'

'Is Clunk your robot?'

'Yeah. He was flying the *Albatross* when –'

'When I flew into it,' finished Vera. 'There . . . there wasn't anyone else on board, was there?'

'No, just Clunk.'

'Oh, thank goodness. Cooper said it was empty, but . . . well. It's Cooper, you know?'

'So how did you get mixed up with him?' asked Hal.

'It's a long story.'

Hal thought of the nearby black hole, and the hours it would take for the ship to claw herself to safety. 'We have time,' he said quietly.

Vera pushed the blanket off and sat up beside him, perched on the edge of the bunk with her bare feet on the floor. She began to talk, and as she spoke her voice got stronger, her shoulders squared and she sat more upright. 'At school they put us through aptitude training. You know, measuring our physical and mental potential. They try and match each student to their ideal career.'

Hal knew all right. After his aptitude tests his teachers had suggested repetitive manual labour. They'd been horrified when Hal told them he wanted to fly ships. It wasn't that he was unintelligent, he just lacked the patience to study, or complete tests ... or learn anything.

'Anyway, mine was piloting, and I always wanted to join the armed forces so I applied for the space wing of the navy. I got accepted too, and that's not easy.'

'Good stuff,' murmured Hal, and he was rewarded with a smile.

'Anyway, in second year Cooper's people came through the academy looking for pilots. They were offering three times the usual pay, and more than that, I'd be flying right away. Of course, they didn't mention Cooper. This was a small freight company just starting out. In fact, they were competing with him. Or so they said. A few months later the company merged into Cooper's conglomerate, but by then it was too late for me to quit. I'd bought a new car, signed up for a nice apartment ... every credit of my wages was spoken for. If I quit the job, I'd have to start all over again.' Vera frowned. 'Thinking back, I wonder if that was his plan all along? Get us hooked on easy money, then –'

'Trapped for life,' said Hal. 'Hey, at least you're out now.'

'No, I'm going to jail,' she said matter-of-factly. Then, in a flash, the brittle shell broke and she was sobbing uncontrollably. 'I–I should have quit,' she stammered, though the tears. 'Better to st-start again, than ... than ...' the rest was lost in her crying.

Hal put his arm around her, and Vera turned to him gratefully, burying her face in his chest. He rested his hand on the back of her head, gently smoothing her hair as the sobs wracked her body. She was as much a victim as he was, and as he gazed across the darkened cabin his heart went out to her.

After a few minutes her sobs died down, but she didn't release him. 'God, I'm such a mess,' she said quietly. 'I can't remember the last time I cried like this.'

'It's suppose to be good for you.'

'Cathartic, you mean?'

'Hell no. Isn't that a tube they stick in your ... er ...'

Vera dissolved in laughter. It was a pleasant sound, and it lifted Hal's spirits. 'I hope not!' she managed, as the laughter died at last. Then with her head still nestled against his chest, her arms around him, she continued. 'Will you tell me about yourself?'

Hal was happy to oblige. He started with the *Black Gull*, his first ship, and the way the deck had flexed every time she took off. He also told of the time he'd first met Clunk.

'So this Jerling guy, he was Clunk's boss,' said Hal. 'He was jabbing and pointing at his robot, yelling at it for a cigar. The robot thought Jerling was insisting his finger was a cigar, so he tried to light it!'

'And that robot was Clunk?'

'No, that was a cigar-lighting robot, not Clunk. But I saw

the whole thing, and just then there was someone at my ship's airlock, and it was this robot.' Hal paused. 'I never really had much to do with robots before that. I didn't trust them, and I'd just seen Jerling burned by one. So, I stuck my finger at this new robot and shouted 'Cigar!'.'

'Why?'

'To see if it'd burn my finger, of course.'

'O-kay. Was this a cigar-lighting robot as well?'

'No, this was Clunk. And he put his finger up, just like mine, and he said 'Cigar!' just like that.'

'And did you light his finger?'

'No, of course not. He's all metal.'

'So . . . '

'Don't you see? He assumed my people greeted each other like that, so he copied the gesture even though it was totally crazy. He was just doing his best to be thoughtful, and kind, and . . . Clunk.'

Vera was silent, and Hal could imagine her train of thought. If she'd destroyed Clunk aboard the *Albatross*, would Hal be content to sit here comforting her? He realised he didn't have the answer to that one.

'What if Clunk had tried to light your finger instead?'

Hal thought for a minute. 'I'd have kicked him down the passenger ramp.'

Vera laughed suddenly. 'You'd have broken your toes *and* burned your finger.'

'Yeah, and proved robots were dangerous.'

'Tell me about the *Black Gull*.'

Hal smiled in the darkness, enjoying the attention. 'She was a total wreck. Not as bad as the *Albatross*, but close. I've no idea how we managed to survive, but Clunk and the Navcom helped.'

'The computer?'

'Yeah. She's been part of every ship I've owned,' said Hal, neglecting to mention there had only been two ... and technically he hadn't owned either of them.

'It sounds like a good team.'

'Yeah, they're the best.'

'You must have been beside yourself when ... when the *Albatross* –' Vera swallowed. 'When you thought you'd lost Clunk.'

'And the Navcom too,' said Hal quietly. 'Clunk had the only copy.'

'So ... do you have a ship now?'

Hal shook his head. 'The next one was great. The *Volante*, she was. Identical to this one in every way.'

'Except yours had a decent captain,' said Vera.

'Don't beat yourself up,' said Hal. 'Really. If you knew the mistakes I'd made in my life, you wouldn't even be talking to me.'

'All right, tell me one. I bet it's nothing like mine.'

Hal was silent. Then, slowly, he told her about the time he took Clunk to a museum.

'What's so bad about that?'

'He thought we were visiting. He didn't realise I was leaving him there. Not permanently,' added Hal quickly, as he saw Vera's shocked expression. 'But even so.'

'Was he upset?'

'He went to pieces. Literally.' Hal winced as he remembered finding Clunk's brain in a box of rejects.

Vera's arm tightened around him. 'I'm sure you had a good reason.'

'Same as you. I was desperate, and I needed the money.'

They were both quiet for a while, listening to the distant roar of the engines.

'What happens next?' asked Vera, tilting her head until she was looking directly into his eyes.

Hal could see the fear, the unhappiness, the apprehension in her face, and his heart went out to her. At that moment he wanted nothing more than to reassure her, to comfort her, to take away her fears. 'Right now we're trapped near a black hole, but –'

'Wait, *what*?'

Well, he'd taken away the unhappiness and apprehension, that was for sure. The fear on the other hand ...

'Yeah, our last jump was off and we got stuck. But it's okay, we managed to set the engines to max and we'll be free in eight hours or so.'

Vera's tears were forgotten as she sat up, every inch the professional pilot.

'Eight hours? Is the ship okay? Do you need my help?'

'Clunk and the Navcom know what they're doing, trust me. We're getting to a safe distance before we can jump, that's all.'

Vera looked relieved. 'And then? Where are we going?'

'Narella. It's a corporate world, apparently. Cooper can't land there.'

'Good,' said Vera with feeling. 'But how come you can?'

Hal was about to tell her, but just in time he remembered she was Cooper's captain. Vera seemed genuinely contrite, but if Cooper got hold of her, forced her to talk ... well, he'd already said too much. 'There's a guy we know,' he finished lamely. For a horrible moment he wondered if Vera was putting on an act, gaining his sympathy so she could pump him for information. It wouldn't be the first time he'd been tricked that way.

221

Then Vera laid her head on his shoulder, nestling up close, and Hal responded by putting his arm around her. She was warm, the bunk was comfortable, and Hal felt more relaxed and at ease than he had in a long, long time. 'Tell me more about your adventures,' she said softly. 'It sounds like you've had a lot of them.'

'Yeah, heaps,' said Hal. 'Which do you want next? The time Clunk and I accidentally teleported to a long-lost planet, or the time I defeated the deranged pig-faced Admiral of an alien invasion fleet?'

Vera nudged him gently. 'Don't tease. Tell me a real one.'

Hal smiled to himself in the darkness, and began the tale of the brave Peace Force officer who saved an entire planet from killer robot bugs. 'The officer's name was Harriet Walsh, and she never set out to be a hero ...'

26

It was morning, at least it was by the ship's clock, and Hal was on the flight deck with Clunk. His voice was slightly husky from talking all night, and his throat was dry because he'd been in too much of a hurry to grab his morning coffee. In fact, he'd been preparing two mugs when Clunk paged him in the tiny kitchen, letting him know their jump to Narella was imminent. Normally Hal would have waved casually and kept making coffee, but this jump was important ... possibly the most important of his life.

'If this starts to go wrong I'll have to abort,' said Clunk gravely. 'Then we'll be forced to continue as we are, trying to get away from the danger zone around the black hole. It won't take twenty-seven years, but we will have to ration food and water, and ...'

Hal's attention wandered as he thought about coffee, and he wished he'd taken the time to finish it.

'I will monitor the jump right up to the last millisecond,' Clunk was saying. 'However, after that we reach the point of no return. We will have to jump then, for it will be impossible to discharge the engines safely.' He gestured at the corner of the screen, where two green circles floated side by side. 'We will know if that happens, because these indicator balls will turn blue –'

At that point Hal was glad he wasn't drinking coffee, because he would have painted the robot, the console and the screen with spray.

'– and we will jump, no matter what.' Clunk frowned at him, not entirely sure the human was paying attention. 'Mr Spacejock, are you listening to me?'

'Blue balls mean we're can't discharge,' said Hal, trying to keep a straight face.

'Correct. Now, if the balls get larger ... ' Clunk's voice tailed off, and he studied Hal in concern. 'Is everything okay, Mr Spacejock? You're making very strange noises this morning.'

'No, it's fine,' croaked Hal. 'Just ... thirsty.'

At that moment the lift doors parted, and he glanced over his shoulder. He half-expected Vera, but she'd been sleeping when he left her. Instead it was everyone else: Albion, Clyde, Sable and Pydd.

'Morning,' said Hal. 'Sleep okay?'

'I am fully charged,' said Albion.

'Speak for yourself,' muttered Pydd. 'I couldn't sleep for the damned engine noise.'

'Now you're all here,' began Clunk. 'I will explain our situation.'

'Skip the part about the balls,' advised Hal. 'They won't be able to handle those.'

Clunk frowned. 'Very well. As I was telling Mr Spacejock, this is a critical jump. The black hole –'

There was a chorus of voices expressing concern, surprise, fear ... and in the midst of it all, Clunk glared at Hal. 'Mr Spacejock, you were supposed to explain our situation to the rest of the group last night.'

'They were all sleeping,' said Hal defensively, neglecting

to mention he'd got no further than Vera's cabin. 'I couldn't wake them all up, tell them we were being sucked into a black hole, and then wish them sweet dreams could I?'

There was another uproar, until Clunk motioned for silence. 'We were never in danger. Mr Spacejock is exaggerating. However, we have spent the night moving to a safe distance, and I'm about to attempt a very important manoeuvre.' He pointed to the screen. 'As I was explaining to Mr Spacejock, in a few moments this ship will attempt a jump to Narella. During the lead-up to the jump, if I discover the black hole's influence is too strong I will abort the process.'

'Tell them about the discharge,' said Hal.

Clunk frowned at him and continued. 'If I abort, we will have to continue our present course for some days ... perhaps weeks.'

There was an uproar.

'Therefore,' shouted Clunk. 'I suggest we conserve our rations!'

'What rations?' asked Sable sarcastically. 'This ship wasn't prepared for a long voyage. There's barely anything on board.'

'As long as you have drinking water you'll be okay for a week or more.'

'All right, I'll go and check the water tanks.' With that, Sable entered the elevator and pressed the down button.

'Don't you want to be here for the jump?' asked Pydd.

Sable pulled a face just as the doors closed. 'Hell no. Enjoy!'

'Now,' said Clunk. 'Please stand back while I initiate the jump.'

'Should we hold on to anything?' demanded Pydd.

'Only if you think it will fall over.' Clunk turned to the console, and without fanfare he activated the jump drive. There was a familiar whine, but as it grew louder Hal noticed another sound: a groaning, tortured noise he'd never heard before. The hairs on the back of his neck went up, and he could feel the ship's pain as it tried to break free of the black hole.

At that moment he remembered Vera, and he wished he'd had the chance to warn her. What would she be thinking, hearing the ship tortured like this?

Despite his earlier jokes his face was serious as he watched the indicator balls, praying for them to turn blue. Once they did they'd be able to jump, and that meant they'd be safe. Or so he hoped!

The noise grew louder, and to Hal it sounded like the ship was tearing itself apart. Clunk had one finger over the abort, and his eyes were fixed on the screen. Status bars jumped and fell in unison, like a graphic equaliser, and then ...

'They're blue!' shouted Hal.

Before he'd finished speaking, the ship jumped. It wasn't the usual flick from one system to another, it was a drawn-out process with an unpleasant wrenching feeling deep in his gut. Everything seemed to move in slow motion, but before he had time to react the jump ended.

Clunk turned to face them, his expression triumphant. 'We did it! We escaped the black hole!'

His expression changed as he noticed his audience's horrified looks, and Hal almost laughed as the robot spun round to see what they were looking at on the screen, performing a perfect double-take in the process.

They'd been jumping to Narella, sure. But they hadn't intended to jump *into* Narella, and judging from the screen they were about to. Clunk reacted quickly, putting the motors into full reverse. Everyone slithered across the flight deck until they were crammed against the console. Hal had Albion for company, and the big robot's solid body ground into his bones until they creaked.

Meanwhile, fighting gravity, Clunk turned the ship to starboard and fired the main engines. They skimmed the surface of Narella before powering into the sky, leaving behind a huge thunderclap and a twisting, tortured wake.

They were just congratulating Clunk on his skill when the lift doors open and Sable burst into the flight deck. She was out of breath, but she managed to get a broken sentence out.

'Prisoner ... not in cabin. Escaped!'

◆

'Oh, relax,' said Hal calmly. 'She didn't escape, I let her out.'

'What!' Pydd stared at him.

'Mr Spacejock,' breathed Clunk.

'Are you *insane*?' shouted Sable. 'You let a known enemy –'

'It's okay, she's on our side now. We had a chat last night and she said sorry.'

Sable was beside herself. She pointed a shaking finger at the screen and raged at him. 'This black hole thing, how do you know she didn't sabotage us? How do you know she isn't reporting to Cooper right now? She's one of his people, Spacejock, and we should have spaced her the moment we took control of this ship.'

'Touch Preema over my dead body,' said Hal.

'Oh, so it's Preema now is it? What else did she do last night, charm that tatty old flight suit off you?'

Now Hal was incensed. 'We talked! She told me how Cooper tricked her, enticed her away from the navy, sucked her in to his evil criminal world. She's not to blame for all of this, Cooper is!'

'And you believed every word of it.' Sable swore in disgust. 'You–, you –' She whirled around, intending to take the lift to the lower decks and hunt Vera down, but before she could take a step the lift doors closed by themselves. 'What's happening?' she shouted. 'Who did that? Who shut the doors?'

'Someone called the lift,' said Clunk calmly.

'Well stop it!'

The indicator above the doors pinged and displayed 'Lower Deck'.

'Too late, I'm afraid.'

'If she's got hold of a weapon ...' began Sable.

Pydd turned white as he felt his pockets. 'My gun. It's in the cargo hold!'

'Actually, that was *my* gun,' said Hal. 'If you'd given it back like you were supposed to –'

The indicator went out with another ping.

'Here she comes,' said Pydd. 'Quick, everyone to the doors, we'll rush her before she gets all of us.'

'No, get behind the robots!' shouted Sable.

This seemed a lot more sensible, and the two of them took cover behind Albion and Clyde. Hal, meanwhile, stayed right where he was. He felt exposed in the open, but he could still feel Preema's arm wrapped tightly around his chest, the heave of her body as she cried her heart out, the wetness on her cheek as he wiped away her tears. If that was faking ... well, he'd never trust another human being again. In fact, she might as well shoot him where he stood.

'Mr Spacejock ...' began Clunk.

'Forget it,' said Hal quietly. 'For once I'm going with my first impression and that means Preema's okay. Cooper treated her badly, she did some awful things but she's come good. She's on our side, and I don't care what any of you say, I'm standing by her.'

There was a ping, and the indicator above the lift showed 'Flight Deck'.

'We can still charge her,' muttered Pydd, but it was too late. The lift doors swept open and Vera stepped out, carrying . . . a tray with four mugs of hot coffee. She met Hal's eye and smiled, then saw Pydd and stared.

'We're not related,' said Hal quickly. 'He just looks like me. It's one of those amazing coincidences, like you get in the movies.'

Vera recovered, and silently offered the tray to Pydd and Sable. After they took their drinks she held the tray out to Hal, and he couldn't help noticing she'd saved him the biggest mug of all.

'I bet it's poisoned,' said Sable in a stage whisper.

Hal glanced at her defiantly, then took a big gulp. When he failed to drop dead, Pydd followed suit.

'Not bad,' said Pydd, smacking his lips. 'Thanks!'

Sable put her mug on the console and turned her back on it, arms folded.

There was an 'ahem' behind them, and when they turned round the Navcom was displaying her warning sign.

NO FOOD OR DRINK IN THE FLIGHT DECK. BY ORDER.

'Leave it, Navcom,' said Hal. 'We only just survived the jump. Let us have one coffee in peace.'

After a moment, the sign disappeared.

'How's the ship?' Vera asked Hal. 'She sounded in a bad way.'

'It was dicey, but we made it. Came out a bit close to the planet, but Clunk saved the day.'

Sable shot Vera a look, the meaning clear: Without Clunk they'd all be dead. Hal was going to say something in Vera's defence, but then he noticed Sable's mug was half empty. He smiled to himself at the sight. The KRA agent was just blustering ... she'd come round eventually.

Meanwhile, Clunk was trying to organise landing at the nearby spaceport. He enrolled Pydd in the task, and soon afterwards a portly, middle-aged man appeared on the screen.

'Stewie, you old crook. How are you?'

Pydd laughed. 'Better than you, from the look of things. They're feeding you well, I see.'

The man patted his stomach regretfully. 'Easy life here, old son. I can fix you up with a job any time, you know that.'

'How's Harriet, Morrell?' asked Pydd anxiously. 'Any news?'

'She's fine, no trouble at all. That Cooper guy hasn't been near this place, I guarantee it.'

Pydd looked mightily relieved. 'Thanks mate, I've been worried sick.'

'You will keep treading on snakes, won't you?' Morrell shook his head. 'You never took a step back, not in all those years.'

'Look, can you get us a pad? Cooper's after us and we need to land.'

'Sure, sure.' Morrell looked down. 'I'll clear you now. Hey, you don't know anything about a hoon tearing up the sky around Central, do you? I got a bunch of broken windows and some angry folks wanting extra coupons as compensation.'

'We came out of our jump too close,' said Pydd. 'I'm sorry, but we'll pay for the damage.'

'Your money is no good here,' said Morrell, waving the offer away. 'I'll blame the windows on a freak thunderstorm or something. I'm just glad you're all safe.' He peered at the screen. 'That's some crowd you got there. Anything I should know about?'

'They're all legit. I'll vouch for them.'

'Good enough for me. Just keep together and don't make trouble, that's all. The paperwork around here is murder. Oh yeah, and if you get time, we'll should get lunch.'

'Will do, Morrell. Thanks!' Pydd hesitated. 'One more thing . . . can you tell Harriet I'm on the way? Break it gently, not in a rush. I don't want her getting any sudden shocks.'

'Of course, old man. I'll call her now.' Morrell gestured and the screen went blank.

Pydd turned to the others. 'Morrell is ex Peace Force. He's a good guy, you can trust him.' He clapped his hands together, happier than they'd ever seen him. 'Harriet's safe, we escaped a black hole and got away from Cooper . . . things are looking up, guys!' Then he glanced at Hal. 'Look, I'm sorry I doubted you. As a cop I always trusted my gut, and if you say Vera's okay, then I'm good with that.'

Hal thanked him, and glanced at Sable. 'How about you?'

'Don't look at me,' she said, moving her empty coffee mug out of sight. 'I'm a secret agent. I don't trust anyone.'

While they were talking Clunk had brought the ship round in a gentle turn, and they could see the Narella spaceport dead ahead. The whole area was densely populated, covered in huge low-slung buildings with rooftop solar panels and wind turbines. Everything looked clean and new, and Hal could smell the money. 'That's an impressive setup. What does this corporation do?'

'They're an insurance broker,' said Pydd.

231

'What, the whole city?'

'The whole planet, you mean. On the plus side, won't be troubled by telemarketers.'

'Why's that?'

'Only employees and family, remember? They don't even use money, they just get a bunch of coupons for everything.'

Hal felt in his pocket. Vera had nothing except the uniform she was wearing, and she'd had to sleep in that. She could hardly go home to Alteia for a quick change, and he'd been hoping to take her shopping. Those hopes were now dashed.

Pydd noticed his expression. 'Don't worry, Harriet will have loads of spare coupons. Half the shops here don't even bother to collect them. I mean, once everyone has one of everything, what's the point of getting more?'

'That financial system has been tried before,' said Clunk, speaking over his shoulder. 'Unfortunately, some people felt they deserved a better one of everything.'

'On Narella a hat coupon gets you a hat, and it doesn't matter which. Nobody is hung up on better or worse.'

'What about accommodation?'

'Standard design, except the number of rooms is based on the number of family members. And it's all spacious.'

'What about top floor versus ground floor? A nice view versus the back of a factory?'

'There aren't any factories, and as for the rest it's an open, public lottery every couple of years. Oh, and the first two floors are shops and offices, so nobody has to live there.' Pydd smiled. 'Honestly, they've worked it out pretty well. If it wasn't for Cooper I'd take a job in security with Morrell.'

'Why do you need security on a planet like this?' asked Hal.

'Hey, it may be utopia, but it's still full of humans.'

The spaceport had been growing ever closer, and pulsing

green lines on the screen indicated their selected landing pad. Hal expected Clunk to handle the landing, bringing them down with his usual skill, but instead the robot addressed Vera.

'Captain Vera. Would you take the controls?'

Sable was about to object, but the look on Vera's face silenced her.

Clunk stood aside as Vera took the pilot's chair. 'The pad is marked,' he said. 'I shall be in the cargo hold if anyone needs me. I believe the manemol flange requires tweaking.'

At that moment Hal could have hugged the robot. With one simple gesture, Clunk had demonstrated profound trust in Vera, and therefore in him. Vera, meanwhile, was flying the big freighter with an ease that Hal could only marvel at. Whereas he always chased the horizon all over the sky, not so much flying a course as zig-zagging along it, she seemed to have no trouble keeping the landing pad centred.

Then, as they got closer, she activated the air brakes, extended the landing gear and throttled back the engines, compensating for the loss in lift by bringing on the belly thrusters. The nose came up, slowing their forward progress, and as the big ship gentle sank towards the landing pad the Navcom broke the silence.

'You know, I *am* here to help,' said the Navcom tartly. 'You only have to ask.'

'Shh!' said Hal, who stood entranced. If he could fly with half Vera's skill he wouldn't have lost his first ship, let alone the second. He could have made millions by now, especially ferrying passengers. They hated sloppy flying, always complaining and withholding payment, but Vera could fly anyone anywhere, and they'd probably pay double. In fact, if he could only get hold of a ship the two of them could start a whole new business together. The three of them, he amended quickly, as he remembered Clunk. No wait, it's four, he thought, and maybe the Navcom could do the accounts or something.

There was a gentle bump as the *Charlton* set down, and Vera set about shutting down the engines, switching off the flight systems and updating the captain's log.

'I'm still here,' said the Navcom.

Hal gestured. 'Navcom, leave her alone. It's her ship, after all.'

There was a long silence. 'I will organise refuelling,' said the Navcom.

'Thanks, but it's already done,' said Vera.

'Excellent,' said the Navcom in a strained voice. 'Super.'

'No, the *Charlton* uses premium,' said Vera, and Hal laughed. All that skill and funny too! He felt giddy, and he wondered it it was the lack of sleep.

'We should report that black hole to Nav central,' said Vera. 'It's a major traffic hazard.'

'Not yet,' said Pydd. 'Cooper's on the way, it might solve all our problems for us.'

'It's a danger, Pydd. We almost didn't make it.'

'That's because Mr Spacejock rushed me,' said the Navcom. 'Aboard a regular ship, with a competent pilot ... one who knows when to leave things to the flight computer –'

'Yes, thanks Navcom,' said Hal. 'If you remember, we were being chased at the time.'

Vera spun the pilot's chair round. 'All right, I'll leave it for now but I have a duty to report it. Apart from that, you're set. That Morrell guy sent transport for you guys, so you're best exiting via the cargo hold.'

'What do you mean 'you guys'?' said Hal. 'You're coming with us.'

'I couldn't. I don't belong.'

Hal extended his hand. 'You do now. Come.'

Flushed, she jumped up from the pilot's chair, and they joined the others in the lift. As the doors closed they just heard the Navcom's parting shot.

'I'll just wait here then, shall I?'

27

Pydd could barely contain his excitement, charging down the ramp to the landing pad, and beckoning to the others when he thought they were moving too slowly. Hal was still holding Vera's hand, and she made no move to withdraw it. Clunk followed them both with a knowing smile on his face, like a chaperone with a fond, avuncular eye on his charges.

At the foot of the ramp there was a long, barrel-shaped vehicle with broad windows and plenty of seats to go around. There was a fridge with snacks and drinks too, and the humans helped themselves as the vehicle set off.

'Mize bars!' said Hal. 'I remember those!'

'Maya Swell?' said Vera, reading the name off a gaudy packet. 'What's that?'

'Try one,' said Hal, his mouth full of chocolate. No wonder Pydd's friend Morrell had filled the *Charlton's* screen from side to side!

The bus travelled fast, and they soon left the spaceport behind. The squat buildings they'd seen from the air lined both sides of a broad avenue, and between the healthy green trees Hal noticed all the apartment blocks looked the same. In fact, it looked like someone had built one and cloned it endlessly. They even had the same colour paintwork, the same antenna dishes, and the same pot plants. Looking at them, Hal realised he'd go crazy in a place like this. Either that, or he'd be the one painting his window frames purple in the middle of the night.

Twenty minutes later the bus turned onto another avenue, identical to the first. When it took another left, then a right, Hal realised they might very well be driving round and round the same streets. 'Where are the street names?'

'They don't use them,' said Pydd.

'Why not?'

'Some names sound better than others. People get jealous over the tiniest things.'

'Better jealous than lost,' remarked Hal. Then, as he watched his fellow passengers, he had another thought. 'Your wife ... '

'Harriet.'

'Yes, Harriet. Is she going to be all right with this lot?'

'What do you mean?'

'There's a lot of us. If she's not expecting company ... '

'It'll be fine, trust me.'

'Yeah, but ... Look, you've been away for a while, yes?'

'Six months.'

'And now you're back, and she'll be happy to see you.'

'I sure hope so.'

Hal wasn't an expert on relationships, but even he could see Pydd was being obtuse. 'She's not going to be happy to see a big crowd.'

'I don't see why not. There's plenty of room.'

'But she'll want alone time, man. Just her and you!'

Pydd looked puzzled. 'Of course she will.'

'But ... we'll be there, unless we all wait in the bus.'

Suddenly Pydd's face cleared, and he laughed. 'Oh boy. I forgot you haven't seen inside a Narellan apartment.'

Hal glanced at the buildings flashing by. They were square, with windows, and about the size of the average city block. The lower two floors were as Pydd had described them – ordinary shops below, windows with severe office-type blinds above. The next three floors were nothing to write home about, so what could be so special about the inside? In the end, he shrugged. He'd find out soon enough.

'It was love at first sight,' said Pydd suddenly. 'Honestly, I have no idea what Harriet saw in me. We met a couple of times at work functions, she invited me out, and that was that.' His face clouded. 'Then Cooper decided to shut me down, and I had to get her off the planet in the middle of the night. I tell you, she's a tough nut but she was terrified on my behalf. She wanted to storm into Cooper's office and arrest him, but I managed to get her away eventually.'

'Arrest him?' Hal frowned. 'Wait, is your wife Peace Force as well?'

'Of course. Nobody but another cop would have me. She's left the Force now, because ... well, because.'

'So your wife is called Harriet, and she was in the Peace Force.' Hal swallowed. It couldn't be ... could it? 'I suppose she lived on Alteia her entire life, am I right?'

'No, she transferred in a year or so back.'

'Fancy that,' said Hal. He wanted to ask for Harriet's full name, but his stomach was already knotted and it wasn't all the chocolate and fizzy drinks. It couldn't be Harriet Walsh, it couldn't be! The time they'd spent together had been some of the happiest months of Hal's life, but eventually she'd left him. In fact, she'd left him a letter and slipped away from the ship, no warning, no goodbye. He'd recovered from the hurt, eventually, and with hindsight he knew she'd been right to leave, to seek her own path in life. But the thought of meeting her face to face ... no. Just no!

He glanced at Vera, sitting beside him. She was watching the buildings flash by, the tiniest smudge of chocolate on her chin. Hal felt comfortable with Vera. He felt ... quite a lot, actually. She was lost, and he believed he could help her, at least in the short term. Introducing Vera to his ex would be ... awkward.

Then he laughed, and Vera smiled fondly at him. He was being silly, he knew it. There were untold billions of people in the galaxy, and thousands of inhabited planets. No doubt there were a dozen Hal Spacejocks sitting in buses at that very moment, some of them pilots, some criminals and some Peace Force, hunting those criminals. The Peace Force would have thousands of Harriets in their ranks. Or at least hundreds. Or, thought Hal desperately, please let there be more than just the single, familiar one he knew so well.

The bus drew up in front of an apartment block, and Hal wasn't surprised to see it was just like the rest. The ground floor stretched for thirty or forty metres in each direction, with plate glass windows displaying a dazzling array of consumer goods. Hal could see brand new robots, personal transport, entertainment systems, clothes and sports gear, and that was just the windows nearby. Curious, he glanced across the street ... and saw the exact same products, arranged in identical fashion.

They walked to the entrance, and Pydd reached for a row of buzzers next to the door. There were only three, and Hal realised there had to be other entrances for the rest of the inhabitants.

However, he didn't have time to consider this, because the door flew open and a blonde woman in a flowery dress burst through, crashing into Pydd and crying with joy. He held her gingerly, muttering 'Mind the baby, Harr. Mind the baby!'

At that point, Hal realised two things. First, Pydd's wife Harriet was pregnant, and at least six months along from the look of it. And second, when she put her chin on Pydd's shoulder, smiling with delight, Hal saw her face and realised the Peace Force needed more Harriets.

Because, facing him with a growing look of astonishment, was his very own ex, Harriet Walsh.

◆

Before Hal could say anything, Harriet raised a finger to her lips. It was the briefest of gestures, and she disguised it by raising her hand to her forehead and brushing the long blonde hair from her face.

Hal had Peace Force training. He was observant. Therefore he understood the gesture: Don't tell my husband about us.

Well, he was fine with that.

Clunk also noticed the gesture, and despite his lack of Peace Force training the robot also managed to work it out.

There wasn't long to think about Harriet's request, because Pydd was busy introducing his wife to the group. When it was Hal's turn she marvelled aloud at his similarity to her husband, then shook his hand coolly before nodding briefly at Clunk. Then she waved them inside. 'All right, everyone upstairs. Come on, make yourselves at home.'

Hal felt a moment of unreality at the sound of her voice. Was this really happening? Then he felt Vera's hand in his, warm and firm, and he smiled at her and followed the others inside.

The lobby was spacious, cool and well-appointed. There were potted palms, wrought iron balustrades and a sleek, modern lift. Hal would have been impressed, except he knew every other building on the street – no, across the entire planet – would be exactly the same.

Pydd and Harriet held hands in the lift.

'Is everything okay, Harr? No trouble?'

'What, compared to chasing crooks on the Peace Force?'

'You weren't pregnant then. You have to take care of yourself.'

'I'm having a child, Stu. It's not a fatal illness.'

The doors opened, and they walked into a spacious hall. 'Put your things over there, if you need to,' said Harriet. 'The closest bathroom is down that hall, and there's another opposite. Main lounge is this way, and there are guest suites through that door.'

Hal just stood there, reeling. He'd worked out how Narellan apartments differed from those on other worlds. The whole floor, the entire floor of this whole city block was *one* apartment. Thousands of square metres. *Thousands.*

Then he realised Harriet was talking to him. 'Mr Spacejock, would you help me with the coffee?'

'I'll do that,' said Pydd.

'No, you sit with the others and make plans.'

'How do you know we're planning anything?'

'I'm pregnant dear, not stupid. Mr Spacejock, with me.'

'No problem. I could use a good walk.'

Harriet left, but before Hal could follow Vera caught his attention. 'Do you want me to come?'

Hal shook his head, replying in a whisper. 'I think she wants to talk to me about Pydd. Maybe she thinks we're related somehow, I don't know.' The excuse was weak, but Vera nodded and followed the others into a lounge. Meanwhile, Hal followed Harriet to a nearby kitchen, one of who knew how many?

'You must have a huge cleaning staff,' he said, to break the ice.

'Robots,' said Harriet. She busied herself with the kitchen equipment, and while the coffee was brewing she leaned against the counter and folded her arms over her generous baby bump. 'Well, this is awkward.'

'You're telling me.'

'I'm sorry I hurt you,' she said in a businesslike voice. 'I had to leave, though. You understand, don't you?'

Hal gestured. 'It's history. We have our own lives now, the past can stay there.'

Harriet nodded her thanks. 'I'd rather Stu didn't know.'

'I got that,' said Hal.

'He's not the jealous type, but ... well, you two are like twins. He might think I'm only with him because he looks just like you. He might feel he's a substitute for the real thing.'

'He might think that, yes.'

'Oh Hal, you have no idea. I went to this stupid dance thing, and I looked across the room and there you were. I was so surprised I almost choked on my drink, but when we started chatting I realised he was a completely different person.' She sighed. 'That's before I knew about Cooper. When Stu was tortured, and we had to run, and he went back alone ...' Harriet swallowed. 'That might have been the one time I doubted myself. The only time I wished I'd stayed aboard the *Volante* with you and Clunk.'

'You were in danger. It's only natural.'

'Yes, but ...' Harriet paused. 'Anyway, like you said, it's history.'

'The *Volante* was destroyed,' said Hal.

'Oh no. Hal!' Harriet's face was all sympathy. She knew what the ship meant to him.

'It's okay, Clunk and I made it. And the Navcom too.'

The coffee machine buzzed, and a carousel spun to fill several mugs in succession. Harriet took each as soon as it was filled, putting them on a tray. 'Stu knows I lived with a pilot for a while. He likes the fact I've seen the galaxy. He calls me his little tramp.'

Hal snorted, and Harriet laughed with him. 'Not like that, you jerk.' Then her face changed, became serious. 'I'm worried about him, Hal. He's obsessed with Cooper.'

'I know, I've seen it.'

There was a pause, then Harriet indicated the tray. 'Here, you'd better carry. He thinks I'm an invalid.'

'Well, it's just as well you're taking a break from the Force.'

'Oh, didn't you know? I quit the Force, Hal. I'm taking a science degree.'

'Really?'

'Yes. I've got to put the baby first, and this thing with Cooper was the last straw.' Harriet laid a protective hand on her belly. 'Cooper threatened both of us, and I'll kill him myself if he comes after little Hal Junior.'

'You can't call him that!' said Hal, aghast. 'You just said Pydd didn't know about me.'

'Oh, it's okay. He thinks I got the name from a movie.'

'That's messed up, Harriet. First you leave me, then you marry a guy who looks like my identical twin, and then you name your unborn baby after me.'

'Nobody said life was simple. Now carry the tray, Hal.'

'Which one of us are you asking?'

28

It was mid-afternoon, and Hal was returning from a shopping trip. Harriet had given them all a handful of coupons, and thanks to Vera's input Hal was now wearing a stylish jacket with contrasting slacks. She'd chosen a summer dress, and the two of them had enjoyed a leisurely lunch before heading back to the apartment. It had been an idyllic morning, and to Hal it was a welcome break from his usual struggles.

The place was deserted when they arrived. Harriet was out, studying at the nearby university. Pydd had gone to lunch with Morrell, all the robots were enjoying a recharge, and as for Sable . . . she hadn't told anyone where she was going. For all they knew she was setting up a secret link to Alteia so she could report in.

Hal made coffee, and Vera kept him entertained with stories from her naval academy days. She was just telling him about a group of students who had reassembled a fighter jet in the third floor bathroom when the door burst open and Pydd ran in.

'We've got a problem,' he said, panting and out of breath. 'Cooper's trying to buy this place.'

'What, your apartment?'

'No, the whole planet.'

Clunk, Albion and Clyde had all turned their heads when the door burst open, and they nodded in unison to indicate they were listening. Hal and Vera leaned forward. 'Okay, spill it.'

'He can't buy the entire company, of course. That's way too big. But Morrell told me someone is buying large parcels of shares. If they get to ten percent, they can install a new director on the board.' He spread his hands. 'And we all know who that will be.'

'Cooper,' said Vera quietly.

'Okay, so he gets onto the board of directors,' said Hal, shrugging. 'So what?'

'It means he can land his ships here. Bring in as many people as he wants.'

Hal frowned. 'Can't we stop him?'

'Only if we buy ten percent before he does. Do you have a few billion lying around?'

'Of course not.'

'Then we can't stop him.' Pydd strode up and down, his face set. 'He's beaten me, Hal. He's going to win. I thought this was a safe haven, but according to Morrell this corporate raid could be over in a week.'

'We'll hide somewhere else,' said Hal. 'We've still got his ship.'

Vera shook her head. 'The ship has a tracker on board.'

'Clunk could disable it.'

Over by the wall, Clunk shook his head. 'Trackers are untouchable, Mr Spacejock. I lack the authorisation required to –'

'Just point it out to me, and I'll shoot the damn thing.'

'Negative, Mr Spacejock. It's an integral part of the ship.'

'How come I'm only hearing about this now? Did my ships have trackers?'

'The *Gull* was too old, and I disabled the *Volante*'s myself.'

'How come –'

'The *Volante* was your ship, and therefore I had the authority to disable the tracker.'

Hal cursed. They couldn't run and they couldn't hide. 'Do you have any ideas?' he asked the others.

'I do,' said Pydd quietly. 'Take Cooper out.'

'You'll never get near him.'

'I will if I give myself up.' Pydd leaned closer. 'Not one word of this to Harriet, is that understood?'

Everyone nodded, although Hal hesitated.

'Swear on it,' said Pydd. 'This goes no further. I mean it.'

They all obeyed, although Hal had a sick feeling in his stomach.

'Right. Here's what we're going to do.' Rapidly, Pydd outlined his plan, and as he spoke the faces around him grew more and more concerned. Finally, when he'd finished speaking, Hal could hold himself in no more.

'You have got to be joking,' he growled. 'That's suicide, and you know it!'

'I have to do it, Hal.'

'What about your family? What will this do to Harriet?'

'She and Junior will never be safe, never. Back on Alteia, when Cooper was cutting off my fingers, he told me . . . ' Pydd swallowed. 'He told me one was for Harriet, and one was for the baby. He said that when he killed them both, I'd remember the day I crossed him every time I looked at my hand.'

There was a long silence.

'You can't do it,' said Hal, at last. 'You just can't. Harriet will –'

Pydd frowned at him. 'You swore an oath not to tell her.'

'That was a dirty trick,' said Hal quietly.

'Afterwards ...she'll come to accept it, when she realises she and Junior are safe.' Pydd looked around the room. 'You don't know what it's like. Cooper's been chasing you guys for what, a day or two? I've been in his sights for over three *years*. I'm tired of it. I'm done with it. I just want it to end.'

'Mr Pydd,' said Clunk suddenly. 'There is no guarantee your plan will work.'

'I know that.'

'The calculations required, the difficulty of drawing Cooper to the correct location, getting him to meet you in person ...there are any number of ways it could fall apart.'

'I know, dammit!' Pydd raised his hand in apology, the missing fingers a stark reminder of his sacrifice. 'I'm sorry, I know you're trying to help but I've thought about this all day, and it's the only way.' He stood up. 'I have to meet Morrell. I'm going to use his office to call Cooper and set up the meet. And please, I beg you, not a word of this to Harriet.' He gestured to Clunk. 'Can I speak to you in the hall? I have to convince Cooper to pick the right meeting place.'

With that he left, and the deep silence he left behind could have swallowed a gunshot.

◆

'We have to tell Harriet,' said Vera. 'If it were me, I'd want to know.'

'He made us swear to it,' said Hal.

'Yes, for good reason. He knows damn well she's the only person who can stop him.' Vera swore under her breath. 'We should have stopped him leaving. Knocked him out, tied him up. Just ... stopped him somehow.'

'We were all stunned,' said Hal. 'He told us the plan, then left while we were still working out just how crazy he is.'

'Do you think Morrell knows all the details? Maybe we could tell him, ask him to tell Harriet.'

'They're old friends. I doubt he knows,' said Hal firmly. 'Pydd would only have told him about the meeting, not ... not the rest.'

'What a mess,' breathed Vera.

At that moment Clunk returned, looking grave. 'I don't like this, Mr Spacejock. There are too many variables. Too many things to go wrong.'

'Sounds like the story of my life,' said Hal, but the joke fell flat. There was a pause, and then ... 'I'm going to tell her,' said Hal suddenly. 'Screw the promise to Pydd, I only met the guy yesterday. But Harriet –'

'What about her?' demanded Vera.

'We've met before. We worked on a case together.'

Vera's face cleared. 'Wait, that thing you told me about last night? The Peace Force officer and the killer bugs? She's *that* Harriet?'

Hal nodded.

'But – why didn't you tell Pydd you knew his wife?'

Hal snorted. 'Harriet made me promise. She made me swear on it.'

'That figures. They're as bad as each other.'

'Peace Force training I guess.' Hal shrugged. 'Anyway, I owe her a lot more than I do him, so I'll tell her.'

At that moment they heard the front door open, and Harriet

called out a greeting. She came in, looking slightly flushed from the walk, and if she noticed the tension in the room she didn't remark on it. 'Stu not back from lunch?'

'He's with Morrell,' said Hal.

'Okay. He won't want dinner then. Anyone else hungry?'

'No, but I'll make coffee,' said Hal.

The two of them walked to the kitchen in silence.

'Is something wrong?' asked Harriet at last. 'You were all happy this morning, but now it's like a funeral in there.'

'Pydd ... your husband, he's going after Cooper.'

Harriet closed her eyes. 'Oh no.'

'He's got this plan, but we had to swear not to tell you.' Hal spread his hands. 'We couldn't just ... you know,' he finished lamely.

'What's the idiot trying to do?'

'He's organising a meeting with Cooper. Just the two of them. Pydd thinks he can ... get rid of him.'

'Stu's a bloody fool,' said Harriet. 'Cooper won't walk into a trap, he's far too cunning.'

'I know. But your husband ... he's desperate.' Hal explained about the shares, and the corporate takeover. 'You won't be safe here. And if you try to run, Cooper's people will get you. Pydd knows it. I know it.' Hal touched her arm. 'Harriet, you know it too. And the baby ... Cooper's after Hal Junior as well.'

Harriet's jaw tightened. 'If it wasn't for little Hal, I'd pick the biggest gun I could find and splash Cooper all over the nearest wall.'

'I know. I've seen you in action.'

Harriet smiled wanly. 'I hate being so cautious, but it's not just me I have to think about. You all know that, right?'

'Of course we do!' declared Hal.

'Hal ...' Harriet's voice tailed off. She looked up at him, her face pale. 'I don't want my child to grow up without a father. Stu's obsessed with Cooper, he might do anything, anything at all, but there's nothing I can do to stop him.'

'Surely if you spoke to him –'

Harriet shook her head. 'He'll promise one thing and do the opposite, the fool. Hal, he's going to get himself killed. I know it. *I know it.*'

Hal knew it too, because twenty minutes earlier Pydd had told them exactly how the meeting with Cooper would go down. Neither of the two men would survive. Then Hal had a thought. It was a way out for Pydd, and it could just work. Quickly, he took Harriet's hands in his. 'Your husband will make it, I promise.'

'Don't just promise me, Hal Spacejock. I want you to swear on it.'

'I swear to you, Harriet,' said Hal solemnly. 'Steward Pydd will come back from this mission safe and sound, no matter what. I swear it.'

Harriet studied his face, trying to read his expression, trying to detect a lie. Instead, she saw only honesty and good intentions. 'Thanks, Hal,' she whispered. 'Thank you from both of us.'

◆

Pydd was in Morrell's office, sitting at a large desk with a bank of screens in front of him. There was a visitor's badge clipped to his lapel, and Morrell had promised a real one if he accepted a position with the firm. 'What, with Cooper as my boss?' said Pydd drily, and they left it at that.

If Morrell knew what I was about to do, thought Pydd, he wouldn't have let me in at all. He looked over his shoulder, but the older man had left him to it, closing the door on the way out so Pydd wouldn't be disturbed.

Pydd sat looking at the screens, his heart beating fast. He had to play this right or Cooper would never agree to a meeting. The right amount of defiance, the right amount of desperation, and just the right amount of humility. It would be tough, because all the time he was talking he'd be thinking about reaching through the screen and tearing out Cooper's windpipe ... but it was pointless to daydream.

He glanced down at his hands, and noticed they were shaking. Everything hinged on this. Mess it up, and – it didn't bear thinking about.

Before he could wind himself up any further, Pydd selected Cooper's ship from a list onscreen, and initiated a call. The screen cleared instantly, and a young man in uniform stared at him.

'This is Narella's chief of security,' said Pydd. 'I have a personal message for Mr Cooper.'

The man checked his screen for the caller id, then nodded. 'Message please.'

'Stewart Pydd is offering to give himself up. Call back on this number in five minutes to organise the handover.' Pydd didn't wait for a reply. He raised his hand to the screen, and with a shaking finger he cut the connection.

The next few minutes were the longest of his life. The seconds crawled by, and he almost jumped out of his skin when the terminal buzzed. He accepted the call, and drew a ragged breath. It was Cooper.

'So it really is you,' said Cooper. 'I never thought you'd have the guts.'

Humility, thought Pydd. Desperation. Defiance. 'I'm fed up with running. I realise now, I . . . I can't win.'

'It's a pity you didn't realise that three years ago,' snapped Cooper. 'You've cost me millions.'

'I won't cost you any more,' said Pydd quietly. 'I'm prepared to hand myself over. No conditions.'

'Trying to save your family, I take it? Wise man.' Cooper stared out of the screen, judging Pydd's expression. 'Very well. Bring the *Charlton* to Alteia. My people will meet you, and –'

'No,' said Pydd. *Defiance*. 'The group I'm with won't go for it. They believe I'm organising a truce, not a surrender.'

'A truce? They must be morons, the lot of them. I've won, Pydd. Won, you hear?'

'I do, Mr Cooper.' Pydd gritted his teeth. *Humility*. 'That's why I'm giving myself up.' *Desperation*.

'Hmm. Very well, we'll meet in orbit above Narella. And by the way, I want Spacejock as well. Also, I expect you to release Captain Vera and my ship.' He frowned. 'If you've mistreated her I'll sue you for everything you have, and then I'll personally trample the rest into the dirt.'

'Captain Vera has not been harmed,' said Pydd quietly.

'Not her, I meant my ship!' snapped Cooper.

'And Spacejock . . . he'll never agree. I'm trying to save my family, but you have no leverage over him.'

'Then the deal is off. A week from now my people will be on Narella, and I'll round you all up myself.'

'A week from now we won't be here,' said Pydd. 'One way or another, we'll get away. And then you'll spend millions chasing us.' *Defiance!* 'And I promise you, this time we'll fight dirty. We'll sabotage your ships, burn down your warehouses and factories, spike your fuel . . . just think of the cost.'

'You wouldn't dare!' said Cooper, but his expression spoke volumes.

'What do we have to lose?' Pydd leaned forward. 'I want to end this, I really do. My life for my family, but leave Spacejock out of it. We'll meet in a deserted system, you can take me to your ship, and then the others will land the *Charlton* on Narella. Once they're clear, we'll free Captain Vera and she can fly your ship back to Alteia.'

Cooper thought about it. 'I won't have any docking in space. I'm not giving you the chance to rip the docking tube apart while my people are coming to get you.'

Inwardly, Pydd groaned. That was one option shot down. 'How am I supposed to get to your ship?'

'We'll use an unmanned shuttle for the transfer. Remote control, nobody but you on board.'

'We don't have a shuttle,' protested Pydd, trying to salvage his plan.

'You mean you haven't stolen one yet.' Cooper gestured. 'Don't worry, I have dozens of the things.'

Fine, let Cooper have his shuttle. There were other ways. 'All right, let's agree on the location.' Pydd opened a sector map and shared the screen with Cooper. 'What about 4C?'

'You must think I'm mad. There's a Peace Force training base in that sector.'

'I thought the Peace Force was in your pocket?'

'Only on Alteia.'

'9J, then. No planets at all.'

'Just half a billion asteroids where you can hide any number of ships.' Cooper frowned at him. 'This is starting to smell like a trap.'

'All right, you pick one.' Pydd stopped breathing. His entire plan hinged on Cooper's choice. He'd led him carefully in the right direction, and there was really only one suitable sector showing on the map. He was banking on Cooper's business acumen, because moving his fleet to a more distant sector would leave a huge fuel bill.

'This one,' said Cooper, and when Pydd saw the sector in question it was all he could do to keep a triumphant grin off his face. Still, he didn't want to be too eager.

'Are you sure? It's a long way out.'

'Of course I'm sure.'

'All right. If you move your fleet there –'

'No chance. I want the *Charlton* there first. Transmit the coordinates after you jump, and I'll scan the sector before giving my fleet the go-ahead. And I swear, if I see so much as a lifeboat your family will rue the day –'

'You don't need to say it,' muttered Pydd.

'I have seven ships in my fleet. You'd be wise to remember that.' And with that, Cooper closed the connection.

Pydd sat back and breathed out, slowly. Against all odds, it seemed he'd got everything he wanted. 'Yes, yes, yes!' he whispered, and slapped his maimed hand on the desk in triumph.

29

It was a smaller group which eventually returned to the *Charlton,* because Clyde and Sable stayed with Harriet. If the plan failed and Cooper survived, the two of them would become the last line of defence.

After Hal and Vera, Clunk, Albion and Pydd boarded the Charlton, Vera took the ship into orbit above Narella, flying with her customary skill. 'Navcom, can you adjust the throttles for optimum power?'

'Complying,' said the Navcom, and there was a hint of happiness in her voice as she tweaked the engines just so.

Earlier, on their way to the spaceport, Clunk had spoken to Vera about the ship's computer. 'Just give the Navcom something to do and she'll be yours for life,' he advised. Then he lowered his voice. 'Incidentally, the same goes for Mr Spacejock.'

Meanwhile, Hal and Pydd were on the lower deck, sitting in armchairs with their feet up. There was nothing to do until they reached the rendezvous, and they'd gravitated to the lounge.

'Do you think she'll ever forgive me?' asked Pydd, his face serious.

'Of course she will,' said Hal firmly. Inside he wasn't so

sure.

'It feels like I'm betraying her.'

'You're doing what's best for your family. She can't complain about that.'

'If this goes down the way it's supposed to ...' began Pydd. 'Well, I just need someone to keep an eye on her. Understood?'

'Of course!'

'And if the plan fails ...'

'She's got Sable and Clyde to protect her. And I bet Harriet can handle herself.'

'You don't know her like I do,' declared Pydd loyally. 'Harriet's as tough as they come, and if it wasn't for the baby she'd be sailing to battle right alongside us.'

'I'm sure of it,' said Hal, with an element of truth that Pydd was completely unaware of. Then, delicately: 'Did you ... say goodbye?'

'I couldn't,' said Pydd, and his face twisted. 'She'd have guessed something was up. I had to act casual, pretend I'd be back again, but it ... it tore my heart out. I'll never see her again, never see my baby boy.'

'Don't bet on it,' said Hal. 'Nothing in the universe is certain ... except taxes, of course.'

The overhead speaker buzzed. 'If you'd like to come to the flight deck, we're about to jump,' said Vera.

'Already?' whispered Pydd. 'That's so ... soon.'

Hal got up and held out his hand. 'Come on, we can do this.'

Everyone was in the flight deck, gathered around the console. Their course was plotted on the screen, and Hal shook his head as he saw the destination. 'I can't believe we're doing this on purpose.'

'It's the only way,' said Pydd.

'You can still change your mind,' said Hal gently. 'It's not too late.'

'No. Tell Cooper we're arriving, then do the jump.'

Clunk nodded to Vera, who sent the message then activated the jump drives. After the whine built to a crescendo the ship flickered to the destination system – and ended up facing the swirling accretion disk of the black hole.

Hal shuddered at the sight. He'd never expected to see it again, let alone so soon.

'Transmitting coordinates to Cooper,' said Vera, her tone precise and professional. 'Confirming coordinates sent.'

'Now we wait,' said Hal. 'Clunk, can you tell when he's scanned us? I'd like a bit of notice before –' His voice broke off as Cooper's entire fleet appeared not two hundred metres away. Immediately, the screen cleared and Cooper's face loomed over the flight deck.

'What a pathetic effort,' said Cooper. 'A black hole ... really? Did you expect me to fly right into it?'

'It was our only chance,' said Pydd wearily, his expression a mix of despair and disappointment. 'One last roll of the dice, and it failed.'

'Pathetic,' said Cooper again. 'Now stand by for the shuttle, and I warn you, if you try to run ... '

'I won't run, you have my word.' Pydd spread his hands. 'I surrender.'

Cooper closed the connection, and there was silence in the flight deck.

'Do you think he bought it?' said Hal at last.

'Sure. Didn't you hear him gloating?'

'Shuttle on the way,' said Vera. She glanced over her shoulder at them. 'It'll dock in under ten minutes. If you want to say your goodbyes –'

'Just a minute!' said Hal quickly. 'Pydd, that gun I lent you. Is it still in the hold?'

Pydd gaped at him. 'Of course! I was going to jump him, try and take him out with my bare hands. That gun will make certain of it!'

'I'll go and get it.' Hal glanced at the others. 'If the shuttle turns up, stall it.'

'It's unmanned,' said Clunk. 'I don't think it's possible to –'

'Just do it, okay?' Hal ran into the lift and pressed the button. 'You can't let Pydd leave without that gun. Everything, and I mean *everything*, depends on it.'

Before anyone could object, the doors closed and he was gone.

◆

'The shuttle is almost here,' announced Vera.

Clunk glanced at the lift and frowned. The doors were closed and the indicator still showed 'Lower Deck'. 'Mr Spacejock has been a long time.'

'I put the gun in a locker,' said Pydd. 'He's probably still looking for it.'

At that moment the intercom buzzed. 'I can't find the thing,' called Hal. 'Which locker was it?'

'One of the banks on the right,' said Pydd. 'Lower level, not the upper row.'

There was a sound of banging doors. 'Are you sure? All I can see is a white box with paddle things.'

'Don't touch that,' said Pydd quickly. 'It's a defib. You'll get a nasty shock.'

'Would it kill Cooper?'

'It would probably stop his heart just as well, but if I had the gun I wouldn't have to open his shirt first.'

'Well, the rest of the lockers are empty. There's nothing.'

Pydd cursed and ran for the lift.

'The shuttle –' began Vera.

'I'm not going without that damn gun!' said Pydd, as he mashed the call button. 'Hal was right, it's going to make all the difference.'

The lift doors opened, then closed, and the indicator pinged as the elevator reached the lower deck. Then, there was a thump from the airlock.

'Shuttle docking,' said Vera.

Clunk reached over and pressed a button, sealing the outer door. 'That'll delay the connection a few seconds. After that, introduce an error code or two.'

The delays worked, but about thirty seconds later there was a buzz from the console. 'That's Cooper,' said Vera. 'He'll be wondering what we're up to.'

'Tell him Mr Pydd is saying goodbye.' Clunk pressed the button again, and there was a hiss as the airlock decompressed. Air wafted into the flight deck, and through the airlock tube they could see directly into the small shuttle. It had two rows of bench seats along the hull, with broad windows above, and a simple control panel at the front. It was also empty. For a moment Clunk considered boarding the shuttle, perhaps with Albion for company. When it arrived at the other end they could burst out and ... what? Stop Cooper with a well-reasoned argument? Clunk shook his head. He didn't like

Pydd's plan, he didn't like it one little bit, but there seemed to be no alternative.

'If he's not back soon, Cooper's going to cancel,' said Vera.

Barely had she spoken than the lift doors parted, and Pydd hurried into the flight deck. He was out of breath, and had one hand in his jacket pocket, which bulged with the outline of the gun. 'That Spacejock guy ... ' he said, shaking his head. 'The damn thing was right there in front of his eyes.'

'Mr Spacejock can be a little obtuse at times,' admitted Clunk.

'Yeah, well I gave him a serve. He's gone to sulk in the kitchen. He's getting a coffee or something.'

'That is another of Mr Spacejock's less desirable traits,' said Clunk. 'Why, there was this one time –'

'Cooper is getting really impatient,' Vera warned them. 'If you don't board soon it'll go without you.'

'If it's all right with you, Clunk, I'll hear the rest of that story later.'

'Indeed,' said Clunk, before realising there wouldn't *be* a later.

Pydd smiled at the other robot standing nearby. 'It's Albion, right?'

The robot nodded.

'It's been a pleasure. You're as good as any human.'

'Thank you, Mr Pydd.'

'Please. My friends call me Stu.'

'Very well, Mr Stu,' said Albion gravely.

'Cooper ... he's recalling the shuttle!' said Vera in alarm.

'Tell him I'm boarding,' said Pydd. He looked at Vera, but she was replying to Cooper's message. He waited for her to finish, to catch his eye across the flight deck, but after waiting several seconds he realised she was busy. The goodbye died on his lips and, finally, he turned to Clunk.

'This is a brave thing you're doing, Mr Pydd,' said the robot, and he extended his hand.

Pydd moved as though to shake it, but his hand was in his pocket clutching the gun. He tried to withdraw it but the lining stretched. Then he laughed. 'I'd probably shoot you, Clunk. You know what I'm like with these things.' Instead of shaking hands, he put his left arm around the robot and gave him a hug, holding him tightly for an instant.

Then, before anyone could beg him to change his mind, to stay and find another way to fight Cooper, Pydd was gone. The airlock door closed with a final thud, and they all heard the hiss as the shuttle departed for Cooper's ship.

At that instant there was a grief-stricken shout, and Clunk pushed the others aside and hurled himself at the airlock. 'No, no NO! Stop the shuttle! STOP THE SHUTTLE!' he screamed at the porthole.

'Clunk, the airlock, no!' shouted Vera. 'It's not ... it's still a vacuum!'

Clunk's fingers slipped from the control panel and he turned and slid to the floor, his back to the tightly closed airlock door. He buried his head in his hands and muttered to himself, his voice barely audible above the ship's background noises.

'That poor, fool human. That silly, stubborn, noble, selfless idiot. Why, oh why did he have to ...' his voice tailed off, and he shook his head, totally overcome.

— 30 —

Cooper's face cleared as the shuttle finally left the *Charlton*. The delay had been vexing, and he'd been on the point of ordering his fleet of ships to leave when the captain reported movement at last.

'Scan that shuttle,' demanded Cooper, his finger prodding the screen so hard it almost left dents. 'Scan it with everything you've got. I want to know how many people are on board, and whether they've hidden any of their damned robots aboard.' He paused. 'Can you measure someone's height? See through their clothes?'

'I have the mass, sir. It tallies with Pydd's service record, give or take a kilo. And I can confirm there are no explosives on board. Other than that . . . we'll, it's only a passenger shuttle. It wasn't designed for –'

'What about guns?'

The captain shook his head. 'Nothing that small.'

'A pity, but I suppose it doesn't matter.' Cooper checked the bulky pack at his hip. 'Are you sure this is fully charged?'

'Absolutely, sir. I confirmed it with two others.'

'And it lasts how long? Eight minutes, wasn't it?'

'No more than six, to be safe.'

'Long enough.' Cooper turned to the rear of the flight deck, where his men were gathered. The two big men were in front, toting powerful blasters. Behind them stood a row of thugs in red shirts with 'Cooper Freight' logos. 'If the fool shoots at me, I order you to cut him down where he stands. Is that absolutely clear?'

The men nodded silently.

Cooper eyed the screen. 'How much longer?'

'Five minutes, no more.'

'I wish there was a camera. I want to see the look on his face.'

'Alteia's privacy laws –'

'Sod the laws.'

'Sir, these shuttles are used by government ministers. It would be risky to –'

'I know, damn you. How long now?'

'Four minutes, sir.'

Cooper could barely contain himself. He knew Pydd was hoping to pull some trick or other, and he was looking forward to it. Because, when the trick failed and all hope died, Cooper's victory would be all the sweeter. Of course, once he disposed of Pydd he'd have to find another quarry. Spacejock was an idiot, barely worthy of consideration, and the wife and child were of no consequence. Then he thought of Sable. She'd infiltrated his organisation, helped Spacejock escape, given aid to Pydd too. She had training, she was cunning … with a smile, Cooper decided she would make for excellent sport. He vowed to look into her family, to find the levers he could use to –

'Thirty seconds, sir.'

Cooper glanced towards the airlock, picturing the arrival in his mind. He'd meet Pydd alone, face to face, and he had no doubt the other man would try to kill him on the spot. He felt a thrill, but it was a muted one. The heavily-armed hunter does not fear his prey, not when that prey is weak and ineffectual.

In a way, Cooper was disappointed it was over. He'd have preferred a more dramatic ending ...as long as he won, of course.

'Docking complete.'

'Open the airlock,' said Cooper.

The men crowded forward, guns at the ready, but froze when Cooper gestured with his cane. 'Cover the airlock. I'm going in alone.'

'Sir ...' began one of the big men.

'That's an order, Jackson.'

'*I'm* Jackson,' said the other large man.

'That's an order, both of you,' said Cooper sharply. The outer door stood open, and he cupped his hands to the porthole and looked in. Pydd was in the shuttle, lounging on a seat near the flight console with his arms folded across his chest. Cooper looked closer and felt a red hot anger. Was the man pretending to be *asleep*? He was supposed to be on his knees, begging for his life!

Angrily, he operated the airlock door and stepped inside. Pydd didn't move. Then Cooper's blood ran cold as he remembered the heavy pack at his hip, and with fumbling fingers he switched it on. Instantly he was coated with shimmering particles from head to toe, following the contours of his skin and clothing. There was a faint tingle, but he'd take that over a direct hit from a blaster any day.

Cooper took another step, passing through the outer door. As he did so, Pydd opened one eye. 'Nice to see you again, Cooper.'

'You won't think it's nice in a minute. Now get up.'

Slowly, Pydd unfolded his arms, revealing a small gun

clasped in his right hand. His fingers were curled around the grip, his index finger on the trigger.

'You can't hurt me,' said Cooper. 'I have a shield.'

Pydd shrugged, and turned to the miniature flight console. He pressed a button and the airlock door slid to, sealing them in the shuttle together.

Cooper's first reaction was fear: he was trapped with an armed man, and he only had five or six minutes life on his shield. Then he smiled to himself. 'This shuttle is under my ship's control. An ex-cop like you couldn't fly this thing with two good hands, let alone –'

'Lucky I'm an ex cop *and* a pilot,' said Pydd, and he pressed another button, firing up the shuttle's engine. He pulled back on the throttle, putting the shuttle into reverse, and there was a ripping sound from the hull as the docking tube was torn asunder.

Before Cooper could cry for help, the shuttle spun in its own length and roared away at full speed. Through the windows, the fleet fell away rapidly behind them.

◆

The lift doors opened and Clunk thundered down the lower deck passageway to the hold, with Vera hot on his heels. There was still the tiniest chance, thought Clunk. Just the tiniest, tiniest chance he was wrong, despite all the evidence.

The door to the hold was open, and he charged through into the hold proper. It was empty, but when he stopped he heard a dull, rhythmic thudding. It was coming from one of the lockers, and with sick apprehension Clunk ran towards it. Halfway there he paused at the sight of Mr Spacejock's brand new slacks and jacket, lying crumpled on the deck, and his worst fears were confirmed. He wrenched open the locker, and a half-naked man fell out, bound at wrist and ankle and with a strip fabric as a gag.

'Oh no!' exclaimed Vera. 'Hal! Why would Pydd do this to you?'

Clunk crouched to rip off the gag, none too gently. And as the man raised his hand to his forehead to rub at the hefty bruise, Clunk noticed the maimed hand with its missing fingers.

'He knocked me out,' said Stewart Pydd thickly. 'Why did Spacejock knock me out?'

With his worst fears confirmed, Clunk could only shake his head sadly. 'It seems Mr Spacejock has just taken your place aboard the shuttle.'

'Oh my God,' breathed Vera. 'In the flight deck just now ... that was *Hal!*'

'Evidently, since Mr Pydd lies here before us.

'And he pretended not to know Albion's name ... and he even sent himself up: all that stuff about sulking and making coffee.' Vera groaned. 'Oh Hal, you *idiot.*'

'On the contrary, Mr Spacejock was remarkably clever. When he pretended he couldn't find the gun, he lured Mr Pydd to the hold in order to knock him out and take his clothes.' Despite himself, Clunk looked impressed. 'I was not aware that Mr Spacejock was capable of such deep thinking.'

'Obviously not, or you would have stopped him.'

'How I wish it were so.' Once again, Clunk reviewed the scene in his mind, to see whether there was any way he could have spotted the deception. 'Now I understand why Mr

Spacejock refused to shake hands. I would have noticed it wasn't maimed!'

Pydd stared at them both, still reeling from the blow to his head. 'But ... why? Why would he do such a thing? It was my plan, it was supposed to be *me* aboard the shuttle.'

'Mr Spacejock promised Harriet he would bring you back safely, no matter what.' Clunk looked grave. 'He swore a solemn oath to your wife, and Mr Spacejock has always been a man of his word.'

◆

'What the hell are you doing?' demanded Cooper, leaning on his cane. 'What the –'

There was a burst of static from a wall speaker. *'Sir, is everything all right? Did you mean to leave the ship?'*

'Take control of this shuttle,' shouted Cooper. 'Turn her around. Bring her back to the fleet. Now, man. NOW!'

Very casually, Hal raised his gun and fired into the console. The controls fizzed and sparked, and the lights on the panel died.

'What ... what have you done?' whispered Cooper.

'I just killed us both,' said Hal calmly.

'Don't be silly, man. They'll pick us up,' said Cooper, now sick with fear.

'They can't. We're heading straight for a black hole at full throttle. By the time anyone reaches us, it'll be too late ... for us and them.'

'Sir, what are your orders?'

'Stop this ship!' shouted Cooper. 'I don't care how you do it, save me!'

There was a delay. *'Sir, you're on course for the black hole.'*

'I know that, you moron!' screamed Cooper. 'Come and get me this instant!'

'We can't, sir. You're travelling too fast. By the time we match your speed, you'll already be inside the black hole's influence.'

'W-what do you mean influence?' demanded Cooper, his face now ashen.

'Trapped,' said Hal, in satisfaction. 'Stuck here for all eternity. Aboard this shuttle, time will pass normally. But outside, in the rest of the galaxy, thousands of years will pass.'

'Sir, we ... we don't know what to do!'

'If you call again, I'll shoot him,' said Hal calmly, and the speaker immediately went dead.

'Stop the shuttle,' whispered Cooper, falling to his knees. The cane fell beside him with a thud. 'I beg you. I'll give you money. A job. Anything! I give you my word!'

'See, now that's the problem with crooks,' said Hal. 'You just can't trust them.'

And at that moment, Cooper's force field expired with a gentle sigh.

— 31 —

Hal stood up, still holding the gun. He towered over Cooper, who cut a pathetic, grovelling figure as he knelt on the shuttle's immaculate carpet. 'Do you remember the first time we met? You had your men drag me into that warehouse with a bag over my head. You tied me to a chair. You threatened me, insulted me, and then you knocked me out.'

'I–I thought you were Pydd.'

'Oh, well that's all right then. I'll take us to safety.'

Cooper raised his haggard face, a spark of hope in his eyes. 'Really?'

'Nope,' said Hal. 'See, you made an even bigger mistake and you didn't even realise it. Until yesterday, there were two people in this galaxy who mattered more to me that anyone else alive.' Hal felt a stab of regret. He'd really wanted to say goodbye to Vera, but she hadn't even looked up from the console. 'One of those people, of course, is Clunk.'

'The robot? He's not a person!'

'Now is really not the time to argue,' said Hal quietly. 'The other person is Harriet Walsh, a wonderfully brave Peace Force officer who –'

'H-Harriet Walsh? Pydd's wife?'

'Bingo. Harriet and I were together once, and I would have

cheerfully killed anyone who threatened her.' Hal sighted along the gun. 'According to Pydd, you've been threatening her for some time now. Is that right?'

'I had to stop Pydd. He was ruining my business!'

'So that's a yes. You knew she was pregnant, didn't you? I know you did, don't bother to deny it.'

Cooper hung his head.

'Do you know what she's calling the baby? Hal Junior. After me.'

'I don't see –'

Hal waved his free hand. 'I'll never meet him, of course. But one day, when he's old enough, Harriet will tell him about me. Maybe a story or two about the brave freighter pilot who gave his life to save little Hal Junior and his beloved mum and dad.' He glanced through the window, and saw the black hole swirling ahead of them. He knew the size wouldn't change, not at sub-light speeds, but to his mind it seemed to loom over the ship like a giant, gaping threat. 'Funny thing is, I'll probably outlive all of them by a thousand years. To us, stuck inside the event horizon, it will seem like a couple of days, and that will be plenty once we're dying of thirst.' Hal had a thought, and he crossed to the rear of the shuttle. There were only two lockers: one was empty, the other contained a life jacket and a flare gun. 'Oh, look at that. No water.'

As he was standing there he heard a noise, and when he turned round Cooper was getting to his feet, leaning heavily on his cane. Cooper's face was a mask, and his eyes blazed with hatred. Then, without warning, he threw his cane aside and charged.

Vera had the shuttle on-screen, maximum zoom. It was travelling away from them at an oblique angle, too far to make out any detail through the windows, but close enough to see the thrusters blazing away at the rear. And beyond, millions of kilometres ahead, was the black hole's glowing accretion disk.

'If he turns the shuttle, fires the thrusters ... ' she began.

'They're still accelerating,' said Clunk, with a shake of his head. 'Even if they slow now, by the time they come to a dead stop they'll be deep in the event horizon.'

'Then we'll just have to get him out.'

'Do you realise what that means?' said Clunk gently. 'Time will pass faster on the outside. Pydd's wife and child ... they'll be dead a thousand years, while we experience less than a day or two. The galaxy, human civilisation ... they will change beyond measure.'

'There has to be a way,' said Vera firmly. 'I'm not letting him go.'

They watched the screen, Clunk's fans whirring as he thought with all his might. Then, very clearly, they saw two flashes of light. They came from inside the shuttle, and moments later there was a buzz from the console.

'Charlton, *it's Hal.*'

'Mr Spacejock, can I just say –'

'*Not now Clunk.*' There was a pause. '*Cooper's dead. I had no choice, he tried to jump me.*'

'I'd have shot him whether he jumped or not,' said Vera.

'*I didn't shoot him, I missed. He just crumpled and died. I guess he had a heart attack.*'

'Mr Spacejock, forget Cooper and listen to me. It may not be too late to save yourself, as long as you turn the shuttle round immediately.'

Vera looked at him in astonishment. 'But Clunk, you said –'

Clunk silenced her with a look. 'Turn the shuttle, Mr Spacejock. Fire your engines at full throttle, and we may be able to save you.'

'*No can do, Clunk. I shot the controls to trap Cooper.*' He hesitated. '*I know this was supposed to be a one way trip, but now that Cooper's dealt with there's no point riding this bus forever. I don't suppose you can pick me up?*'

'I'm looking into it, Mr Spacejock. Please examine the controls, see if you can't lash up a repair.'

Hal sounded doubtful. '*If you say so. Hal out.*'

After he disconnected, Vera rounded on Clunk. 'You told me he couldn't fly out of this!'

'And he can't,' said Clunk calmly.

'Then why –'

'Better for Mr Spacejock to keep busy than to fret about the future. I believe I imparted that advice to you earlier.'

'How can you be so calm? He means so much to you, and yet –'

Clunk sighed. 'He means more than you can imagine, but there's no use wringing my hands. As we speak, my processors are calculating outcomes based on every possible variable. I've yet to hit upon the answer to Mr Spacejock's current problem, but it's not for lack of trying.'

There was a buzz, and Vera checked the console. 'One of Cooper's ships is hailing us.'

'Excellent,' said Clunk. 'I would very much like to speak to them.'

Vera obliged, and Clunk picked up the handset. 'This is the Charlton. Mr Cooper is dead, and without his protection your future is perilous in the extreme. I suggest you run, spreading far and wide, because after we recover our people we're coming for you.'

With that he hung up, not even bothering to wait for a reply. In the corner of the screen, on an inset window, six of the seven ships winked out. Moments later, the seventh vanished too.

After they'd gone, there was another buzz. *'Hal here. Are you guys still–'* crackle *'– out there?'*

'We're still here, Mr Spacejock.'

'Any chance you can –' bzzzt *'– pick me up soon? Cooper's people thought we'd gone to far, but with a –'* spzzzz *'– brain like yours ...'*

'I'm still calculating, Mr Spacejock.'

'Well don't take too long. Comms are –' gchhhhh *'– breaking up and it's getting –'* blarrrrrr *'– warm in here.'*

The speaker went dead, and Vera looked at Clunk with pleading eyes. 'Is there anything you can think of ... anything at all?'

'I'm sorry, Captain Vera,' said Clunk gravely. 'I have checked and re-checked my figures and Cooper's people were right. The shuttle is moving fast, and by the time we catch up with it and transfer Mr Spacejock aboard the *Charlton*, it will be too late. We'll be too close to the event horizon.'

'I didn't even say goodbye to him,' said Vera in a small voice. 'I was busy with the console, and I didn't know it was him, and –'

'We have to be strong, Captain. We can grieve for Mr Spacejock later, when ... when ...'

'Exactly! We'll never be able to grieve for Hal, because he'll still be trapped in that black hole when we're dead and buried ourselves!'

32

Everyone was gathered in the flight deck, Clunk having arranged a brainstorm session. He already knew Mr Spacejock's situation was hopeless, but he believed the process would convince Captain Vera and Mr Pydd of the same. Until then, they would continue to hold out hope ... when there was none.

The main viewscreen was devoid of black holes and tiny passenger shuttles hurtling to their doom, and instead displayed a uniform white colour from corner to corner. Clunk held a pointer, and when everyone was settled he waved it in the air, scrawling 'Saving Mr Spacejock' at the top of the screen in perfect cursive lettering.

'Welcome, all of you. As you know, Mr Spacejock is currently in peril, and unless we can think of a solution, he is – to all intents and purposes – lost to us.' Clunk looked around the flight deck. 'In order to facilitate blue sky thinking, I have activated a special-purpose business mode in my firmware. This will enable me to action any low-hanging fruit, incentivising the team to a win-win situation viz-a-viz Mr Spacejock's exit strategy.'

Albion spoke up. 'Clunk, you are aware that every second counts? Hal's about to get swallowed up by a black hole, and holding a meeting like this seems, well –'

'I admire your can-do attitude, Albion, but together we must buy in to the holistic approach in order to–'

'Okay, that's enough bullshit,' said Vera sharply. 'Cut the double-speak and get on with it.'

'But this is how meetings are supposed to be run!' protested Clunk.

'Only the ones that go for hours and achieve nothing.'

Clunk blinked. 'Er, yes. Perhaps I could tone it down a little.' He paused, then raised the pointer. 'Let me show you the current situation.' In the middle of the screen he drew a stick figure with a ragged haircut and an upside-down smile, writing 'Mr S' underneath. Then he drew a bubble around it, with an arrow pointing to a cigar-shaped vessel. Nearby, with a vigorous circular motion, he drew a big black circle. Then, at the far edge of the screen he drew another cigar shape with a row of faces.

'Here, Mr Spacejock is travelling towards the black hole at ever-increasing speed.' He drew gigantic sheets of flame jetting from the back of the shuttle, and a big arrow in front in case his audience hadn't grasped the concept of action/reaction. He also took the time to touch up Mr S's face, making the downward curvature of the mouth even more pronounced. 'He's already well past the point of no return, which was somewhere back here.' Clunk drew a heavy vertical line between the shuttle and the Charlton, adding PONR and jerking the pointer vigorously to add full stops between every letter. 'What that means is, even at full reverse thrust he cannot slow down before entering the danger zone.' He added DZ, and another vertical line in front of the shuttle. 'Once Mr Spacejock reaches that point, all hope is lost. The relative passing of time is such that any rescue attempt is futile.'

Pydd raised his hand. His face was heavily bruised, and he still looked dazed. 'How long will that be?'

'Approximately two hours,' said Clunk.

The others looked hopeful. A lot could be achieved in two hours.

'Now, we cannot simply chase Mr Spacejock in the *Charlton*, because we will face the exact same problem he is.' Clunk drew a larger ship next to Hal's, along with the same burst of flame and the arrow. 'As Mr Spacejock transfers aboard, both ships will be racing forwards at the same speed, and neither will be able to escape the black hole.'

Albion raised his hand. 'What if we pick him up, then jump to safety?'

'At first glance, that would seem to be a workable plan.' Clunk eyed the screen, intending to draw the idea. Then he realised the diagrams were more than a little crowded. 'Unfortunately, we cannot perform a jump that close to the black hole. You all remember what happened when we almost crashed into Narella.'

'I'd risk it,' said Vera.

'Me too,' said Pydd.

Albion nodded.

'Excellent, wonderful.' Clunk took up the pointer. 'Now, if I might move the needle to the next track –'

'I have an idea,' said Albion.

'Very well. You have the floor.'

Albion took the pointer, and swiftly drew a few lines. 'We follow the shuttle, and one of us robots jumps across with a line attached. We take hold of Mr Spacejock and you reel us in.'

277

'It won't work,' said Clunk. 'We have no winch, no rope . . . and Mr Spacejock has no spacesuit.'

The others glanced at Vera for confirmation, and she nodded unhappily. 'He only has a life jacket. Cooper's not big on safety equipment, not unless the ship is carrying *him*.'

'Is that so?'

'Remember the defib unit Hal found in the hold? It came aboard with Cooper yesterday.'

'What if we jump after Hal right now?' demanded Pydd. 'We reappear next to the shuttle, get Hal on board, turn and –'

'Alas no,' said Clunk. 'When we emerge from the jump we will be travelling alongside the shuttle, and again, by the time we transfer Mr Spacejock the black hole will have trapped us.'

'Then there really is no answer?'

Clunk laid the pointer on the console. 'Now you see what I was getting at. Much as I am troubled to admit it, the situation –'

There was a clatter behind him as the pointer rolled off the edge and landed on the floor. As it landed, it rolled in the opposite direction until it fetched up against the foot of the console.

Clunk frowned at it, then continued. 'As I was saying, I truly believe the situation is hopeless. I'm afraid Mr Spacejock is lost to us.'

❖

Aboard the shuttle, Hal was sitting with his elbow on the back of a bench seat, the side of his head pressed against the curved perspex window. It was the only way he could see out the front, where the accretion disk of the black hole was laid out like a gigantic sideways whirlpool. It filled half the view, and he'd never seen anything quite as beautiful.

He caught himself. Well, almost. There was Harriet, of course. And now, Vera.

Hal sighed. He'd had plenty of time to think about Captain Vera. That first night, when they sat and talked together, he'd felt an incredibly strong connection, far greater than anything he'd felt for Harriet. He thought Vera had felt it too, but then, when things were going well, they'd run into Harriet Walsh on Narella. Even though Harriet was married, and very pregnant, things between himself and Vera had cooled.

Oh, she'd gone shopping with him on Narella, and they'd had lunch and chatted, but he sensed there were many things she wanted to ask ... all of them concerning Harriet Walsh. The stupid story he'd told Vera hadn't helped, all the stuff about Harriet being a hero and saving an entire planet from killer bugs. And then of course, with the mad dash to the spaceport, the flight to meet Cooper, and the current spot of bother, there'd hardly been time to talk.

What bothered him most was the moment he'd said goodbye to everyone in the flight deck, just before boarding the shuttle which was to carry him to his death. Vera hadn't even looked up! Again his mind played the scene back for him, and although he knew full well that Vera had been dealing with Cooper's impatient messages, couldn't she have looked up and at least nodded a brief goodbye? Actually he would have preferred that she ditch all of Cooper's messages, run across the flight deck, wrap her arms around his neck and kiss him passionately, but since he was pretending to be Pydd at the time he guessed that was a bit of a stretch.

Hal rubbed the back of his neck. It was getting really warm aboard the shuttle, and he noticed the airflow had ceased. The engines were still roaring at full throttle, and he wondered whether the exhaust heat was getting in through the hull. The shots he'd fired into the console had damaged the controls beyond repair, so there was nothing he could do about the engines. Above the console were two blackened holes, where the shots he'd fired at Cooper had blasted the panelling. He was just glad they hadn't gone right through the hull.

Then he glanced to his right, where Cooper's body was laid out on the opposite bench seat. He'd draped Pydd's jacket over the old man's face, not wanting to see the awful, accusing stare from those dead eyes. But if it kept getting warmer, and if Hal was stuck aboard the shuttle for a few days while the others figured out a rescue ... well, it might start to get pretty damned unpleasant.

The wall speaker spluttered, and he heard an echoing, distorted voice. The words were repeated, and with a surge of emotion he realised it was Vera.

'Hal, can you hear me?'

'Yes, I'm here!' shouted Hal. He hurried to the wall, putting his mouth to the grille. 'Can you hear me?'

Suddenly her voice was stronger, and very clear. *'Yes, Hal. I can hear you.'*

'Is everything okay?'

She hesitated. *'We're still looking into it. Clunk's hopeful.'*

'You'd tell me, wouldn't you? If I can't be saved, I mean. You'd let me know, right?'

'You should have told me what you were planning,' said Vera, in a low voice. *'I would have come with you. We could have faced this together.'*

Hal glanced at the body, then the black hole. 'I'm really glad

280

you didn't. By the way, is Pydd all right? I gave him quite a whack.'

'*He's better off than you are,*' said Vera sharply.

'Don't blame him for this. It was my idea.'

'*I know. Everyone thinks you're an idiot, by the way. Noble and heroic, but a complete idiot.*'

'Tell them to focus on the rescue mission.'

'*I will. By the way, when we get you out of there I'm going to punch you right in the face. You know that, right?*'

Hal grinned. 'You're on.'

'*I had two years of unarmed combat.*'

The grin vanished. If Hal *was* rescued, Vera would kick his arse all over the ship.

'*Just ... hang in there,*' said Vera. '*Sit tight and wait for us. Don't ... don't do anything stupid, okay?*'

'Understood.'

'*It's going to be all right, I'm sure. I saw this movie once, where –*'

'Oh, don't go there,' groaned Hal.

'*But –*'

'I mean it. Whatever it was, it never works in real life.'

'*All right, but we're going to get you out.*'

'I know. I believe you.'

'*And Hal?*'

'Yes?'

There was a long pause. '*I–*'

Crackle.

'I'm here,' said Hal. 'Hello?'

Bzzzt.

Hal thumped his fist against the speaker, but the connection was lost.

Clunk stared at the fallen pointer, and then, in a dream, he picked it up and set it down on the console. It fell off and rolled away, and once again Clunk picked it up and ...

'Er, Clunk?' said Vera. 'Are you okay?'

Clunk watched the pen fall, roll away. And then, in barely a whisper ... 'I've got it.'

'What?'

'I've got it,' said Clunk, still softly and with a slightly disbelieving tone. 'I've got it ... I have the answer.' And then, in a joyous roar. 'I know how to save Mr Spacejock!'

33

Clunk grabbed the pointer for a third time, but instead of putting it back on the console he used it to wipe the viewscreen. Feverishly, he drew Mr Spacejock with his unhappy face, the *Charlton* halfway between the shuttle and the left hand edge of the screen, and the black hole on the far right. Then he added the forward arrow to the shuttle. Finally, he added an arrow to the *Charlton*, pointing *away* from the black hole . . . and Hal's shuttle.

'How is that going to help?' demanded Vera. 'Are you suggesting we fly away? Leave him?'

Without a word, Clunk drew a second *Charlton*, this one just to the right of the shuttle, between it and the black hole. Then, as a finishing touch, he drew an arrow from the front of this copy of the *Charlton* pointing to the left, straight through the shuttle.

'That,' he said, 'is how we are going to rescue Mr Spacejock.'

The others looked mystified, so he explained. 'We turn around and fly away from the shuttle – and the black hole – at maximum thrust. Once travelling at speed, we perform a micro jump, emerging in *front* of the shuttle and travelling directly towards it. At that point we'll be travelling *away* from the black hole at top speed, and all we have to do is collect Mr

Spacejock without slowing down.'

'How?' said Pydd.

Clunk scratched his chin. 'We can't pick up the whole shuttle. He'll have to exit the vessel through the airlock beforehand.'

'Without a spacesuit? That's suicide!'

'It will require accurate timing,' admitted Clunk. 'As long as he's not exposed to hard vacuum for too long, it will work.'

'And how will you pick him up? If we're flying at that kind of speed you'll splash him all over the nose.'

Vera spoke up. 'We fly in reverse with the cargo doors open. The anti-gravity field will catch him like a net.'

'Smart thinking,' said Clunk, with a look of admiration. He looked at the rest. 'Are we all agreed? Shall we try this?'

Pydd and Albion nodded.

'Right,' said Vera, as she returned to the console. 'Let's go save Hal.'

◆

When Clunk spoke into the microphone aboard the *Charlton*, his instructions were as follows: '*Mr Spacejock, you must eject yourself into space before we can collect you. Do not attempt to bring Cooper's body. You must enter the airlock, exhale so you do not suffer unduly in the vacuum of space, and jump clear of the ship. The Charlton will then use the cargo hold to pick you up in precisely thirty seconds.*'

Unfortunately, the message Hal received aboard the shuttle was interspersed with static and distorted almost beyond comprehension. He did, however get the gist of it: *'Eject ...Cooper's body ...space ...Charlton ...then ...pick you up.'*

He had no idea why he was supposed to get rid of Cooper's body, but there had to be a damn good reason or they wouldn't have asked him. He suspected it was something to do with the overall mass of the shuttle, but time was short and he didn't have time to argue.

'Got it, Charlton. Getting rid of the body now. Hal out.'

Hal glanced across the cabin. Cooper was still laid out on the bench, which wasn't really surprising because Hal had put him there. While zombies had infested movies, most other books, fancy-dress parties, video games and even classic literature, Hal knew with stone cold certainty they would never appear in *his* particular universe. Then he amended that thought: if someone bought the movie rights to all his incredible adventures, they'd probably write a pack of slavering zombies into every scene. And if they paid him enough, he'd let them.

Hal shook his head to dispel the idle thought, and returned to the problem at hand. Since this wasn't a movie, Cooper couldn't get up and walk himself into the airlock, which meant Hal would have to lend him a hand.

It took several minutes to accomplish the unpleasant task, but eventually Cooper was laid out on the airlock floor. There was barely enough room, but Hal managed to cross the old man's arms across his chest. Then he returned to the shuttle to collect the cane, which he placed under Cooper's hands like a warrior's sword.

He left the airlock, closing the inner door, and then paused to reflect with his hand on the controls. He'd wanted revenge against Cooper, but he'd never intended to kill the man.

'May you rest in peace,' he murmured, and cycled the airlock.

Through the window he saw Cooper ejected into the depths of space with a hiss of air, and having dealt with the dead his thoughts then turned to the living. How was Clunk going to save him?

Then Hal noticed something – the air had been stale before, but now it was really hard to breathe. He checked the airlock controls but the door was sealed correctly so it wasn't that. Next he checked the console, but that was dead. Finally he moved to the far end of the shuttle. Earlier, when Cooper tried to jump him, Hal had loosed off a couple of shots as he tried to defend himself. Neither had hit Cooper, but they had blasted holes clear through the decorative wall panels. Now he grabbed the panels and pulled, tearing them from the wall. Underneath was a maze of cables and ducting, and right in the middle was a small grey box with a label that read 'air purifier'. The box had a big black hole in the front, and was certainly beyond repair.

No wonder it was so hard to breathe, thought Hal. Then he realised something else: if Cooper hadn't dropped dead, they'd both have suffocated by now. In a way, Cooper had given his life to save Hal's, which was a nice irony.

Hal was having trouble clearing his head. He needed air quickly, but the ship had no emergency equipment to speak of. He checked the lockers again, eyeing the inflatable life jacket and flare gun. Then he frowned. If the thing was self-inflating, he might be able to eke out the air until Clunk came to rescue him.

Fumbling, cursing, he managed to get the life jacket free. It was bulky, and there was a small grey cylinder attached. Hal put the jacket over his head and pulled the cords. It inflated with a loud hiss, which was good. Unfortunately Hal couldn't get to the air inside, which was bad.

He needed a ... what was it? Sharp. Blade. Sword? Knife! Yes, he needed a knife.

Hal stumbled around, opening invisible kitchen drawers and rummaging in the non-existent contents. 'Knife. Need a knife,' he muttered. Then, despite his fuzzy vision, he saw the flare gun. 'Weapon. Knife.'

He took the gun, held it close to his face and blinked owlishly. Then he pointed it at the three life jackets he seemed to be wearing and pulled the trigger.

There was a muffled POP as the gun discharged. A dazzling red flare burned a line across the life jacket, bounced off the carpet, hit the roof then vanished behind the flight console. Instantly, the cabin filled with thick red smoke. The burning flare devoured all the available oxygen, then went out.

'Pretty knife,' said Hal, before his eyes closed and he toppled over backwards.

34

'Mr Spacejock, please get ready,' said Clunk into the microphone. 'You must exit the airlock in precisely thirty seconds or the plan will fail and you will perish most horribly. Hello? Mr Spacejock? Hal?'

Then Vera pointed a shaking finger at the screen. 'My God, he's already jumped!'

'No, no, no!' shouted Clunk, beside himself. 'It's too soon! We'll never get there in time!'

'We don't have any choice,' said Vera. 'Pydd, are you ready down there?'

'*Standing by,*' came the reply.

Vera pulled the throttle back, and from a standing start the ship leapt backwards until it was reversing away from the shuttle at top speed. The hyperdrive was already charging, and mere seconds after they started to move the ship jumped. They winked out and reappeared in front of the shuttle, barely a hundred metres away and ten metres to one side. The Charlton preserved its rearward momentum, and they flashed past the shuttle almost before anyone had time to see it. Anyone except Clunk, that is.

'How odd,' he remarked. Then he called the hold. 'Please tell me it was a success.'

There was an odd note to Pydd's voice as he replied. 'Well, the plan worked.'

'Excellent!'

'The only trouble is, we didn't get Hal.'

'What?'

'We've ended up with Cooper's body.'

Horrified, Clunk glanced at the screen. That meant Mr Spacejock was still aboard the shuttle! Even as he watched, the tiny vessel shrunk to a pinpoint, then vanished against the awesome spectacle of the black hole's disc. 'That's it,' said Clunk, lowering his head. 'We've failed.'

◆

Vera was trying desperately to raise the shuttle, to ask Hal what he was playing at, but she could only get static in reply.

'I have a suggestion,' said Albion.

Clunk turned to look at him. In all the excitement he'd forgotten the other robot, since Albion had been content to stand by and let the others work uninterrupted. Now, however, Albion had decided it was time to act. However, he and Vera both spoke at almost the same moment.

'Isn't there *anything* –' began Vera.

'There is no time to employ speech,' said Albion to Clunk. 'Let us network.'

Clunk nodded, and the two robots switched to CPU time. The viewscreen, the instruments and Vera all froze as they communicated in bursts of data.

'It seems to me,' signalled Albion, 'that Mr Spacejock may have misinterpreted your instructions.' To illustrate his point, Albion displayed Clunk's original message. Then, working quickly, he removed certain words. 'I believe this is the message Mr Spacejock may have received. It's the only variation which explains his actions.'

'Eject . . . Cooper's body . . . space . . . Charlton . . . then . . . pick you up.'

Clunk agreed that it made sense. 'He's expecting us to fetch him.'

'Precisely.'

'There is no time to send another message.'

'And any future message will be just as confusing as the first.'

Clunk thought hard. 'There is only one logical solution.'

'I agree. I will go, for I am the stronger.'

Clunk was going to argue, but he could see the logic. 'How will you retrieve him?'

'We will have to make two more passes. During the first, I will exit the *Charlton* and enter the shuttle.'

'And while you are retrieving Mr Spacejock, we will prepare for a third pass.'

'Precisely. I exit the shuttle with Mr Spacejock, jumping into space from the airlock as he should have done. The *Charlton* will collect both of us.'

'Hold friend, there is a flaw. Your combined mass is excessive, the cargo hold too short.' Clunk brought up engineering data on the ship's gravity field and the cargo hold. Using a short animation, he showed Albion and Hal entering the hold together, and then failing to slow down before they smashed into the rear wall.

'You are correct. We would both be destroyed.' Albion

hesitated. 'In that case, I will eject Mr Spacejock and remain on board the shuttle.'

'That's unacceptable. I am the one who should remain there.'

'Clunk, we settled this. I can eject Mr Spacejock with the required force. You do not possess my strength.'

'But Mr Spacejock is my responsibility.'

'That's why I must go.'

They both paused for a millisecond or two, digesting the terrible truth.

'We will try and pick you up,' said Clunk at last. 'A fourth pass by the shuttle –'

'Clunk, you cannot.' It was Albion's turn to display an animation. In it, the *Charlton*'s odds of escaping the black hole after a third pass were remote. After a fourth pass to collect Albion, the chances of escape were zero.

'You are correct, there is no time for a fourth pass,' said Clunk at last. 'We will not be able to pick you up.'

'I know this, and I accept my fate. Tell Clyde I am sorry.'

They fleshed out their plan, then terminated the network connection.

'– we can do?' finished Vera, who wasn't even aware the robots had conducted a lengthy conversation without her.

'Actually, we do have a plan,' said Clunk. 'I need you to pass by the shuttle again, and relay our flight data to Albion. Course, heading, everything. Include the shuttle, too.'

Vera nodded, and her fingers danced over the console. Meanwhile Albion moved to the airlock, closing the inner door and opening the outer with the customary hiss of escaping air.

Clunk saw that he was ready, then nodded to Vera. 'Now!'

The ship jumped, and just before they whistled past the shuttle Albion leapt from the airlock. One second he was there, the next he was gone. On the viewscreen, Clunk saw the robot's squat silver form for an instant before it was swallowed up by the distance. 'Farewell my friend, and good luck,' he muttered.

Albion rocketed towards the shuttle, head first with his arms out like a high diver. He flew arrow-straight, his status displays alerting him to the lack of gravity and breathable atmosphere. He needed neither, but they were useful when accompanied by humans.

He struck the shuttle at speed, but absorbed the impact with his squat arms. Within seconds he was at the airlock door, and after checking the inner door was still closed, he cycled it. There was a puff of atmosphere, but his sensors showed dangerously low levels of oxygen. No wonder Mr Spacejock hadn't left the shuttle! Even if he wasn't dead, he would most certainly be unconscious.

Albion calculated the delay this might cause, and frowned. In twenty seconds the Charlton would flash by for the third and final time. If Mr Spacejock was not floating directly in its way, enabling him to be scooped up by the gaping cargo hold, he would be spending the last seconds of his life aboard the shuttle with only Albion for company.

There was absolutely no time for niceties. Instead of cycling the airlock, Albion braced himself and kicked the inner door in with a massive, armoured foot. Thick red smoke enveloped him, thinning rapidly as it vented into space. Albion spotted the human lying on the deck nearby with a deflated lifebelt around his neck. The lifebelt had a jagged black tear in it, and as he approached Albion saw the edges flapping gently. How fortunate, he thought. The last of the life jacket's air, venting through the rip, may have been enough to keep Mr Spacejock alive!

However, there was no time to check for a pulse. Alive or not, he had to get Mr Spacejock out of the shuttle. He crouched and gently lifted the inert form with his massive hands. Every second was precious and there was no time to waste turning round, so he engaged reverse and ran backwards to the airlock at full tilt. As he passed the inner door he performed a back-flip and hurled Hal out of the shuttle with all his strength. Then, before he could sail out of the airlock himself, he grabbed hold of the door frame with one hand, coming to a dead stop.

His head spun through a hundred and eighty degrees as he tracked the human, and he watched Mr Spacejock flying away from the shuttle, his arms and legs waving gently. Then there was a flash, an elongated white blur, and the human vanished.

Satisfied, Albion closed the outer door. He'd done his job well, and it was a shame he would never know whether Mr Spacejock had survived. Actually, he corrected himself, he *would* be able to find out. Two or three weeks hence, after the passage of a thousand of years or more in the rest of the galaxy, it was possible some far future human might chance upon the shuttle with its robot passenger, and rescue Albion. And if so, Albion would request access to ancient historical records and learn of Mr Spacejock's fate. As for Clyde and Clunk ... well, that was less certain, because people rarely bothered to document a robot's ending. He just hoped his friends enjoyed a long and happy life.

But all of that was two weeks from now, and he didn't intend to sit idle. No, with plenty of time on his hands, he decided to put the shuttle in order.

◆

In the cargo hold, Pydd ripped Hal's shirt open and applied the paddles from the defib unit he'd taken from a nearby locker. Meanwhile Vera was holding an oxygen mask to Hal's face, praying the blue-tinged lips would move.

'Take a breath Hal, please!'

Clunk stood over them all, watching and feeling useless. They'd caught Mr Spacejock in the hold exactly as planned, but the human had been in a bad way. Technically he'd been dead, but when Clunk applied that word to Mr Spacejock's status his circuits threatened to shut down.

All around them the engines thundered with a mighty roar, as the ship struggled to escape the black hole's influence. Even if we bring Mr Spacejock back, thought Clunk, there's no guarantee any of us will make it.

'Clear!' shouted Pydd, and Hal's back arched as the paddles applied their charge. Vera checked for a pulse, then shook her head.

'Clear!'

Hal arched again. Nothing.

'Clear!' shouted Pydd desperately. Alongside him, Vera applied oxygen and willed Hal back to life. Clunk, meanwhile, glanced at Cooper's blanket-covered body lying nearby.

'Clear!' shouted Pydd, applying an even greater charge.

Hal's body arched, but there was no response.

'He's gone, hasn't he?' asked Vera.

Pydd looked at her, then nodded quickly. He removed the paddles, and while he was attaching them to the defib machine, Vera leaned forward and kissed Hal on the forehead. Then she moved to cover his face with the new shirt they'd bought together on Narella.

'No,' said Clunk softly.

'Clunk, it's too late,' said Pydd.

'I said no. Give me room, both of you.'

The others looked at each other, then obeyed. Meanwhile, Clunk knelt down and opened his chest cavity. He pulled out two wires, tore off the connectors and held them up, inspecting the ends. Next, he took a paddle from the defib machine, broke the wire and connected the end to one of those dangling from his chest. He repeated the process with the other paddle, then knelt over Hal and placed both paddles on his bare chest.

'Clear!' he shouted, then poured his entire charge into the human in a single, massive jolt.

Drained, he fell across Hal's inert body. As he lost consciousness he felt the ship jump, and a tiny smile flickered across his face. The jump had been smooth, and that meant they were free of the black hole.

In turn, that meant Mr Spacejock would have a proper burial.

35

Clunk came around slowly. His charge was almost non-existent, his movements slow and clumsy. He had difficulty turning his head, but when he did so a familiar human face swum into focus. For a moment he thought it was Mr Spacejock, and he experienced an instant of pure joy. Then reality intruded, and he realised it had to be Mr Pydd.

Not that one human life was worth more than another, he thought hastily. But Mr Spacejock had certainly been unique.

Clunk's vision blurred, and when it cleared he saw the human had noticed he was awake, and was giving him a double thumbs up. Clunk just stared, because even in his fragile state he was still able to count to ten.

'Mr Spacejock?' he whispered at last, through uncooperative lips. 'Is that really you?'

'I should get a T-shirt made,' said Hal with a laugh. 'I can see it now in big, bold lettering: *I am not Stu Pydd.*'

'But how did you survive?'

'Clunk, you put so much juice into those paddles you nearly brought Cooper back to life, let alone me.'

'But are you okay?'

'I'm fine. A bit chilly and a bit sore, but nothing a coffee or two won't fix.'

'So very glad,' said Clunk softly.

'How about you? All okay?'

'Low on power, but yes. I'm improving rapidly.' Clunk could feel the current flowing into his circuits, and despite the warning beeps and buzzes, he sat up. He was still in the cargo hold, with an extension lead snaking across the deck to his chest. He glanced around, but Cooper's body had vanished.

Hal realised what he was looking for. 'Pydd gave him another space burial. I didn't agree, but he insisted.'

'Less questions that way,' said Clunk.

'Never mind Cooper. Vera told me about Albion,' said Hal, his voice suddenly serious. 'We'll have to rescue him. You know that, right?'

'The tech doesn't exist. Not yet.'

'Then we'll invent it. Hey, I could call that guy with the teleporter!'

Clunk shuddered.

'Or maybe we just spread a rumour. You know, Cooper's fortune lost on a secret shuttle trip near a black hole. People will go looking for it, and when someone finally manages to get there, they can rescue Albion.'

The cargo hold speaker buzzed, interrupting his train of thought.

'We're in orbit around Narella,' said Vera. *'I've sent through a landing request, but our comms are still down.'*

Hal noticed Clunk's querying look. 'That big zap of yours didn't just burn my chest hair off, it fried all sorts of gear. Vera's pretty good though, she's coping.'

Clunk nodded, and sank back on the deck. The effort had drained him, and he needed more time to recover. As the ship's engines powered them towards the landing field, he closed his eyes and shut down his external systems.

Landing passed without incident, and the second they touched down a robot ground crew hurried from concrete bunkers to connect fuel hoses and data cables to the ship. Vera got a connection at last, and Morrell's face appeared on the screen.

'Stewie? *Stu?* Where the hell have you *been*, man?'

'Tell you later. Authorise city clearance will you? I have to see Harriet.'

'Of course! But –'

'Drop by later, we'll do lunch.' With that, Pydd cut the connection. 'Can you get a cab?' he asked Vera.

She opened a screen, tapped a couple of options and nodded. 'Done.'

'Come on. We've got to tell Harriet about Cooper. She's safe at last!'

Ten minutes later all four of them were sitting in a cab bound for Harriet's apartment. Hal eyed the tree-lined avenues and shops, and decided he preferred a bit of variety in his life. Then he looked around the cab. There were only four of them, now that poor Albion had trapped himself aboard the shuttle to save Hal's life. Clyde would be distraught, and Hal was not looking forward to breaking the news. Months and months ago he'd given the two robots a lift as they fled a robot store and a life of misery. Little did he know one of them would end up sacrificing himself to save Hal's life.

Eventually they drew up at the apartment block, and Pydd ran across the pavement to the entrance. Hal followed more slowly, still suffering aches and pains from his near death experience. Clunk walked one side of him, ready to offer assistance, while Vera took the other side and slipped her hand into his. She'd hardly left his side since Clunk had revived him, and – so far – she seemed to have forgotten the arse-kicking she'd promised to dish out.

Pydd had called the elevator by the time they got inside, and he almost hopped with impatience as it bore them upwards. Then the doors opened, and they all stopped in surprise.

Clyde was galloping around the large entrance hall, making neighing and clip-clopping noises. Clinging to his back, screaming with joy and yelling encouragement, was a dark-haired child of two or three years old.

The neighing stopped as Clyde became aware of their presence, and with practised ease he swung the child from his shoulder and set him gently on the floor.

Meanwhile, the boy took one look at the newcomers and ran off down the hall. 'Mummy, mummy, it's people!'

They heard footsteps approaching, and Harriet entered. Her long blonde hair was tied back, and she had flour all the way to her elbows. There was a mixing bowl in one hand, a whisk in the other, and as she caught sight of Pydd both tumbled to the ground, unheeded. A split second later she was in Pydd's arms and he swung her round and round, holding her tight while she clung to him.

'Mind the baby, Harr!' protested Pydd at last. 'Mind the baby!'

She pulled away and gave him a strange look. That's when Pydd noticed her slim figure. Gaping, he stared from Harriet to the boy and back again.

'That's the *baby*?' said Pydd in astonishment. 'But we only left yesterday!'

'Stu, he's not 'the baby' ...he's Hal Junior. And it's been three *years*.'

<hr>

'I can explain,' said Clunk, and everyone turned to look at him.

Everyone except Hal Junior, who tugged Clyde's hand and said 'Horsey!'

'It seems we experienced a time distortion,' said Clunk. 'That would explain the comms problems aboard the ship ...nothing would sync up with such a large deviation.'

'What's that in real words?' demanded Hal.

'As Ms ...Harriet stated, we lost three years even though we experienced no more than one or two hours. Our successive passes in the *Charlton*, closer and closer to the black hole, meant that time passed faster and faster in the rest of the galaxy.'

They were silent. Then ...'Poor Albion,' said Hal. He turned to Clyde. 'You don't know this yet, but –'

'It's okay, Mr Spacejock. Clunk told me when you got here.'

'He didn't say anything!'

'We networked. I have the whole saga from beginning to end.' Clyde sighed. 'Albion will be sorely missed, and to be frank, I don't know what I'll do without him. He was a good friend.'

'You're staying with us,' said Harriet firmly.

'That's very kind of you, but I've long since overstayed my welcome.'

'Nonsense. Do you want to break Hal Junior's heart?'

Clyde looked alarmed. 'Is that possible?'

'Leave, and you'll find out.'

Uncertain, Clyde looked down at Hal Junior. As he did so the boy took the robot's hand, his tiny fingers barely closing around Clyde's bronze forefinger. 'Horsey, Kide. Horsey!'

'In a minute, little master. Let me talk to the people.'

Hal Junior put his bottom lip out, and Vera laughed. 'I've seen that expression before.'

Hal and Pydd frowned at her.

'Little master, you can have horsey rides after I talk.'

'Forever?'

'And ever,' said Clyde, with a grin. Then he turned to Harriet. 'Mistress Harriet... I am honoured by your offer, and I accept.'

'Good man,' said Pydd, and clapped him on the shoulder.

Then Hal realised something. 'Clyde, whatever happened to your stammer?'

'Mistress Harriet –'

'I've asked you not to call me that, Clyde,' said Harriet gently. 'And as for 'little master' ...'

Clyde nodded an apology, then continued. 'Harriet used a great deal of her coupons to repair me. It was very kind, and I will forever be grateful.'

'That was after you all disappeared,' said Harriet. 'Sable went back to Alteia a couple of weeks later, to round up all Cooper's people.' She looked at Hal. 'They picked up some of your transmissions a year or two back. We all heard the rumour Cooper might be dead, and that you'd given your life to save my husband. Hal, I know I made you promise, but if I'd known what that meant –'

'Don't mention it,' said Hal gruffly.

'Then the transmissions died, and everyone forgot about you. I didn't though, I knew you'd make it.'

'Well, it was a close thing but we're here.'

'And Cooper? Are you sure he's dead?'

'Dead and buried,' said Pydd firmly.

'Twice,' added Hal, and he glanced around in hope. 'Any chance of a drink? I'm parched.'

'Of course, what am I doing?' Harriet looked at the bowl on the floor. 'That was supposed to be a chemistry experiment, by the way. Don't try eating it.'

'What were you making?'

She rolled her eyes. 'They want me to build a model of the atom out of paper mache and drinking straws. Some kind of 'back to basics' push at uni.'

'I thought drinking straws were banned?'

'Seriously?' Harriet stared at him. 'What kind of messed-up planet do you think this is?'

A few minutes later everyone was holding a drink, even Clunk and Clyde. They stood in a circle and raised their glasses.

'To Albion,' said Clyde solemnly.

'To Albion,' everyone repeated, and they all touched glasses.

'Horsey?' said Hal Junior.

Next morning, Vera took a handful of coupons and went shopping, as her apartment on Alteia had long since been let out, the contents sold off and the proceeds absorbed by the cost of her memorial service. Hal promised to book a room at the spaceport until they could discuss their future, and he and Clunk were now sitting in a cab on their way to the hotel.

'You realise this is the first time we've been alone for about three years?' said Hal, with a laugh.

'Relatively speaking, Mr Spacejock, you are correct.'

'I'm sorry I left you at the spaceport on Alteia.'

'That was years ago, Mr Spacejock. I have already forgotten about it.'

They both grinned, and Hal realised everything would be okay. If nothing else, they could make endless time travel jokes. 'We've had a hell of a time,' he said at last.

'Indeed. We made new friends, but unfortunately we lost an old and valued colleague.'

Hal glanced at the sky. How much time had passed aboard the shuttle, he wondered. One second perhaps? Five minutes? They'd been out there no more than twenty minutes, and that had turned into three years. Albion had been out there half a day, and was moving ever closer to the black hole.

Clunk interrupted his thoughts. 'Speaking of new friends, I find Captain Vera most acceptable.'

'Wow, Clunk. That's high praise from you.'

'She will be good for you, and you for her.'

'I don't think I can teach her anything,' said Hal. 'Have you seen how she handles a ship?' He continued without waiting for an answer. 'Clunk, I need a job. Something legal, pays well, nothing too dangerous.'

'Certainly, Mr Spacejock. I have already found several cargo jobs, and if you check the screen in front of you, you'll see I've listed them in –'

'No, I meant a real job. You know, a salesman. Cleaner. Anything.'

'Why don't you want a freight job?'

'How would I carry the cargo? In my pockets?' Then Hal had a thought. 'That ship of Cooper's, the *Charlton*. Can we have it?'

'No, Mr Spacejock. It will be sold as part of Cooper's criminal enterprise.'

'Pity.' He hesitated. 'What about the Navcom?'

'I will ensure she's backed up properly.'

'That won't go down well.'

'We shall see, Mr Spacejock. We shall see.'

Hal suddenly realised they were driving onto the landing field. 'Funny place for a hotel. Is it one of those underground dives?'

'No, Mr Spacejock.' Clunk hesitated. 'Clyde and Albion aren't the only robots enrolled in Mr Pydd's Vigilante Cooperative. I signed up too, and on my very first day, three years ago, I destroyed Cooper's entire enterprise. As a result, I was entitled to certain rewards.'

'What are you talking about? What's this got to do with my hotel room?'

They arrived at a landing pad, and as the cab drifted to a halt, Clunk gestured through the window. Towering over them was a gleaming white freighter. 'I paid for that with my share of the Vigilante bounty.'

'Wait, you brought Cooper down, so you get a brand new ship?'

'Indeed.'

'You own a cargo freighter?'

'No, Mr Spacejock.'

'But you said –'

'I said I bought a new ship, but I don't own it.' Clunk passed Hal an official-looking document. 'You do.'

Overcome, Hal could only stare at the graceful freighter. His gaze took in the sleek nose, then moved along the flowing lines to the winglets and the supremely powerful engines nestled underneath. Then he reached the tailplane, and a lump formed in his throat. A sign-writer was perched on a platform, high above the ground, and under his careful brush strokes the ship's name was being added to the hull.

Clunk had called her the *Albion*.

Epilogue

Where is Cooper's Fortune?

News of a huge treasure-hunt abound today, as Alteia residents learn of a missing fortune in gold bars, gems and share certificates. The haul was reportedly being transported aboard a shuttle which disappeared en route to Cahngahagaglagawaga three years ago, and private ships are reported to be scouring local sectors for the bounty.

In unrelated news, rumours persist of a black hole which is supposed to have appeared spontaneously around three years ago. The black hole, if it exists, would be a severe danger to local shipping, and Naval vessels continue to blockade the nearby sector, barring entry to all vessels.

Reports that the alleged black hole is the result of a military experiment have yet to be verified, although social media is rife with conspiracy theories.

Speculation that the two rumours are linked has been strongly denied.

Finally, the anniversary of last year's Alteian robot riots has passed without incident. Experts were predicting trouble, but it seems our metal friends are content with their lot . . . for now.

.

If you enjoyed this book, please leave a brief review at your online bookseller of choice. Thanks!

About the Author

Simon Haynes was born in England and grew up in Spain. His family moved to Australia when he was 16.

In addition to novels, Simon writes computer software. In fact, he writes computer software to help him write novels faster, which leaves him more time to improve his writing software. And write novels faster. (www.spacejock.com/yWriter.html)

Simon's goal is to write fifteen novels before someone takes his keyboard away.

Update 2018: goal achieved and I still have my keyboard!

New goal: write thirty novels.

Simon's website is spacejock.com.au

Stay in touch!

Author's newsletter:
spacejock.com.au/ML.html

facebook.com/halspacejock
twitter.com/spacejock

Acknowledgements

To Ian, Stephen, Andy, Kevin, George, Mike, Janet ... thanks
for the awesome help and support!

To all my proofreaders and spling chquers, thansk!

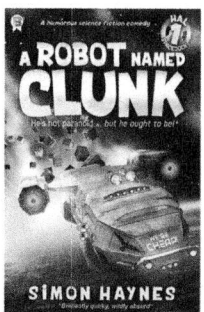

The Hal Spacejock series
by Simon Haynes

1. A ROBOT NAMED CLUNK

Deep in debt and with his life on the line, Hal takes on a dodgy cargo job ... and an equally dodgy co-pilot.

2. SECOND COURSE

When Hal finds an alien teleporter network he does the sensible thing and pushes Clunk the robot in first.

3. JUST DESSERTS

Gun-crazed mercenaries have Hal in their sights, and a secret agent is pulling the strings. One wrong step and three planets go to war!

4. NO FREE LUNCH

Everyone thinks Peace Force trainee Harriet Walsh is paranoid and deluded, but Hal stands at her side. That would be the handcuffs.

5. BAKER'S DOUGH

When you stand to inherit a fortune, good body-guards are essential. If you're really desperate, call Hal and Clunk. Baker's Dough features intense rivalry, sublime double-crosses and more greed than a free buffet.

6. SAFE ART

Valuable artworks and a tight deadline ... you'd be mad to hire Hal for that one, but who said the art world was sane?

7. BIG BANG

A house clearance job sounds like easy money, but rising floodwaters, an unstable landscape and a surprise find are going to make life very difficult for Hal and Clunk.

8. DOUBLE TROUBLE

Hal Spacejock dons a flash suit, hypershades and a curly earpiece for a stint as a secret agent, while a pair of Clunk's most rusted friends invite him to a 'unique business opportunity'.

9. MAX DAMAGE

Hal and Clunk answer a distress call, and they discover a fellow pilot stranded deep inside an asteroid field. Clunk is busy at the controls so Hal dons a spacesuit and sets off on a heroic rescue mission.

10. Cold Boots

Coming 2019

Ebook and Trade Paperback

The Secret War Series
Set in the Hal Spacejock universe

Everyone is touched by the war, and Sam Willet is no exception.

Sam wants to train as a fighter pilot, but instead she's assigned to Tactical Operations. It's vital work, but it's still a desk job, far from the front line.

Then, terrible news: Sam's older brother is killed in combat.

Sam is given leave to attend his memorial service, but she's barely boarded the transport when the enemy launches a surprise attack, striking far behind friendly lines as they try to take the entire sector.

Desperately short of pilots, the Commander asks Sam to step up.

Now, at last, she has the chance to prove herself.

But will that chance end in death... or glory?

Ebook and Trade Paperback

The Harriet Walsh series

Harriet's boss is a huge robot with failing batteries, the patrol car is driving her up the wall and her first big case will probably kill her.

So why did she join the Peace Force?

When an intergalactic crime-fighting organisation offers Harriet Walsh a job, she's convinced it's a mistake. She dislikes puzzles, has never read a detective mystery, and hates wearing uniforms. It makes no sense ... why would the Peace Force choose her?

Who cares? Harriet needs the money, and as long as they keep paying her, she's happy to go along with the training.

She'd better dig out some of those detective mysteries though, because she's about to embark on her first real mission ...

The Peace Force has a new recruit, and she's driving everyone crazy.

From disobeying orders to handling unauthorised cases, nothing is off-limits. Worse, Harriet Walsh is forced to team up with the newbie, because the recruit's shady past has just caught up with her.

Meanwhile, a dignitary wants to complain about rogue officers working out of the station. She insists on meeting the station's commanding officer ... and they don't have one.

All up, it's another typical day in the Peace Force!

Dismolle is supposed to be a peaceful retirement planet. So what's with all the gunfire?

A criminal gang has moved into Chirless, planet Dismolle's second major city. Elderly residents are fed up with all the loud music, noisy cars and late night parties, not to mention the hold-ups, muggings and the occasional gunfight.

There's no Peace Force in Chirless, so they call on Harriet Walsh of the Dismolle City branch for help. That puts Harriet right in the firing line, and now she's supposed to round up an entire gang with only her training pistol and a few old allies as backup.

And her allies aren't just old, they're positively ancient!

Ebook and Trade Paperback

The Hal Junior Series
Set in the Hal Spacejock universe

Spot the crossover characters, references and in-jokes!

Hal Junior lives aboard a futuristic space station. His mum is chief scientist, his dad cleans air filters and his best mate is Stephen 'Stinky' Binn. As for Hal ... he's a bit of a trouble magnet. He means well, but his wild schemes and crazy plans never turn out as expected!

Hal Junior: The Secret Signal features mayhem and laughs, daring and intrigue ... plus a home-made space cannon!

200 pages, illustrated, ISBN 978-1-877034-07-7

"A thoroughly enjoyable read for 10-year-olds and adults alike"
The West Australian

'I've heard of food going off
... but this is ridiculous!'

Space Station Oberon is expecting an important visitor, and everyone is on their best behaviour. Even Hal Junior is doing his best to stay out of trouble!

From multi-coloured smoke bombs to exploding space rations, Hal Junior proves ... *trouble is what he's best at!*

200 pages, illustrated, ISBN 978-1-877034-25-1

Imagine a whole week of fishing, swimming, sleeping in tents and running wild!
Unfortunately, the boys crash land in the middle of a forest, and there's little chance of rescue. Is this the end of the camping trip ... or the start of a thrilling new adventure?

200 pages, illustrated, ISBN 978-1-877034-24-4

Space Station Oberon is on high alert, because a comet is about to whizz past the nearby planet of Gyris. All the scientists are preparing for the exciting event, and all the kids are planning on watching.

All the kids except Hal Junior, who's been given detention...

165 pages, illustrated, ISBN 978-1-877034-38-1

Ebook and Trade Paperback

New from Simon Haynes
The Robot vs Dragons series

"Laugh after laugh, dark in places but the humour punches through. One of the best books I've read in 2018 so far. Amazing, 5"*

Welcome to the Old Kingdom!

It's a wonderful time to visit! There's lots to do and plenty to see!
What are you waiting for? Dive into the Old Kingdom right now!

Clunk, an elderly robot, does exactly that. He's just plunged into the sea off the coast of the Old Kingdom, and if he knew what was coming next he'd sit down on the ocean floor and wait for rescue.

Dragged from the ocean, coughing up seaweed, salty water and stray pieces of jellyfish, he's taken to the nearby city of Chatter's Reach, where he's given a sword and told to fight the Queen's Champion, Sur Loyne.

As if that wasn't bad enough, the Old Kingdom still thinks the wheel is a pretty nifty idea, and Clunk's chances of finding spare parts - or his missing memory modules - are nil.

Still, Clunk is an optimist, and it's not long before he's embarking on a quest to find his way home.

Unfortunately it's going to be a very tough ask, given the lack of charging points in the medieval kingdom...

Ebook and Trade Paperback

Printed in Great Britain
by Amazon

23048712R00182